Thoughtreal

By Michael Gryboski

BOCH Publishing edition / August 2018

ISBN 13: 978-1949350029
ISBN 10: 1949350029

Table of Contents

I.

They lived normal lives on the day that it arrived. It was like a bright shooting star, traveling across the daytime skies. Scarring the eye and the air at once, it had a radiance that lit the darker shades of the afternoon. A brilliant sight high above the village, it drew the attention of all those in the rustic area. Folks of all stripes beheld it in wonder, halting their idleness, their games, their occupations, and their conversations. Before it came, all was typical.

Youths were outside of the small collection of buildings. Many boys were kicking around an old soccer ball with hexagonal patterns with faded colors. They used backpacks for posts, with some bickering at the start to determine whether the two goals were equally wide. The first goal renewed the debate briefly. Many of them were too young for either beards or acne. Two boys of a similar height and weight played together, scoring a few shots. Every success brought a wry smile. Some were keeping score, most were just playing for fun. They all ceased their leisure along the grassy hills when it came.

The glow of the sky drew the focus of the elders and distinguished, grayed in hair and wrinkled in flesh. They turned their balding heads, many wearing caps to hide their follicle deficiencies, to see the blinding force above. Board games of chess and checkers stood in stalemate. Outings with long acquaintances, which occurred since the days when they went back and forth on the hills in sport, had become tamer due to stiffened bones and withered muscles. They also watched in wonder and then in horror.

The middle demographic, those older than the players on the hills yet younger than those of a senior age, worked various jobs on that day. Businessmen, mothers, fathers, carpenters, workers all. Their actions halted, tipping up their faces, hands to foreheads, squinting eyes in faint pain as they attempted to view the shining vessel. As with the others in their humble settlement, they saw the object as though it were an otherworldly creation, a meteor, a comet, a great ship from some as yet undiscovered civilization. Then came the revelation.

Every being within and around that village beheld the entity, even those taking naps being awakened by the luminosity and the growing noise. How could such a great ball of gas, millions and millions of miles away, ever compete with the wondrous awful sight? No sun of any day has the ability to shine forth with such diverse and swift reaction as that creature.

No villager, not along the cobbles or the dirt streets, not within the modest homes and quaint shops, not among the fair number of automobiles or near the numerous radios and televisions that inhabited numerous rooms could miss the sight. None of these, not the old nor the young, not the man nor the woman, not the clergy nor the laity, were inattentive to the fast-moving bright machine, its fiery line translating from blaze to smoke, a darkened ink pen written upon a blue paper folded over their rooftops and spires. Few cloistered in the peaceful valley, with its solemn mountains, haunting forests, and plain dirt routes ever thought they would see such a magnificent dread sight. No object could protect them from the rocket that drove across the sky and then journeyed downward, in a smooth arc, to the very center of commerce.

II.

She was a woman of her times, captive to the trends of the age. Before her arrival, all was still for the moment. Walls were white, their cleansed appearance colored with the inclusion of vibrant posters. There was no central theme to the imagery. Clear tape was applied to each corner of each image placed on the white painted borders between inside and out. One was a band from yesteryear, another a photo of some classic artwork in Western Europe, still another a bizarre stream of consciousness. They were selected at various times and held up through the years and multiple moves. A couple of them betrayed their age through folding creases and little white blemishes on the texture.

There was furniture, mostly darkened wooden objects. At the urging of a cousin, the couches, chairs, and book shelves were placed along the walls, usually below the level where posters hung. This created a nice open space for the wood-paneled floors. The bedroom was different, having a carpet floor of light blue installed by the previous owner. Otherwise, the paneling was the constant, with a couple of pseudo-Oriental rugs to add a level of high class beauty to the plebian environment. In the bedroom a vanity mirror was in the corner, on top of a desk with drawers full of various products. A window, sometimes settled by cut flowers in a water-filled glass, gave the room a respectable view of the urban outside while also providing a nice glow at twilight.

  The kitchen and the living room had no wall between them, but a countertop separated the space for cooking and the space for leisure. A freezer and refrigerator were present, with a frame almost as white as the walls. The interior was sparsely populated, with alcohol the majority drink in the fridge. Frozen dinners dominated the upper level, one of them to meet its doom in a matter of minutes. All the modern amenities were counted among the objects present: a microwave, electric stove, toaster oven, and, for the living room space, a flat screen television that was a few feet wide with high definition pixels, a box that provided wireless internet, a laptop whose standby status was evidenced by its slow flashing light. Nothing spectacular was present in the 800 square foot space, all typical: a few shelves of books mostly comprised of bestsellers fiction and nonfiction, a closet full of clothes ranging from a dinner dress to sweats, several kinds of shoes for any possible fashion, and the strategically-placed digital clock to better track the passage of time.

  A key inserted, a bolt shifted, and a knob turned. The door opened and swung into the combination living room and kitchen. Immediately the portal was slammed shut and the door bolted from the inside. Once again the bronze knobbed door was impervious to being opened. An overpriced jacket unbuttoned, a popular shade of red its hue, was removed and discarded upon the arm of a wooden clothes tree positioned by the door. The removal of shoes, nothing too fashionable but more practical for the occupation, were also discarded not far from the clothes tree that held a few jackets including the one recently added.

Removing some other minor items from her person for the sake of comfort, Brittany Johnson took some relaxing breaths as she went about her unofficial routine. She placed her light gray purse upon the vacant countertop. Opening the freezer, a box was selected and one end of it torn. Freezer shut and the microwave opened, the instructions were unread as the chef had memorized the proper preparation. Placed in the device with film intact, the frozen meal was briefly obscured within the microwave before a few buttons were pushed, last among them the fading start button. After the inaugural beep, the light went on to display the black container for the meal, which slowly turned in circles.

Trusting the machine to its warming task, Brittany unzipped the main pocket for the filled purse. Pushing some objects aside, she found the zipper for a smaller pocket within the black-hued interior of the purse. From the smaller pocket came a bright green rectangular phone with a screen that included a couple of small thin cracks. Brittany hooked the oft-used pocket technology to a charger in the living room. By instinct she pushed a button to view the screen and saw no new messages. There was no indication that any had been sent, but she always double-checked and double-checked again. After all, it was always possible that one slipped through the alert system, right?

A click of the remote and the television was on, stationed at a local news channel just in case. Watching the screen, she saw a local talking head on the left side of the moving image and some footage of a large crater on the other. There was talk about some blast in Siberia, or a comet impact, or something of that ilk. The world kept moving and it kept happening. While by no means callous to the tragic, comedic, and positive events of the modern day, Brittany decided in seconds that this one did not warrant intense attention. Russia was farther away than the most recent brutal crime scene she saw a few metro stops away from her living quarters. Not an uncommon sight for her.

As she searched for a drink within the malnourished shelves of the fridge, the paced beeps of the microwave sounded. The small screen on the corner said "DONE" and Brittany concurred, opening the door and carefully removing the hot container of food. Pulling away the film, she saw the steam rise as she took out a plate and some utensils. It was not long before she sat before the television, a glass of water for drink and a hot meal for eating, placed on a small yet sufficient dinner table. She rarely had people over and when they were there, it was usually just to gather before hopping on the metro to get to U Street NW, where the best nightlife abounded. If she had more sustained company, there were other small dinner tables that could be brought out and used.

It was a few more clicks before she found some sitcom on TV to watch while she ate. A rerun, she somehow could tell it apart from the others. They all seemed the same at first: pretty, single 30-somethings who get into wacky situations, sleep around, argue loudly, and yet by the credits all was well again. Commercial hits and a brief advertisement for the news stories that evening were mentioned. Again, there was talk of the big explosion in Siberia, with the expected promise of a statement from the Russian government. They sure beat little things to death, she thought as another commercial began.

The television was a nice companion for her. She often ate her meals in front of it, letting the screen draw her attention as she consumed the food. It was also usually on while she folded laundry, wrapped birthday presents for family, or did various chores. It was a minor distraction, a bit of artificial light and noise that made the space more festive. At least to her, anyway. She was not an addict per se and while at work or on vacation had little interest in turning on a screen. Yet it was good company, providing a modicum of entertainment without cleaning out her fridge or messing up the bathroom.

For the next hour, she performed other menial tasks. Cleaning dishes, checking some work-related matters on the laptop, and then unhooking the now fully charged phone from the wall. On and active, she was searching, not for treasure, not for some random trivia, Brittany was looking on some app for dates. She was feeling especially lonely these days, having gone awhile since she last went out with a man. There was little interest in her for something concrete, just a casual matter for now. Just to have something more tangible than a TV set. The app had a simple design, with basic descriptions of men with profile photos. She skimmed through their ranks. Some profiles had multiple photos, some had none. Some had lengthy descriptions, others not so much.

There was one fellow. Nice looking, blonde and freckles. Going to his profile she saw the information on age, height, and what not. Only 5 foot 8? Her finger pushed down upon the screen, shifted left, and the profile was gone. Next one had no profile picture, a generic sounding description, and a cell phone contact. A little too shady in her opinion. The finger motioned again towards the left and the profile disappeared. Several more met a similar fate, various reasons accounting for the rejections. The quality of an entire life and the possible future of two beings stood at the mercy of a single fleshly digit.

A profile caught her eye. The fellow looked decent, had a few photos, and seemed to have good information present. 6 foot 1 so no worry there. Making $70,000 to $100,000 a year, so maybe he'll pay. Finally, the icon by his profile picture implied he was online at that very moment. This will do, Brittany thought. Rather than shift her finger leftward as before, she scrolled upwards, towards the contact button. A nudge, a simple notification of contact, and with that he was informed. Not expecting much, she returned to the television. Maybe something passable was airing.

Sound from her phone drew her away from the tube. He did not take long. So, she continued the communication. Another little show of interest and then another brief amount of time waiting. He was interested. She replied and he replied. Soon they were communicating in words. Tonight? Sure. How about this bar? Fair enough. What time? I can make it. See you there! It was simple textual small talk, some of the words being shortened for expedience. Still, from that paucity of language arose a date. Like that, technology was going to bring Brittany some company.

Now to prepare. Good thing she got to pick the time of the meeting. In front of the bedroom closet, Brittany began the careful discernment process. Pushing the hanging clothing aside to make clear for other options, she found a decent outfit for the occasion. Locating the right shoes for it came soon after. As she changed in front of the mirror, two tattoos became visible. Brittany got them both in college. As with the posters, they held no passionate significance. One was a butterfly and the other a black rose. Both were no larger than a palm print. She got them partly out of adolescent rebellion and partly because they looked cool. At this point in life, she neither hated nor loved them.

More deodorant and a small amount of makeup on the cheeks and the lines of the eyes were applied. Nothing too extravagant. Lip gloss was added, the lips puckered together for full application. She combed her dirty blonde hair, which over the years had been dyed a few different colors. A quick smile in front of the mirror and she checked the time. Plenty of time; no need to rush. Grabbing her purse, double checking some things, Brittany unlocked the door, exited, and closed the portal. Locked secure, the apartment was again motionless.

....

It was not the worst place in the Southeast. Defying the decades-old stereotype, the place was not a collection of slums or affordable housing. Crime was not a common occurrence, nor were drugs being consumed on every corner. Rather, it was a decent place, full of large brick buildings dating to the building boom of the Second World War. Some of that democracy arsenal still remained, with civilian businesses having supplanted the martial commerce from decades ago. Shipping and storage were the lots for most of these edifices, worn but unbroken, retro yet fitted with the occasional modern device.

One such device was on one such building, huddled among the industrial brick creations lined up and in formation. A small piece of technology, it was a memory and an eye, an ocular aid to the preservation of order and the punishment of disorder. Grayish in hue save its eyepiece, the device stood still among the buildings. Its range of vision black and white, its auditory comprehension was nonexistent. Still, it saw much and could witness constantly, undeterred by slumber or drowsiness. Late evening, the urban electricity covering the presence of most of the stars, it saw things.

For the time, the stage was vacant, with the grid formation of the walkways connecting to streets absent of car or man. On the bottom corner of its screen there was a stamp of constantly changing numbers, specifying date and time down to the second. Digital imagery, while lacking a diversity of colors, the shots of a moving world were quite detailed. Small wonder crime was seldom an issue there, for many comrades in mechanical arms dotted the various brick buildings, silently standing during the night when so many were asleep. A couple of them even moved around, slowly directing their gaze in a half-circle, watching over even more streets, walkways, and storage facilities. An additional aid was a human guard; who, because of the other security measures, walked a scarce beat.

Despite the measures for succor, there were weaknesses in the network of vigilance. No camera could turn a full 360 degrees, no screen panoramic enough to view all its immediate vicinity simultaneously. No mechanism was flawless in its activity, with periodic shortcomings to video feed, blind-spots in its range of vision. A well-educated local could properly dodge the machines and their watch. Experience with the blind-spots, the timing of the guards, and the weaknesses in the systems; these matters were exploitable by the less than honorable among society and at times to great effect.

So, it was that in the shadow of a blind-spot, between two great rugged brick buildings, between the long gap of time before the next law enforcer arrived for his rounds, there were nefarious folk about. They abounded in euphemism, shunning the overt vices of the street life. No jeans and few visible tattoos, three of them stood in a row. Suits were their uniform, the weather mild enough that additional protection was unnecessary. Each man had a loaded handgun holstered to his side. Two were right-handed, one was left-handed. They were not clean-shaven, each sporting the trendy three-day beard, varying in dark brown or black hues as it dotted the chin and cheeks.

Facing them was one man. Face unseen, body size normal, head bent downwards at the glistening paved ground. He was not as properly dressed as the trio; his attire was normal for a casual appearance. Had he not wanted to be found, they may have failed to find him in that late hour. It had been raining for most of the day, clearing up by sunset and thus adding some coolness to the climate. All four men were from the same location, the same general region far beyond the borders of the free world. At that moment all four men were silent in the alleyway starving for a good camera.

A moment from the silence passed and at once all three of the suited men drew forth their handguns and aimed them at their mysterious guest. Each weapon made the clicking noise that sounded its readiness for usage, barrels pointed no more than fifteen feet head of them at the tacit figure. A wry smile came across the face of the man who raised his head up, and thus had his dark eyes level to the three guns held by outstretched arms.

The man knew none of them personally, but he knew each suited individual by name and appearance. Such information was given to him by a third party, a figure similar to those with the weapons drawn yet different in his motives. The thuggish triumvirate and their unwanted guest were different, yet similar. Dark hair and dark eyes, accents identical enough to confuse outsiders, and names structured in their lettering as to betray a common origin. Yet there was a longstanding contempt, a hatred that transcended time and was drenched in heritage. They spoke similar tongues, had similar faces, and prayed in similar churches yet were they different, so very different, in each other's eyes.

The quiet night was broken by the loud chatter of the firearms, the clips being emptied of their loads by the three men in the direction of the stranger. The bright muzzle flashes signaled the origins of the shots, aiding the vibrations of sound waves in exposing the site of their volleys to any potential witness. Indeed, had this episode of violence been set closer to the apartments and homes elsewhere in the southeast, phone calls would have overwhelmed switchboards at the nearest police stations. As it were, few heard the loud noises; yet another benefit courtesy the setting of the malicious meeting.

Sound and flash halted, the last of the casings flying out the sides of the three weapons. Yet there he was, still standing, still unharmed, and still with the wry smile. Save the occasional blinking as the bullets sped towards him, his position remained unchanged. The carefully aimed and delivered projectiles lay all around him, having the whizzing straightforward journey directed away from their intended target.

Eyes widened, hearts pulsed, sweat began to bead, and confusion consumed. Knowing nothing better, all three men desperately went for their second clips. Slamming the payloads into the body of the guns, the three repeated their previous action, filling the air with more directed lead and ear-splitting noise. Again, the bullets whizzed in straight lines towards the stranger only to suddenly veer off course and puncture the ground. Again, the sounds and flashes halted, the man still standing and his company frightened.

"Do you want to try again?" he asked them, shadows obscuring the fullest view of his face. Only that smile, that wry smile, purely visible.

Too afraid to think yet not afraid enough to flee, the three men reached for their third clips, the last of their supply. As they did so, the figure walked towards them, formally, as though in procession, his dark clothes seeming to blend with the vesper air. No passion, no intensity, simply a cool look at the professional thugs. Snapping the clips into place the three men began to fire, the bullets falling to either side of the approaching man like rose petals tossed at a wedding. They backtracked as they continued to fire, each shot becoming a miss even as the distance between the two parties narrowed to a mere couple of feet.

Now in the main roadway, the place where trucks descended, were loaded, and then departed, the three men were sweating lines of perspiration, their hearts pumping all the faster. The firing continued with the same result. Then the man raised his left hand and each firearm discontinued its action. Each of the trio wanted to run, they wanted to turn and race away. But no, not now.

"Your carnal weapons will not work against me," said the man in a whispery voice, a British edge to his words. Each man breathed hard, each brow glistening with sweat. None of them could move. This stance was not of bravery nor blinding fear. The man did not let them move. Each joint ready to bend and each muscle ready to stretch remained stagnant. His smile became sinister as he enacted the next stage of his late evening performance.

III.

    Good thing she had ample time to arrive at the meetup. The Red Line was on delay; a frequent occurrence. Being the first of the metro lines completed decades back only gave it the honor of having more fundamental structural problems. Still, even this train eventually showed up and made up for its tardy arrival by being fast, which reminded the passengers why they opted out of automobile travel. Brittany had not owned a motor vehicle since college, when enrollment led her to a more natural desolate space. However, given the standards of her occupation, her abilities behind the wheel were well honed and tested.

    As the train slowed to a stop at DuPont Circle, Brittany rose from her window seat and walked towards the doors even before the train was entirely halted. After a few moments, the double doors pulled back to open, allowing her and several others to step on the platform while people waited on either side of them to enter. Checking her phone, her only time piece, she was not tempted to outpace the lengthy escalator at the DuPont exit. The great opening to the surface was beautiful during the day, a perfect shot of the sky with stone-carved quotes along the sides. However, at night all was darkened to a blur.

At least the music was present. As the moving stairs lifted Brittany towards the surface, brass instruments met drums in a jazzy message of welcome. The upbeat notes and the swinging melody made a good appetizer for the preplanned meeting place. As she stepped off the escalator, she got the full view of the enthusiasm: brass players moving their bodies along with the tune, swaying their trombones and trumpets with the beat, the drummers shaking their heads up and down while feeling the sound waves. A small number of folk stood around, nodding with the beats and applauding the music. Donations came in the form of green bills dropped into open instrument cases.

Amidst the glowing street lights and neon, the roving taxis and the chattering people going to and fro, Brittany walked a couple of blocks. She had been to the place previously, the windows showing a dark interior punctuated by perpetually changing colors. A heavy-set black man stood by the door. Brittany took out her driver's license, which the bouncer took and stared at for a few moments before handing it back. Giving a nod, he let her join the loud music, alcohol, and dancing within. A local band was playing at the far end of the open space, comprised of two guitar players, a drummer with the usual kit, a lead singer, and one fellow who kept beating the wooden box he was seated on.

It was hard to see in the crowded space, the noise of the band making a challenge of picking up auditory cues. Brittany approached the main counter, manned by four bartenders of varying age, size, and gender. They had a recurring theme, however, with the black clothes, tattoos and unconventional hair styles. Amid the musical layer of noise, Brittany successfully placed an order for a beer and waited. She was a little early. She handed the bartender, a skinny gal with shoulder-length purple hair, one of her credit cards to open the tab. Soon after, the bartender gave her the order, a medium-sized glass full of fermented concoction. It was a golden brown shade with a foamy crown.

Sipping the contents as she looked around, Brittany wondered if he would show up. Loud laughter erupted in the background. At first Brittany thought it was something of concern, but soon it died down and things continued in their loud, dark habit. Another sip and she wondered, checking her phone once more to see if there was a cancellation message. Nothing. It might have been a ruse; on past dates with men she met online they had failed to appear. One time, Brittany and a fellow were to meet at a cafe inside a bookstore. She waited and waited, ordering three dark coffees with cream before giving up. Later, she learned that he misread their online correspondence and assumed they were meeting outside of the bookstore rather than inside at the coffee house. One strike and he was out.

As she sipped again, detailing in her mind the past failures, she gazed outside the big window at the front. There the hefty fellow was checking someone's identification card. The man had a three-day beard, well rounded jaw, and a dark complexion overall. After studying him she realized it was her date. Arising from the counter, she ventured towards the entrance as he entered. A simple "Hey" and a smile alerted him to the presence of the woman he met online. He responded with a simple "Hi," stretching out his hand to shake hers; she awkwardly shook his hand and they both made their way to the counter.

"How are you doing?"

"Fine, am I late?"

"Not at all. I was early."

"Okay," he said, nervously smiling. To make him feel better, she smiled back. That way he would know he was not that out of line.

"So, um, did you get here alright?"

"Oh yes. Some delays on the Red Line, but what else is new?" he said with laughter, which she reciprocated. He glanced to the bartender and ordered a different beer, turning in his card for his tab.

"Nothing really. You from here?"

"Is anyone?"

"Yeah, good point," replied Brittany with a laugh. "So where you from?"

"Upstate New York."

"Not New York City?"

"Nope."

"Ever been there?" asked Brittany, still exploring the possible topics for first date conversation. He got his drink and started imbibing between statements.

"A couple times. It's okay," he said with a smile.

It was similar banter for the first beers. The local band played their last song and generic background tunes were piped in to keep the party going. Brittany and her company watched the members unplug the guitars, pack the drums, and get the aid of a tech person to properly place the microphones where they were meant to be.

When they were each on their second beer, they talked some more about where they were from, what brought them to DC. Work was the answer for him. He was an analyst for some consulting firm. Brittany asked what a consulting firm did exactly, which prompted a lengthy and meaningless mission statement. Realizing this, the date was keen enough to laugh afterwards.

Some more people entered, including some younger females. They were probably college students, maybe seniors assuming their IDs were not forged. Brittany was adept at recognizing the little nuances between real and faked ones. That, before reaching age 21, she had an effectively fabricated one adding three years to her then teenaged life probably helped in her knowledge. Practice makes perfect? Brittany did not talk much about herself. It seemed awkward whenever she brought up the subject; besides, her company seemed most comfortable chatting it up about himself.

"But yeah, parking sucks here."

"It does," she responded with a smile.

"Glad I took the metro."

"Yup."

Another local band was taking the stage. They only had three members, but the lead singer did double duty as vocalist and lead guitarist. The bassist to his left had longer hair than both Brittany and her date.

Another beer for each of them, some idle conversation, and a few songs from the locals. Brittany wondered what time it was, but feared looking less she offend her company, who she noted occasionally looked off at people as they passed by. Maybe it was an innocent reflex to the sense of presence of other people. It looked however, like he did it whenever another woman walked by.

"This band sucks. Can we leave?" he said, causing people near them to turn their heads.

"Okay."

They each got a bartender to get their tab. He did not pay for her drinks. It was three beers each. Given the two people's drinking habits, neither was particularly intoxicated. Just more of a buzz. A small sheet of paper was handed to each of them. For lack of pens, they had to share. She wrote her signature first, then handed the blue pen to her date. Signing in big, swinging form, he handed the check back to the man behind the counter. They left, first him and then her, through the entrance. Outside, they made their way past the bouncer and another hefty

22

fellow who looked to be an assistant to the main enforcer.

As they gathered themselves outdoors, Brittany's phone went off. The smile the man had on his face weakened. Out of the gray purse came the bright phone, made brighter by the contact alert. After she tapped the screen a couple of times with her finger, Brittany saw that it was a coworker. The man looked curious as he saw her read the text message.

"Who is that?" he asked.

"Just a friend," Brittany answered casually, though she could see her date was still skeptical about the pure nature of the message. Taking an annoyed breath, she walked a few steps to be closer to the date. She showed him the message. The photo of a young woman was next to the text, which simply read "How's it going?"

"Oh, sorry. Bad experiences," said the man with a smile and a faint laugh as Brittany looked down at the phone and texted a reply.

"I am with someone right now," she sent back, adding an immediate second message of, "is it work-related?"

"Yes."

"Do I need to come in?"

"Not yet."

"Keep me posted," she said out loud as she texted it and sent it off, her company pacing around outside a couple feet away.

"Ok!" texted the friend. Adding "Is he cute?"

"STFU"

"Ok bye!"

The phone was put back into the purse and Brittany looked up, making amends by smiling at the less than patient man before her. "Sorry, work stuff."

"It happens."

"A lot."

"So," he began to say, drawing out the word some.

"So?"

"So where to next? Another bar, your place, my place?"

"Your place."

"Alright."

The two walked side-by-side to DuPont Circle metro, people walking around them, past them, near them, and away from them. They saw the lights from the bars, the shops, and the streets, the cars going by, and finally that jazz band. They were still at it, though it seemed they had fewer players and fewer listeners than before. Brittany and her date went down the long escalator and waited for about ten minutes before the next Red Line came. More idle chatter, this time with no alcoholic sips between comments.

Because of the hour of night, they had their choice of seats. Both went for the window-side seat at the front, but Brittany's date let her have it when he realized that she wanted it. Two stops later and he rose from his aisle-side seat, Brittany following suit. "You are not far from me."

"That's good."

The doors opened and the two went towards the exit; each using, as with past trips, their plastic metro card to exit the facility. He was low on his amount. "You are low," observed Brittany.

"Yeah, I'll deal with that soon."

"Are we almost there?"

"Yes, just about."

"Apartment?"

"Yup."

"Same here."

Brittany's date also lived in the Northwest, his apartment building looking about the same as hers. It was a similar basic cubic model, nothing too extravagant but more beautiful than the typical dormitory. He was on the third floor, a reddish painted doorway with brass golden numbers nailed to the front. The door unlocked, the man entered first, turning on a light near the entrance that brought everything into view.

It was not particularly tidy, with a laundry basket full of crumpled, dirty clothes off in the corner. The sink had a dozen or more different dishes waiting for a cleansing, as well as a few glasses. A black trash bag two thirds full of stuff was off in the corner by the entertainment system, a flat screen television with DVD player and two medium-sized speakers attached to the monitor. The space appeared larger than Brittany's living room, though it could not have been by more than a few feet in width and length.

"Sorry for the mess, I wasn't expecting guests," said the man, who took off his jacket and threw it onto the nearest furniture. After Brittany took off her jacket, she handed it to him and he tossed it upon the same piece. "Let me just get a couple things out of the way," he said as he grabbed hold of the basket. "There's beer in the fridge."

Brittany looked around. It was not too bad a place. A few posters of notable bands and musicians were on the wall. No family pictures to be found, but then again, they might have been in his bedroom only. Or maybe he does not have a family. Or maybe he is not particularly close. Brittany could relate. After moving out of her parents' house for college she never moved back. She saw them once every few weeks or so. An only child, there were no siblings to keep in touch with and no nieces or nephews either. Friends had mostly fallen out of touch also, as they all moved on, some even getting married.

He returned to the living room and moved a couple more things, again apologizing for the condition of the space as he exited again. After pacing around a little bit more, she opted to go towards the fridge, opening the door to view the liquid contents. Looking through the bottles, she turned some of the cold thin frames, only to discover that none of her preferred brews were present. The door closed, she walked to the couch and waited for her host to return, which he did about a moment or so later.

"If you want a beer, I have some in the fridge."

"Yeah, you told me."

"So …"

"Yes?"

"You mind if I get one for myself?"

"No, go ahead."

Without hesitation, the man rose from the seat he just took and ventured to the fridge, where he took out the first bottle he touched and, using an opener magnetically placed on the side of the refrigerator, popped the cap off. The first sip seemed to give him some courage, as he asked if he could sit next to her on the couch. Brittany consented. Gradually as they spoke, his right arm made its way around her shoulders. She was aware of it but was in no mood to protest. The topics of conversation were starting to blur together. They were becoming even more irrelevant as lust controlled them both.

"Want to see my bedroom?"

There was a slight pause, perchance a moment of awkwardness at the proposal. The moment was not long. "Sure," she replied.

"You'll love the sights."

"I believe it."

Phone noise erupted.

"I don't believe it."

"I should check that."

"Do you need to?" asked the man, a slight whine to his voice.

"It might be important."

"Oh, fine."

The phone rang again. It was not as loud as it had been outside the bar, because it, along with the purse, remained in the living room on the couch. A clear look of frustration came over him, passing judgment on the woman in his bedroom. Brittany exited the room, feeling much the same way as her date. The noise repeated itself, another message coming. Unzipping the main pocket and then unzipping the next pocket, the dark hole of stuff was lit bright as the device was taken out of the purse. Brittany saw that it was her coworker once more.

The first message read "You should come in," followed quickly by "Sorry!"

Brittany texted back as her date slowly walked out of the bedroom.

"This better be important," she typed then sent.
"It is, 3 dead."
"3?"
"Yes. My plate's full. Can you look into it?"
"Yes."
"Thanks!"
"NP"
"Well?" spoke up the man.
"I am really, really sorry, but I have to go."
"You sure?"
"Yes, work and all that."
"Fine."
"Tomorrow night?"
"Same time?"
"Sure. Yeah."

"Sounds good," said the man as he unlocked his door and opened it for Brittany, who grabbed her jacket and hastily put it on.

"Like I said, I am really sorry about this."

"Its alright. I'll take a cold shower," he said with a smile.

"Bye," she said, kissing him on the cheek as she exited with jacket and purse. The man smiled as

he closed the door. Tomorrow night, he thought.
Tomorrow night.

．．．．．．．

A stream ran by the road in that rustic setting.
Beautiful clear water, flowing smoothly along the
twisted route. It bonded with other blue venules
connecting to veins which connected to major
rivers that connected to the Black Sea and the
Mediterranean. In ancient eras, the Greeks and
the Romans sent armies into places like these,
conquering the world for the cause of civilization.
During the Medieval Era, the Byzantines made
their aged empire last in this land, fending off
invaders through commerce, diplomacy, and war.
Mongolians rode through these parts, dipping
their vast domain into the corners of Eastern
Europe. By the Renaissance, the Turk had
arrived, annexing the territory as they blasted
away the mighty walls of Constantinople. For
centuries they ruled the land, battling assorted
Christian kingdoms. Amongst the conquered
peoples were Tarans and Tayrayans. While not
as numerous nor as known as the Serbs, the
Croats, the Bosnians, or the Albanians, these two
peoples were nonetheless a people subjugated to
the Muslim power's will.
    Many Tarans and Tayrayans dipped their
buckets into this fair stream, known for its
exceptionally beautiful sable-hued peony flowers.
Considered elegant by both peoples, the black
peonies were found in the wild and in the homes

of wealthier families throughout the generations. This stream, like others, was also stained with blood. Blood from numerous battles waged not only between Turk and Christian, but also between Taran and Tayrayan. As the Ottomans took control of the region, the Tarans called for resistance against the infidel imperialists. The Tayrayans, by contrast, sided with the Ottomans, drawing the conclusion that the tide of history was in the Turk's favor.

So the people once brethren and kindred, once bound by marriages and trade, tore themselves apart in the grand conflict of civilizations. Their enmity and violent contempt appeared to only grow with the centuries, transcending any particular era of history as newer conflicts and disputes placed them on opposite wings. During the Second World War, the Tarans aided the German invaders and had a Fascist commander placed as puppet leader of the region; the Tayrayans fought a partisan war while receiving arms from the British and the Americans. When the Iron Curtain descended the Tayrayans embraced the Communist ideology and proceeded to crack down on anti-socialist groups largely comprised of Tarans. They seemed to take turns dominating and massacring each other. By the late twentieth century, each people could claim a register of offenses.

By the peacefully rushing stream, indifferent to the race of any who trod through it, the road curved along a hill. It was paved with markings, albeit faded ones. Seldom used, it had a number of cracks and potholes that made it subpar for a modern road. In some parts, wild grass had even emerged from the wounds. Sounds of nature, the birds, beasts, and bugs, all filled the air that day. Thrilling noise of water, soothing yet active, filled that forested space as a new pair entered the scene.

Huffing and puffing, desperate and frightened, the young boys tumbled into the natural setting. Similar in height and weight, neither having passed the five-foot mark yet, they ran with throbbing chests and fast hearts. Neither face populated by acne, neither chin sprouting a hair, they moved as rapidly as their sore legs could bear them, going up and down the rolling hills that were found by the stream and the road.

There was no particular direction but forward, a meaningless shifting aim that at times felt more arced than linear. Trees and branches, hills and water, bugs and beasts, birds above and dirt below. It was the same, it felt the same, it was as going nowhere and now here were the two boys, to the point of collapse, to the point of fear and beyond, racing against an invisible all powerful force. It had taken so many others, so many they knew and loved, so many they played with, schooled with, and prayed with every Sunday and special holy day of obligation. All was gone in a twinkling.

They stopped at the stream, falling to their hands and knees, coughing and breathing hard. One was crying. Both eventually rolled to their backs in great gasps and throbbing heart, lungs, and legs. Everything was in pain, everything was in terror. Was it possible they were going to be next? They must be next. All the others had gone away, burned or poisoned. It was just them, only them, two lost frightened boys. Who could they turn to? Strangers were of no help; it was strangers who did this to them.

Breath being caught, recovery being noted, the sun was hindered that morning by its placement in the sky and the bushiness of the branches. Green leaves and brownish arms blocked most of the beams, making even that rising morn a bleak perdition. The other one was crying, filled with the hopelessness of their lot. Others had tried, they all failed. There was no escape, no treatment, no cure, and no way to survive. All these thoughts of melancholy cascaded over the two boys.

"What do we do? What do we do?" said one to the other, exasperated in his dolorous temperament, shouting in the wild. "What are we going to do?"

The other could not answer; he was equally ignorant. They started to return to a standing position, looking around to see if there was any danger. No predator, neither man nor beast, was around them. They turned and turned, seeing if any were close. No human being was on the road, by the stream, or the forested hills. Only them. The breathing slowed and the calm came. Seconds became minutes, tears decreased, and one of them had an idea.

"I know what to do."

"What?" asked the one who had shouted the previous queries.

"We can do this; we use what we have."

"What?"

"You know, this," he said, pointing to his head. "We both have it, we both use it, and maybe, just maybe something will happen."

"Like what?"

"I don't know! It's better than not trying, I know that."

"Okay, whatever you say."

They stood facing each other, forcing themselves into a strict posture, as though at attention. The mouths stayed closed as their breathing calmed, their heartbeats slowed, and their bodies throbbed less. The boy with the idea raised his right hand, the arm from the shoulder to the elbow touching his side, while from the elbow to the hand it was horizontal and pointed in the direction of the other. While the arm maintained its form, it turned and the hand went from the tips pointing towards the other boy to facing the skies, as though readying to ask a question in class or to do a high five. The other boy did likewise until he was a mirror image of the boy in front of him.

They began to focus, to center themselves first on the individual and then on the other. They concentrated, not sure of what would happen or what they were doing to one another. Their initial glance toward each other became a stare. The stare grew in intensity as the seconds passed, seemingly drawing away all sights and sounds around them, the birds themselves hushing like the stream before the two minds. Lips began to quiver, eye lids began to move rapidly one centimeter up and then down, though not closing to a full blink. The hearts pumped harder, the mouths opened to breathe harder. The energy was as though they were running, sprinting as they had been before. It was becoming painful; it was becoming piercing. Neither halted their pose, neither halted their posture. Neither knew what was going on, if anything. How does one determine the undetermined?

Then in a flash both fell backwards, the sounds of the stream and the forest returned. Each boy was on his bottom on the dirty ground, panting as before. however, something felt different. Something was different. They slowly got up and looked at the stream, wondering if any physical alteration had occurred. Seeing that none had done so, they wondered. They drank from the water, absent of any other potable liquid. They crossed the unimposing waterway, which never rose above their knees, and ventured onto the road.

After walking for a few miles, a random car went by and stopped. The boys took the ride to the city and their pursuers, regardless of their intentions, were unable to track them down that day.

. . . .

Buildings of brick in the Southeast stood in silence as another car appeared. Meeting the driver was a group of about a dozen police officers, a coroner, and a photographer. Also present was a middle-aged night watchman. This was not the first macabre display he had uncovered during his decades-long career. Indeed, a few instances in his evenings the watchman had taken fire from assorted outlaws; however, never had he seen multiple dead arrayed upon the ground, brutally disposed of by an unknown menace.

Flashing red and blue added sporadic visual texture while the yellowish white glow of the street lights provided sight in the eventide. The car keys were turned and the vehicle was off, lights exiting soon after the engine. Stepping out of the driver's side was a well-dressed and dolled-up single woman. The men working around her briefly saw her coming, but then returned to their various tasks. The notable exception was the coroner, a graying man about the age of the security guard. Lab coat distinguishing his profession from the others, he rushed to meet the newly arrived woman.

"My, my you sure look pretty this evening," said the coroner, a native of what his Northern Virginian friends dubbed "Rest Of Virginia."

"Please cut the wisecracks, Mike. What do we have?"

"We just finished taking the photos and we were about to move the three bodies to the morgue. Before we do, I got some preliminary information."

"Sounds good," replied Detective Brittany Johnson of the District of Columbia's Metropolitan Police Department. They walked over to three gurneys, each carrying one of the men discovered on the paved ground. The coroner removed the three sheets covering their bodies down to the lower chest, giving Brittany a perfect view of the head, neck, and shoulders. "So what happened?"

"The watchman was doing his usual rounds and found them over there," said Michael, pointing to the corner of one of the brick warehouses. "I will know more about the cause of death when I get them back to base, so to speak."

"Did they have ID?"

"Yes, they did. Also a policeman recognized two of them. Apparently, they are muscle for a hood named Viktor Makovnor."

"The Tayrayan mobster?"

"Yes, that one."

"Do you think it was a hit?"

"I doubt it. The side arms we collected where the three men were found didn't have any silencers attached."

"An ambush?"

"The evidence does not seem to say that."

"What do you mean?"

"I will probably know more when I do the autopsies, but it does not appear that they were surprised by their killer. And that's not the only weird part. May I show you the scene?"

"Definitely."

"Then let me show you, pretty lady," smiled Michael, who placed the sheets back over the faces of the three dead men. Brittany and the coroner walked over to where the bodies were found. Meanwhile, a few of the officers departed the sight, being needed elsewhere. Brittany and Michael stopped before the scene of the crime.

"So what happened?"

"Very strange. Basically, the three men were found here. All three in a row on their backs. They each had basic handguns, no silencers."

"Okay," said Brittany, attending to what Michael was saying but also looking around with her own ideas. She sought evidence pointing to the series of potential events, studying each little detail between the warehouses.

"We found a sizable number of bullet casings here," said Michael as he moved into the alleyway, "and here."

"So they fired at the killer or killers at fairly close range."

"That's where it gets weird," said Michael. "If they did, they sure were horrible shots. There are no traces of blood or skin tissue or even ripped clothing."

"Excuse me?"

"I'll get the lab to double check, but the bullets collected didn't appear to be aimed at the direction of a person. They impacted on the pavement."

"Okay," said Brittany with an equally perplexed expression, made more expressive because of the makeup she wore for her date. "Why would they shoot into the ground when the killer or killers was right in front of them?"

"You got me."

"Let me know what you find out from the autopsies. They might have been drugged or something," said Brittany as they both exited the alleyway.

"Yes ma'am."

"I'll see what the lab says about the bullets. It's possible you missed something."

"Maybe."

"Or maybe that could help," said Brittany, directing her vision to the still operational camera device perched upon the brick warehouse. She summoned one of the other police who was still on sight. "Has anyone seen about getting the footage from that camera?"

"No detective, I don't think so."

"Then I will look into that."

Over the next several minutes each of the small crowd dispersed to their respective places. The coroner went with the bodies to the morgue, the police went to either their station or another call on the blotter, and the watchman went to his bed when his replacement arrived. Brittany returned to her apartment and did some work on the new case, learning the name of the company who owned the warehouse and getting, even at that late hour, permission to view the security footage. She planned to look into the matter more the following day, going to bed with some frustration over the interruption of the pleasures of her personal life.

Her date sent a couple of messages to make sure they would meet tomorrow evening. She agreed. He then sent an emoticon. As she drifted to sleep, a light rain dropped thin lines of water on her bedroom window, bare of any object other than the curtains. Working on the weekend was not a foreign idea for Brittany, but it was not welcomed. Coupling this with the rest of her caseload, Friday was looking to be too brief a shift to finish it all.

IV.

    They did everything right. Or at least, they thought they did. It was hard to tell for Willard and Abby Gaskins. The two spouses were from different parts of the country, having both moved to the Washington, DC area after college. He was from the Midwest, she was from the South. He had gotten a job with the State Department; she worked as a business contractor with the federal government. They were introduced by mutual acquaintances and months later were engaged. After the wedding, they spent a few years in different apartments before they found a suburban dwelling across the river in Alexandria.

    It was a nice house in a nice neighborhood, found within walking distance of an elementary school. This was sensible as the two already had one child when they moved to the house and another a year later. Now in their late thirties, their elder child was enrolled at that very elementary school and was, as is typical of youngsters, oblivious to the pressing problems of the parents. The younger was in preschool and in a couple of hours one of them was going to drive to the church-run establishment and pick him up.

They were both in the dining room, Abby seated at the ovular table while Will paced back and forth. Around them were photos of the kids, the entire immediate family, grandparents, and some cousins. Each was framed and two were hung on the walls while the rest leaned, standing atop a few furniture pieces. The table base was on a carpet, which covered the whole floor and extended into the adjacent living room. The stairs leading to the second floor and the hallway upstairs were likewise carpeted. It looked so beautiful and properly domestic, each room filled with enough items to be livable, personal effects that may have lacked the proper elegance but held personal sway. Picturesque could describe the house's interior, a dream nearing its waking point.

The couple had borrowed quite a bit to get the place, the total being several thousand above their originally planned maximum. It was a gamble. Even with the healthy government salary of Will, they were going to be basically living paycheck to paycheck. This was especially the situation once Abby quit her occupation to look after the children. Will asked for and got a raise, which took effect the following year. They cut back on certain things, from presents for the children to alcohol for themselves, little things here and there to meet the interest-laden payments.

Yet even these various measures were becoming too much. A muddied economy and a troublesome market was leading to a greater financial tightening. The Gaskins family struggled to cut more from their budget and also to delay payments. Things were coming to a head. By now holding three weeks' worth of vacation time, Will asked for a couple days off to resolve the mess. As he and Abby hammered out their finances, it was realized that they were going to lose. Soon after, the bank called and arranged a meeting. A representative was coming that morning. No hope, no joy, and no relief. The Gaskins' knew exactly what was coming with the bank employee.

Talk was sparse while they waited in the dining room. It was a little after nine in the morning, the bank having only opened a few minutes ago. Dread kept them from doing anything else and limited their breakfast intake. With both kids at their respective schools, nothing on the agenda remained between their moment in time and the visit from the bank. Will ceased his pacing, moving towards the big window with its drapes pulled to the sides. Picturesque, he thought, glancing at the well-paved street laden with decent-looking homes on either side. The green lawns, the occasional picketed fence, the driveways with minivans and sports cars. It was their notion of that much heralded and much envisioned American Dream, of having made it in that world.

"He's here," said Will stoically, peering out the window to see a dark compact pull up to the curb and stop in front of their house. Silently Abby got up from the dinner table and joined her husband by the window to see a bespectacled man wearing a gray suit and red tie get out of the driver's side. The car door slammed with a dull thud, the bank representative walking in front of his halted vehicle before opening the passenger side door to get his briefcase. Closing that door with a deep note, he made his way to the lightly-hued walkway that led to the main entrance of the Gaskins residence. Without further prompt, the two walked to the front door, knowing that the man was about to request entrance. As the pounding began, Will shouted a "just a moment" and unlatched the lock, pulling the door inwards to behold a man colored by the glass of the screen door.

"Mr. Willard Riley Gaskins?"

"Yes. That's me."

"I am Mr. Samuel Wanstead with the bank. I believe we have an appointment today," responded the man, who lacked significant height or weight. Such dreadful news to come from so minute a creature.

"Yes. Of course," said Will, pushing the screen door open and holding it for the bank representative, who expressed his minor gratitude at the gesture.

"Would you like anything to drink?" asked Abby.

"No, thank you. This should not take long," responded Wanstead, who was directed to sit at the dining table along with Will and Abby. As they each pushed their seats to the preferred placing on the carpeted floor, the couple noticed that Wanstead appeared to share their level of discomfort. "Before I start, I want you to know that I do not take any joy in visits like these. I wanted you to know that."

"Okay."

"Anyway, I knew you wanted this to be over with quickly, which is why I did what I could to come as soon my day began."

"Thank you."

"I will cut to the finish. You cannot afford to live here anymore, unless you can pay off the rest of the debt plus interest by Monday."

There was silence among the couple. They looked at Wanstead, then they looked at another, and finally back to Wanstead.

"Monday?" asked Abby.

"I am afraid so, Mrs. Gaskins."

Will took a hard exhale. He and his wife both knew the total amount in advance of the meeting. Sliding his fingers through his hair, he did what he could to understand the situation. "So they won't extend it, then?"

"I am sorry, no."

"Why not?" interjected Abby, as though such a question might change the course of history.

"The board concluded that your credit was not good enough," explained Wanstead. "You are too much of a risk, I am afraid."

"So is there any other option?"

"I am sorry, but no. You must pay the $14,000 by close of business on Monday. And it must be by check or cash, not credit," replied Wanstead.

Abby and Will returned to silence, they returned to looking at each other and in sorrow looked back at the bank representative. They wanted to ask again, they wanted to see if the answer was going to change. They wanted to shout, to scream at the little bank employee and demand an extension. To what purpose? None. They kept struggling, the two of them, to figure what was to come next. Samuel was aware of their internal struggles regarding the news he was tasked to bring.

"Given your situation, I think it would be best if I leave now," said Wanstead as he got up from the table, prompting the Gaskins' to rise also. "I will leave some information about how the foreclosure is going to work and the timetable for your removal from the property," he continued, taking a folder with various papers and pamphlets explaining the complicated process of removing the Gaskins family from suburbia.

"Thank you for the information, Mr. Wanstead," said Will, who forced himself to shake the hand of the bank representative.

"No problem, Mr. Gaskins," he said as the couple escorted him to the front door. "And I am very sorry about what is happening."

The two nodded as Wanstead exited the house and made his way down the walkway, being watched by one person standing on the sidewalk. The door closed and still unlocked, Abby buried her face into the chest of Will, who embraced her with one arm around her back and the other on the back of her head. Will squinted as though in piercing physical pain and then looked around the interior visible from his stance.

Samuel continued down the walkway, briefcase handle grasped by his left hand, shaking his head at the appointment. It was not a pleasant meeting. He remembered these types of sit-downs being very common years earlier during the Great Recession. In those days, it seemed all he did was go to houses and ruin peoples' lives. He looked to his left side briefly, just checking to see if anyone was walking his way in the neighborhood. It was then that he noticed a figure approaching. His glance, meant to be fleeting, held and stopped his walking as the stranger was clearly making eye contact.

   "Good morning," said the stranger, whose average height made him stand a couple inches higher than Wanstead.

   "Good morning, um, can I help you?"

   "Maybe I can help you."

   "Not sure I understand."

   "Well, I am just fleshing out this matter a bit myself," replied the stranger, wearing blue jeans, sneakers, and a hoodie jacket with the hood resting on his upper back. "You work for the bank, correct?"

   "A bank, that is."

   "So you were on business at that house, right?" asked the stranger as he looked at the house, where from their position outside they could faintly make out the Gaskins' talking in misery about the brief meeting. They were seated, shuffling through the papers that Wanstead had left.

   "I am sorry stranger, but that is privileged information," said Wanstead, opening the passenger side door and placing his briefcase on the seat.

"It was not a pleasant meeting, was it?"

"Excuse me?"

"Your meeting with the family there," said the stranger, again looking at the dining room window and seeing the couple in their distress. "You gave them bad news. News that you did not want them to have."

"Well, if you need to know, yes. Yes, it was bad news," responded Wanstead. "They will be losing the house."

"How come?"

"That is confidential."

"What do they owe you?"

"That is confidential."

"Can someone else pay it?"

Wanstead laughed some. The jeans and hoodie did not bring to him any image of wealth. The clean-shaven man looked even younger without a beard. Negative perceptions about the lad abounded in his mind. "Why yes, of course if someone steps forward and pays it, then they can keep their house."

"How much?"

"You stepping up to the plate, batter?"

"How much?"

Wanstead paused for a moment of drama and then let the stranger know the total. "Fourteen thousand dollars. And it needs to come to the bank by five o'clock PM on Monday. That's probably more than you make in a year."

Wanstead was done talking with the optimistic soul. It was not a personal offense, but rather a casualty of his occupation. Samuel had seen how overconfidence poisoned people who came to his bank. They were the ones who took out loans and mortgages they could never pay back all on a whim. His job was drear because of people like that, whose number always came up. He walked in front of his vehicle turning his sight away from the stranger. As he pulled open the door, he turned rightward to see the young man, who to his surprise was standing only a couple of feet away.

"Will this cover it?" he asked, handing Wanstead a bundle of $100 bills. "Go ahead and count them." Surprised, Wanstead did just that, taking out a counting machine that he had in the glove compartment. A minute later he confirmed that the amount was the exact amount necessary and no forgeries were among them. "Unbelievable. How did you know to have that much available?"

"Sow to yourselves in righteousness, reap in mercy; break up your fallow ground: for it is time to seek the Lord, till he come and rain righteousness upon you."

"That's from the Bible, right?"

"Hosea 10:12."

"Thought so."

"I think you should tell them first before going back to the office."

"By all means," said Wanstead. "They will be thrilled to meet you."

"They do not need to meet me."

"You sure?"

"So when you give to the needy, do not announce it with trumpets, as the hypocrites do in the synagogues and on the streets, to be honored by others," quoted the stranger with a wry smile. "But when you give to the needy, do not let your left hand know what your right hand is doing, so that your giving may be in secret. Then your Father, who sees what is done in secret, will reward you."

"Fair enough, can't argue with that. Take care," said Wanstead, who earnestly shook the hand of the stranger.

"Go in peace," replied the stranger, who walked away from the house as Wanstead rushed back up the walkway and knocked on the door. The stranger continued down the sidewalk, looking back once to see the soundless moving images of the dining room. There, an excited banker informed the home owners that their debt had been paid by a stranger. The news brought expressions of confusion, then joy from the couple. Such was the lifted burden that the Gaskins couple nearly forgot to pick up their youngest from preschool.

. . . .

Brittany had a quick step as she walked towards the entrance of the building for the Eighth District of Metro PD. She was not running late, but still felt an obligation to get where she needed to be as quickly as possible. It was a common mentality for people in that realm, speeding through red lights or darting across busy streets because of a gap in traffic. In front of her was a wall and doors made of glass, with black trim outlining each large pane. Up a few steps with an ignored railing and she went for the door, which was opened as a couple of people, including one released on bail, exited the facility.

The noisy, crowded place had a diverse amassing of folk inhabiting its surging interior. Obscured by the occasional private office or medium height cubicle, beat cops and detectives, lawyers and arrestees, suspects and witnesses, those with handcuffs and those in handcuffs, shared the space. Televisions and computers projected bright high definition screens at various places, with the former tuned to local and national news stations.

"Hey!" said Detective Tracy Ramirez, whose cubicle was across from Johnson's. Ramirez had shoulder-length black hair put into a pony tail, a medium build, and could outrun anyone in the precinct. She wore glasses when reading and at no other time. Tracy joined the force at the same time Brittany did and they endured the training and the classes simultaneously. She was the one who bothered her during the date night and was one of the few not outranking Johnson who did so with impunity.

"Hey," replied Brittany as she maneuvered over to her computer and pushed a button so as to begin the process of loading the system.

"Sorry about the interruptions last night."

"No big deal," said Brittany. "And to answer your question, yes, he is kind of cute. Not really big on much else."

"Does he want a second date?"

"Don't they always?"

"Well that's something, I guess," responded Tracy, providing the last comment before the two were distracted by a small group of older individuals leaving their superior's office. Mostly male and mostly gray haired, their journey was a serious one. Each of them had an ethnic look and even with modern American clothing appeared to have a foreign feel about their walk and demeanor as they passed by the cubicles.

"Who are they?"

"Representatives from the Taran and Tayrayan immigrant communities."

"Oh no, this isn't about my case is it?"

"It's been on the news cycle all morning," said Ramirez, who directed Brittany to the nearest television and turned up the volume. "I think it's about to come up yet again. You know how it is, beat a story to death."

Tracy and Brittany both looked at the high definition screen, showing the head shot of a talking broadcast news anchor. She was a regular and both women could identify her by name, having listened to her narration since teenage years. Keeping focus on the camera, a teleprompter off screen directing her words, they caught the anchor at the tail end of another story that she was covering before the one that interested them.

"Russian and American scientists are expected to release a joint statement in the coming weeks regarding the mysterious Siberian explosion … and in local news, last night three men were found murdered outside a warehouse complex in Southeast DC. Not much is known at the present time regarding the victims or the cause of death, but they are believed to have been executed possibly as a vendetta killing over a centuries-old conflict between two Eastern European ethnic groups. The three men, all of whom were Tayrayan …"

"We had that place sealed off," said Brittany with annoyance as the anchor lady continued her laconic descriptions. "How do they learn these things?"

"Well, we never did find that missing radio months back," quipped Tracy. "Oh by the way, Mike told me that he needed to see you asap. It's about the case."

"Okay, thanks."

. . . .

It was a high-end location. Sidewalks were crowded with pedestrians while streets choked with cars. The edifices on this stretch of Connecticut Avenue Northwest were top quality. Suites and hotels for those coming in from all over the world dominated the blocks, each with their own touch of luxury. Suits were the typical attire for men as dresses and pantsuits were for the women. Business casual was an acceptable compromise and plenty donned service economy uniforms. Tourists of all ages came in jeans and shorts, their children wearing shirts of the most popular cartoon characters and action heroes.

The Magna Colonial Hotel and Residence fit well with these places. The twenty-story building stretched half a city block, flanked on either side by highly rated restaurants. It traced its lineage to the nineteenth century, with its many rooms once used to house Union soldiers both healthy and wounded. Since then it had been renovated and expanded three times. Minor alterations, like the addition of top notch climate control and improved cable, followed as well during the past few decades. Magna Colonial owners prided themselves on fusing tradition and progress into their business.

Its exterior was predominately white, porous with rectangular windows offering a perfect view of the major street below as well as other towering buildings nearby. A wide red carpet adorned the main entrance and led to an interior with carpeted floors of various hues. On the ground floor, one found marble and elegance, as well as several large rooms used for various gatherings ranging from political meetings to academic conferences. It also had the usual hotel qualities: bellhops and luggage carriers, valets and janitors; a counter for check-in and check-out, artificial fountains and well-trimmed plants.

A couple of days ago a person checked in. Clean shaven and fairly young, he traveled alone. He kept to himself, having his meals delivered to his room. Paying with cash, he secured for an undetermined time a suite that had a king-sized bed, a walk-in closet, and full bathroom. He bore with him only a single suitcase of clothing and toiletries. His conversation with the help was genteel but minimal, offering no more words than mandated by good manners. Oftentimes the "Please Do Not Disturb" sign was placed on his door knob and some passerby hotel employees swore they heard him talking loudly to himself. Then again, peculiar people had visited their hotel in the past. As far as the staff was concerned, so long as his menacing was restricted to himself, no problem existed.

The man also went about town, leaving his suite for long hours each morning and afternoon and sometimes late evening. There appeared no true pattern for his going out and coming in save that he ate all three square meals at the hotel. He ordered just about anything, from surf to turf, soup to salad, and always left a near empty set of dishes. He also gave the deliverer a tip that was double the total price. Merely an eccentric one-percenter, concluded many on the staff. A rich boy who probably inherited an ample sum of money courtesy the death of a well-heeled relative. Probably never worked an honest day's labor, concluded others. Speculation was kept to a whisper level, as were so many talks amongst the help about their customers.

After a modest breakfast that morning, the man exited his suite on the top floor and via the elevator descended down to the streets. Sporting a light long-sleeved shirt, jeans, and black sneakers, he went into the metropolis. Apparently meandering, possibly searching. He talked with some people, including one figure that he had talked to the day he arrived. Their discourse was important and will hopefully lead to a meeting soon.

Going through the District of Columbia was like traveling the world, with the cosmopolitan nature of the capital apparent at every turn; Indian cab drivers, African-American crossing-guards, Latino street cleaners, kufiyah-wearing Arabs, turban-wearing Sikhs, several languages spoken in person and over the phone by passing pedestrians. There were hijab-wearing Muslim women, Catholic and Episcopal priests with Roman collars, hoodie-wearing youths of several races, and wrinkled veterans with caps bearing their respective theatres of war along with the occasional downtrodden beggar asking for aid along the sidewalk, and business folk of various shades all waiting for their meal orders outside a colorful fleet of food trucks. Young and old sitting in the parks named for historical figures, metro stops occupied by singers and guitar players attempting to earn small change for their musical talents. A vast multitude of nations all in one space.

He returned to the Magna Colonial in time for lunch. Tired by his travels he sat upon his bed and picked up the phone to order whatever he pleased. A half hour later, the knock on the door alerted him to the arrival of his meal. Opening the door and confirming the accuracy of the meal, he gave a wry smile and handed the hotel employee the usual doubling of the actual amount. Exchange concluded, the door was closed, but not before he hung the sign on the knob. Lunch was consumed fairly quickly; he had built a strong appetite during his sojourning around the city. Clearing his plates, he left them outside the door for pickup so no disturbance came while he attempted it.

Double-checking the locking of the door, the stranger ventured over to the walk-in closet. Within the space were his clothes, shoes, and a large bucket with a lid and metal handle. Carrying the bucket with one hand gripping the handle and another holding the bottom, he went to the living room area of the suite. It was the big open chamber for the rented room. The man sat the bucket down near the window opposite the door that opened to the hallway. One of the reasons for his choosing the Magna Colonial was that they had the option of a suite with a room having a wood-paneled floor.

The lid was removed from the bucket, showing its contents. Sand mixed with red ochre, a reddish heavy substance whose origins came from a journey to India. The bucket opened, the man was in good posture. Then he slowly walked to stand beside the bucket. He faced away from it, filled nearly to the brim with the red ochre sand. With a deep breath, he began to walk but in a strange manner, dragging his left foot. The ochre sand shot out of the bucket and followed the dragging left leg. Pouring out of the bucket, the red ochre moved like a serpent as it coursed behind the left leg.

Meanwhile the man entered a bizarre pattern of breathing and heartbeats. His eyelids began to flutter up and down rapidly, his pupils widening as he began to curve the line of red ochre sand trailing behind him. The circle he drew was wide, being at least ten feet around. Initially a perfect geometric shape, rather than complete the circle he directed himself more inward in his trek. Another curved line was created, parallel to the first one, smaller in diameter as it went along its circular journey. Constant eyelid movement, his pupils had widened to the point that his irises were completely covered, giving his eyes a cartoonish appearance of only containing black and white domains.

His breathing intensified as the red ochre sand continued to consistently flow out of the bucket, following the ever lengthening line. A third circle was created with the dragging left foot, then a fourth, and then a fifth. Each one was smaller than the previous, an ever descending spiral arriving to what appeared to be a flat cone. The heart rate was quickening as he began the sixth ring, nearing completion. Eyes completely closed, no more fluttering, but still the pair rapidly moving as he continued his circumambulation. This final circle was only a couple of feet across when he completed it. In a breath and a step, in a beat of the heart and a click of the heels the movement stopped.

All was still. Eyes closed, feet steady, lungs and heart slowed, the red ochre sand halted. The spiral line was complete and at the epicenter was its creator, hands at the side as though in martial attention. His breathing was barely present. Lights were out, the noises of the outside world were becoming dimmer: the honks and motors of cars, the thousands of pairs of feet striking the cement, the bells chiming at nearby New York Avenue Presbyterian Church, the winds cooling the sunny day's temperature. Nature and man, machine and mammal, all was fading away from the senses.

Then the eyes opened with all color and whiteness consumed by a perfect black. The wry smile emerged from the once stoic countenance, the two lips gradually parting to reveal the mouth. No longer did the man see the hotel suite, nor any sign of the District. Rather he was somewhere else, somewhere beyond the scope of most minds to comprehend. The scene was a storm, a nightmarish tempest wherein the whole of the sky and the ground was encased in darkness. Peals of thunder echoed while lines of lightning lit the bleak scenery, dotted with hauntingly solemn ebony trees rooted in a dark field.

Torrential rain followed, resembling spits of fire rather than water, scorching the ground and driving sideways into the targets courtesy a horrid wind that kicked up the black branches of the old trees. Yet the fire created no light, offered no respite from the dark corridors of the mind. The lips fully parted, the man at the center of this nightmare offered a simple query, a question that echoed as a loud whisper, projected across the landscape.

"Do you see me?"

A moment passed and the torrential storm blew away. A few more seconds and all remained silent.

"Do you see me?"

The whisper, filling the void with penetrating sound waves, kicking up the branches as the passing storm had done. Nothing followed.

"Do you see me?"

Again the bluster, the all-encompassing clarion call rippled through the scape of darkness only to produce no response.

"Do you see me?"

So the simple query was delivered over and over, for several minutes it was uttered, and even heard by one not present. The smile was gone, replaced by disappointment. After several minutes, the man felt compelled to cease the anguish. Eyelids fluttered rapidly once more, the pupils returning to their natural borders. The darkness soon faded into diverse shapes and colors, gradually replacing the black with an image, as though the stranger was beholding the development of a photograph from before the digital age. He stood by himself in the suite once more, at the center of the ochre sand. Breathing and heart beats became normal. He walked away from the center of the spiral. On command, the sand reversed its course, going into ever-widening revolutions, the pouring out of the bucket performed in reverse as if time itself was being rewound.

When the last speck of sand returned to the bucket the discarded lid flew upon the top of the container, sealing shut. With a heavy heart the man approached the bucket, took the burdensome entity by its handle and the bottom, and then returned it to the walk-in closet found in the master bedroom. The door closed, he ventured to the bed and wept, gripping the blankets covering the large mattress.

. . . .

It was a cold, bland, morbid place. Colored white and gray and punctuated by the occasional cold multicolored corpse, it was a contemplative place, for it showed the fate of all flesh. Regardless of the wealth, of the status, the reputation, the actions, or the victory, the cold slab was the destiny. The deceased, who made their temporary residence at this place, came because of unknown malicious causes pending discovery. These bodies were not merely the elderly falling to collapse over their tired systems, nor the younger ones departing over an illness or a car accident. Rather these corpses were laid in that room for the extralegal nature of their exit.

"Good morning to you, detective," said Michael as Brittany descended the flight of stairs and pushed open the glass doors.

"Morning, Mike," said Brittany approaching the lab coat-wearing man who stood next to three slabs, each supporting a body. They were nude save the white sheet covering, the eyes and lips closed and the Y-shaped stitching on their chest. Everything had been worked on through the night, a dark hour for such tasks. However, after two decades of performing such work, Michael was desensitized to the process and thought no more of it than any other person thought of cramming late for a college exam.

"Back to normal, I see."

"What do you have for me?" asked Brittany, ignoring the smart comment.

"Strange things."

"What's the problem?"

"Let me show you," said Michael, pulling back the three sheets on the three bodies all the way down to their waists. "Well, take for example cause of death."

"I'm listening."

"Well, I know how their bodies expired. Each of them had severe internal injuries inflicted. The rib cages appear to have broken apart and shards of bone tore up the vital organs."

"So what caused this to happen?"

"I have no idea," replied Michael, giving Brittany an uncharacteristically serious stare.

"Excuse me?"

"I looked for bullet wounds, for knife wounds, for anything. There was nothing. No residue, no imprints of fists or blunt objects," explained Michael as he pointed at the various puncture wounds on the bodies. "From what I can tell, it's almost as though one moment these men were perfectly healthy adults and then, in the next, their bodies started to attack them from within."

"And you have no idea what could have caused this?"

"Well, there is one possibility," began Michael as he drew the sheets back to cover the bodies. "I know of certain artillery payloads, especially during the Second World War, which when exploding could deliver such an intense shockwave that they caused lethal internal injuries to nearby troops."

"So there is an explanation."

"An artillery shell?" responded Michael, stopping his action and staring at Brittany. "I don't recall seeing a crater at that warehouse."

"Good point."

"By the way, that reminds me. This information comes courtesy ballistics. Sure enough, none of the bullets hit anything other than the ground. As I suspected before, none of the bullets had any traces of blood, skin tissue, or even clothing fabric."

"You're right, this is getting strange," said Brittany. "Because you're saying these three men were killed by someone who didn't even touch them yet was never more than a few feet away. Further, when they shot at their killer, rather than hit him they shoot the ground."

Phone noise. It was Brittany's device, which gave off sound and light while in her pants pocket. Taking it out and pushing on the screen to view the message, she saw that it was another coworker. Brittany texted a quick message in response and then put away the device.

"Who dares disturb the sleep of the dead?" asked Michael, lighthearted once again.

"Don, he said he was given a copy of the surveillance footage and that we are both looking into the matter now."

"They don't trust you anymore?"

"Well, there is a lot of politics involved with this one. The press has been claiming some race war or something like that is happening."

"What do you think, Brittany?"

"I think I need to look at the video footage before I draw any more conclusions. Thanks, Mike, as always."

"No problem, detective."

. . . .

Few knew that his first name was Joe. Fewer still knew that his last name was Springfield. He was a fixture on the street, the streets in general for that matter. Typically, he was found in the Northwest, where many of his kind journeyed to benefit from those who are richer and better off. His earthly home was undetermined for such a place was nonexistent. Rather, his regular venue of rest and comfort was wherever his feet brought him and his dignity, what little he retained, bore him.

Joe was a hero. During the First Gulf War he was on the front, in the fast-forward of the advance into Kuwait. He remembered the tall minarets and the desert landscape, the fiery oil fields, and the violent enemy. His unit was in combat for long periods of time, aided by Apache helicopter strikes and stealth bombings. Sometimes the battle memories were blurred by light yellow ground, blue skies, and thick billowing dark gray smoke. Other memories involved firefights, destruction, and casualties. For his part, Joe engaged the Iraqi enemy and suffered minor wounds in return for saving a dozen or so comrades temporarily pinned down by the Republican Guard.

Despite the honors, the memories were strong. Persian Gulf seemed so splendid from afar but up close it was nightmares, dark thoughts, and bloody bodies. Joe struggled with his thoughts, fending off the traumatic episodes with an increasing amount of drugs and alcohol during the 1990s. A time of economic prosperity, Joe worked at an investment firm located across the Potomac in Arlington. Every morning, he navigated the poorly numbered streets and Beltway traffic to work a normal nine-to-five.

Weekends tended to be lost for him. Be it the bars of Ballston, or the dark corners of the DC night life, Joe's self-abuse came as scheduled just about every weekend and some weekday evenings. Things ratcheted up during the holidays. A few times over the years he tried to quit the permissive practices, yet all that appeared to happen as a result were increased withdrawal symptoms. It was those memories, flashbacks, and dreams. If he could only defeat those issues, then the dependency would end.

   The cycles of abuse escalated during the 2000s, fueled by the crushing loss of opportunity following the early recessions. Joe suffered a cut in pay and then in 2007, he lost his job altogether. His superiors, driven by the guilt of firing an army veteran, promised to do what they could to help him find a new occupation. They gave their contact info for references, even directed him to a few job sites that specialized in his abilities. They did what they could, but the Great Recession had other plans.

   More employees were laid off and then the business itself was no more by 2009. Struggling to find work themselves, Joe Springfield's superiors shifted their efforts inward and lost track of him. Having gone months without any income or charity, Joe was evicted from his apartment, already mostly empty due to selling off nearly all his possessions for groceries and substances. When possible, he made money as a day laborer. This allowed him sufficient funds to eat a meal or two a day and, unfortunately, to fuel his habits. He was skipping meals and the damage of the substances was finally taking a grand toll upon his frame. No longer did he have the strength to do most jobs expected of a day laborer, as younger, fitter men lacking his problems supplanted him.

   By 2012 Joe meandered along the District of Columbia with the other destitute, sitting by the street corners and metro stops, begging the throngs of passersby for change. In a typical day, he got enough for one or two meals at the nearest fast food location. In his meandering, he occasionally found a charity to get a free warm meal and even the occasional new used set of clothes. It all felt pointless, as the food inevitably was eaten and the clothes worn away. Winter was the nadir, as there seemed no place to protect him from the near and below freezing temperatures. Nights were often spent at those banks who had in-door ATMs, generic old blankets and trash aiding in the quest for warmth. Even as the drugs and alcohol decreased, the untreated trauma of years past still ripped at his psyche, inhibiting actions that may have aided his recovery.

On a nice sunny day in the busy metropolitan area, Joe was as he had been before. An old empty coffee jar jingled with a small number of coins. People walked by as was the case, ignoring him, awkwardly looking the other way, talking to friends, or looking ever so briefly in pity. A few threw coins and he did his best to thank them verbally. A few more quarters, much desired, thrown in by a young fellow whose friend next to him said within hearing range that the money will only go to drugs. He sat on a small stone ledge that served as a border for the property of some business across the street from a couple of glass buildings of commerce. They reminded him of the facility he used to go to, fully washed and well fashioned, to earn a living despite his vices.

A man walked by and Joe offered his usual half-hearted demoralized plea for change to buy fast food. The clean-shaven man stopped his journey, looking at the poor man with big eyes. It was the first stranger to look Joe in the eyes in years. "Hello there. Can I help you?"

"Change please."

"Where do you want to eat?"

"That place. Just a burger and fries. That's all."

"Okay," said the stranger. "Let's go."

"What?"

"Let us go. I'll pay."

"Okay."

"Do you need help to get up?"

"Some."

The stranger descended to Joe and took him by the hand and the shoulder, gently lifting him up while a few people stared. They turned some heads as they entered the facility, but since many of the customers were working class, the difference in appearance and demeanor was not great. Joe ordered a couple of burgers and some fries as well as a drink. The man with him ordered a medium-sized meal and paid with cash.

A couple minutes later they found a simple booth at the restaurant and after the stranger said grace, they began to eat and talk. Joe was surprised that the man seemed to know much about him. The veteran asked him if he were a psychic, to which the stranger gave a wry smile and assured him that those people were fakes. They stayed a little bit after the completion of their lunch to socialize a bit more.

"It must have been rough, the memories."

"Yes."

"PTSD hits a lot of people. Have you ever sought treatment?"

"Wouldn't know where to go."

"I know a place."

"Where?"

"I will show you."

"Sir, do not take this personally …"

"Yes?"

"I don't, I can't pay for it."

"It's a charity, so no big deal."

"Then let's go."

"I stand at the door and knock. If anyone hears my voice and opens the door, I will come in and eat with that person, and they with me," said the stranger who before a response could be given got up, prompting Joe to rise.

"How far are they?" asked Joe as they exited the restaurant, making way for three people entering for a quick bite.

"Only a few blocks."

"I can't thank you enough."

"No problem."

A few minutes later the two were in front of a modest facility crammed between other various shops and offices. Unprepossessing but beneficial, the place was a shelter run by a religious nonprofit. The stranger held the door open for the veteran, making Joe smile some as he had yet to receive such courtesy in a long time. They approached the counter where a secretary was on the phone. A simple office space with no magazines and only a couple of chairs for sitting, the walls contained a couple of framed posters with inspirational quotes. She then got off the phone and brought her attention to the two men.

"Can I help you?"

"Yes," said the stranger. "My friend here is in need of a bed for a brief time and also one of your experts to treat his recurring PTSD."

"Got it while serving in the Gulf."

"Sure, that can be done. Can you write, sir?"

"Yes, of course," responded Joe, who was given a form and a pen to fill out the data. The effort was quickly accomplished. "Here you go, ma'am."

"Okay, I am going to process this. In the meantime, you can go through that door over there and find a bed to rest if you need to," explained the secretary while outside church bells heralded the new hour.

"Thank you, thank you," said Joe Springfield to the stranger, adding with a laugh "I don't even know your name."

"Not necessary," replied the stranger with a wry smile, waving as the veteran disappeared from his sight with the closing of the door.

As the stranger was alone in the waiting room, a sudden twitch of pain struck him. Gripping his side with his left hand and his eyes shutting tightly in the initial bout of pain, they opened soon after amidst the rush of agony. He gripped the top of the chair with his right hand while his left hand continued to grip his belly. Teeth gritted as the moments slowed and he struggled to maintain his stance.

"Sir? Sir? Are you alright?" he heard from behind. The secretary had returned to the counter just in time to see the episode.

"Yes, I am," said the stranger in grimaced tone. "It will pass, I just need to be, I just need to be alone."

"Are you sure?"

"Yes! I am," replied the stranger. "Is there some place I can be alone?"

"We have a room free that we use for medical exams."

"Please, show me," he responded, following the prompting of the secretary who pointed down another short hallway and noting that it was the door to the left. Nodding, the stranger continued to grip his abdomen as his right hand felt along the wall to steady his advance to the room. Finally there, he opened the door and slammed it shut, his cries of pain being heard down the hall by the secretary. Several minutes later when a doctor finally came at the secretary's request, they found the room empty.

. . . .

Nestled deep in the forests, it was abandoned. The structure was built generations ago with the supplies coming from the surrounding arboreal environment. Long ago, it served as storage space for some local estate, keeping within its walls various harvested crops before being sent to the market along the adjacent worn dirt path. A broken down wagon lay beside the old building, which was a structure about two stories tall and fifty feet long. No one bothered with it anymore, as the estate collapsed during recent political upheavals and other caretakers moved to the cities for better employment.

Much of the wooden beams were rotting away, bent and distorted by the wrecks of time and nature. Several of these elemental building blocks were missing, either eaten away by various lower life forms or stolen by some unknown party. The metals that were part of the building were rusted and needed replacement years ago. Glass panes were shattered or completely missing. Flora grew along much of the exterior and interior, conquering much of the facility once reserved for mankind.

Within the storage space, the flooring was a poor sight. Torn up and worn by past frequent usage and present neglect, the space was a hazard to walk or sit upon thanks to several protruding rusted nails. Grass and vegetation also covered some of the ground, growing through the cracks and fissures within the once solid floor. Lacking any artificial lighting, the interior was dark save the dozens of bright lines of sun. Like the flora, these beams stretched through the formerly impenetrable walls and covered the air, making for a dim yet seeable room once filled with market commodities.

They stood there, the two of them. Young boys with dark hair and dark eyes. Both were old enough to have acne yet lacked it. Each had a pair of jeans on, a T-shirt, and a light jacket. It was autumn and so while cool it was not yet cold. They were on opposite ends of the large interior, the sounds of nature droning outside. The occasional bug flew around them, the occasional vermin scampered nearby. Overturning any of the broken pieces of wood or rusted metal within the facility might well have triggered a mad dash of furry pink-tailed creatures known best for spreading the plague.

"Are you sure about this?" asked one to the other, his thick Slavic accent giving away his present location.

"Yes, yes I am," responded his more confident companion.

"But we've tried before," countered the skeptic, "and nothing happened. Nothing came of it, only pain, the pain you hate so much."

"This will be different," replied the optimist, pacing some around the creaky fractured wooden flooring. "I know it will be."

"How come?"

"Thoughtreal."

The two held their peace after the optimist spoke the word. Like a holy supplication, a word whose very utterance brought sacred devotion. A chant amidst the rotten wooden sanctuary, its parishioners great and small, human and pest, plant and animal. It seemed as though even the noise of bug and bird on the exterior did but for an instant cease their songs out of acknowledgement. Pausing upon the statement, the powerful, powerful statement, the optimist looked wide-eyed at his companion. Initially taken as the whole environment seemed taken, the companion looked down, less inspired by what was delivered verbally to his presence, like mist rising away.

"So?" asked the skeptic. "It's not like we lacked it before when we tried. It was the reason we tried, how we tried. It meant nothing."

"But it's different now," said the other, walking towards his doubtful companion. "We are different now. It has increased. Its power has increased. Have you not seen it for yourself?"

"I have," admitted the skeptic, walking some away from him, yet remaining within the rotting structure. "It is becoming easier to summon things, to create things."

"To destroy things."

"I would not know," said the young man, stopping his walk. "I have yet to use it for such a purpose."

"Yes, yes I know."

"So what then?"

"We are stronger now."

"True."

"Maybe we are strong enough."

"I don't know," said the youth, looking down after speaking. "Maybe."

"I will take a maybe," quickly replied the optimist, "you should also."

"Maybe."

"Yes, maybe," he said with a wry smile. "We have a chance. I refuse to believe any lasting harm will come."

"Are you sure?"

"Of course! Our past failures did not result in anything lasting."

"That was the problem," said the skeptic as the other one walked towards him and put his hand on his shoulder.

"Please, Adi," he said, locking eyes with his companion. After a moment of silence, the skeptic relented with a tacit and repeated nod of the head. "Thank you. Thank you!"

The two positioned themselves in the abandoned locale by walking to different areas of the rough interior. As though preparing for a duel, they ended up about twenty paces apart from each other, standing face-to-face at attention. The breathing of each figure began to slow as they centered themselves. Arms at their sides, all four hands pulsed, repeatedly balling into fists and then returning to a straight fingered pose suitable for clapping. They each began to blink uncontrollably, at first in concert with the balling of the fists and then with greater speed. The rest of their bodies were still.

The world around them began to blur, the browns, grays, greens, and reddish hues of the abandoned building swirling into rays of color. That natural cacophony found in the heart of the woods sounded lower and lower until it was no longer audible. None of the nails or broken beams, nor rays of sun nor crawling plants appeared significant, but rather belonged to the spectrum of shades. The blinking ceased and all four eyes were closed. The hands came to a general stillness as all four were fists. Eyes shut harder, tighter, as the mixing of the various hues became an ever lightless gathering.

The floor flattened perfectly, the walls solidified without window or door. The roof, leaking several rays of sunlight, shut its porous border and became a perfect protector from all outside elements. No more bugs, nor vermin, nothing infesting the space around them. They disappeared as though raptured to glory, forbidden to remain any longer in the once rotten, once forsaken quarters. All was in good order, all was sealed and suffocating. Everything became dark and then dim and then bright.

Harrowing winds rushed around the two teenagers as they stood still, refusing to budge more than a millimeter as the winds got louder and harsher. Unseen at first, the winds became various shades of red, orange, and yellow. They started to hear the sound of screams, the coursing warmth passing about the two youths. Soon the warmth got hotter and hotter, and then the winds of the aforementioned colors became as fire, burning all objects in their midst. They struggled to maintain their closed eyes and stable stature, but both persevered as the fire did no harm to either human.

The entire space was fire, choking smoke peeling away from each tongue. Each wall was a blaze, each corner the source of an intense conflagration. Screams became increasingly human, male and female, young and old. They were returning, they were pulling back the pages of history to an era that defined who they became. Pulling back the environment, the moments, and the great horror as the screams' source became present. Shadowy bodies dancing in pain and fatal misery, their limbs flailing about, their bodies thrown over and around like a tornado. Their differences became more defined, as did the shadows of homes and offices, churches and restaurants. The hills off in the distance, the fallowed farmland north of the village. The streets, cobble, unpaved and paved, the chairs of the outdoor leisurely folk, the vehicles of cart, wagon, and automobile.

Tongues of fire began to recede, pushed away by a beautiful blue sky and a grassy series of hills and valleys. The people stopped their macabre flailing dance and acted as normal, with defined features and characteristics. Other colors appeared, completing the motioned scene of a bygone setting. The two opened their eyes and were standing in the village. Breathing relief, feeling joy, they had returned. Back to the days before, back to the times and places remembered but in dreams. O beautiful world, O lost people.

"We've done it, Adi!" said the optimist. "We've done it!"

"It's beautiful," replied the surprised skeptic. "But is it real?"

"It can be."

The villagers walked by, all unaware of the sudden arrival of the two youths. A young woman smiled at both adolescents as they drew close to one another, nearing an embrace. Despite the cheerful euphoria, the skeptic started to wonder, "What do we do now? We have never gotten this far before."

The optimist's joy turned to concern and then to melancholy. So easily distraught after so effective an achievement. "I do not know ... I guess we do what we did before and will it."

"Just will it?"

"Yes."

"Are you sure?"

"Yes," he said. "We know what we want. Now all we must do is think about it. Will it!"

"Okay, okay," said his doubtful companion, who nevertheless removed such notions from his mind and heart and like his peer began to concentrate on the task.

"Remember them," said the optimist. "Think hard of them ... very hard ... want them ... know they are close ... want them ... want them ... want them ..."

Soon both youths were standing proper, channeling their fullest energies to the people. The village faded away and only the people remained. Various folk based not on fantasy or some crafted fiction but rather the memories of those they knew. Eyes shut harder, fists balled tightly, and the mental forces at work endeavored as never before. Back at twenty paces, the group of figments stood around them, neither talking nor listening, neither running nor walking. Their coloring changed and altered, their solid frames were fading as well. The exhaustion of the two minds was coming, the visions of the villagers was disappearing. Their cries were growing as they tried to keep the images.

Nothing. Nothing once more. Sounds of bugs and birds, buzzing, humming, and chirping, overtook them once more. Broken wooden beams gathered all around them, nailed together generations ago for the benefit of a defunct estate. The old world was gone yet again, the sorrow within them great once more. Eyes opened and postures weakened as the experiment was completed. Around them was the vegetation, the occasional fast-moving mini-beast, and small shadows of avian beings darting through the sun beams. Tears fell from all four eyes as one walked towards the other.

"Never again."

Silence in response.

"Never will we try this again."

More silence, more consent.

. . . .

Brittany ascended the stairs quickly, having done the route countless times since being assigned to that district. Going by the same assortment of folk, the mélange of lawbreakers, law enforcers, and all in between, she made her way back to the collection of cubicles where her desk was located. As she neared her own space, she saw Detective Donald Patrick seated by his computer, a tall, pleasant-looking fellow with a salt-and-pepper mustache. Standing above him was their superior, Commander Ella Patterson. Both directed their gaze towards Brittany as she came.

"I got your message Don. Boss, what brings you here?"

"Politics," she said firmly. "Having just had an hour-long meeting with Taran and Tayrayan community leaders will do that."

"In other words, on this one we need to be careful," added Don before redirecting his view to the screen of his computer. As Brittany joined them, she saw that he had the footage from the warehouse camera on full screen. To the right hand corner were the numbers indicating second, minute, hour, day, month, and year. The overall sight was mute and in shades of black, white, and gray. A modern surveillance device, the image was digital and therefore of high quality detail.

"Now that you are here, Brittany, we can all see this from the onset," said Commander Patterson. "The more eyes the better."

"I had to fast forward through quite a bit before I noticed the three men," said Don while scrolling with the mouse. "I rewound it back some to his point, just before they show up."

"I'm ready if you are," said Brittany, looking intently at the computer screen.

Don left-clicked and the camera's portrait began to move. The silent passage of time initially was noted only by the seconds ticking away in the corner. A still night was documented until about a half minute went by. In the left hand side of the image, the backs of the three suited men were visible as was some of their muzzle flash. Soon after their movements were noted, they became stagnant.

"Has the image paused?"

"No, according to my computer it's still playing."

"Maybe a malfunction with the footage," said Ella.

"No," replied Brittany, pointing to the faint showing of a small rodent scurrying by in the lower right-hand corner. "They are still because they were still. No error."

"Good point."

"Another pair of eyes, right boss?" asked Don rhetorically.

As they kept watching, the scene became macabre. It was not apparent what was causing the sudden expressions of pain and mutilation, but it was apparent that they were being disposed of. Their clothing hid the most gruesome details, yet they saw the bodies convulse in reaction to the damage. Then, after these moments of fracture and rupture, of pain and brutality, the three men fell dead where they were found by the watchman last night. Don paused the video with another left click.

"What do you think?" he asked.

"Not much that we don't already know."

"Yeah, it's still a challenge to see who caused their demise. Much less how."

"Then we keep watching," said Patterson as Don clicked the image and the video resumed. Moments passed when it was just the three bodies, most of their legs obscured by the blind spot of the warehouse side. Their murderer remained absent.

Then it happened. A slow menacing walk, a shadowy image standing over the three corpses. His arrival drew the attention of the three watchers, staring at the corner of the camera footage to hopefully gain a better understanding of the suspect. With slowed movement and a bowed head, he looked at his actions. He stepped a little more out of the alleyway, then took another step closer to the camera.

"Come on, come on," said Don under his breath. "Get closer."

Soon the experienced detective got his wish, as the unknown man took a few more steps, passing the three dead men and going into the main warehouse complex byway. He seemed to ponder, to contemplate his actions. His movement was reserved and concentrated on the murderous deed he performed. With a sense of accomplishment, he lifted his head, but his face was still obscured as he remained centered on the corpses. He took out a phone from his pocket and a piece of paper. Dialing the number, he soon placed the device to his ear and was talking to an unknown party.

Next the turn occurred. He shifted his torso and then the legs followed. A sense of excitement came over Don as the suspect finally turned fully to camera view and was caught with the street lights as an aid. Phone to his ear, his dark eyes were off in another direction as he continued his conversation. The three clearly saw the countenance; its rounded nose, clean shaven cheeks and chin, dark hair and dark eyes. He was probably no older than early thirties, as young as mid-twenties.

"He looks like he's Taran," said Patterson with chagrin.

"Or a Tayrayan; I can never tell them apart," interjected Don.

"Either way, he looks like one of them," said the Commander with a deep breath. "This means the ethnic blood feud theory is alive and well. Not good."

"At least we have a visual."

"True."

As the video continued, the stranger pushed a button and the phone conversation was ended. He slid the device back into his pocket. Rather than flee the scene, he still looked at the three corpses. He even scratched his chin as he peered over them, as curious as he was culpable. These actions perplexed Brittany, Don, and Ella as they continued to watch the silent footage. Then he finally noticed the camera, looking up for contemplation only to be met with the mechanical eye of surveillance. After displaying a small amount of shock, the face became cold and detached. Then a wry smile was given as he kept his glance at the camera. The smile became a vile looking grin and then he disappeared.

"Wait what happened?" asked Brittany as the man who was smiling at the camera vanished from the footage in a second's passing.

"Go back," Patterson ordered Don, who obliged and rewound the video about ten seconds to see the man smiling once more. Left-clicking to press play, the three again saw the smile and again saw the stranger dematerialize.

"Maybe the camera was messed with, damage of some kind."

"Doesn't seem to be the case. Go back and try again, Don," requested Brittany. The third viewing Brittany pointed to the timer at the corner. There was no apparent jump in time from the moment he was there to the moment he disappeared.

"Maybe sabotage?"

"No way," said Brittany. "Neither the watchman nor the police noted any evidence that another party scaled the warehouse to mess with it. And if they did, why leave all that other footage that gives us a clear view of the suspect?"

"This is getting weird," said Don.

"Tell me about it."

"Well, at least we have his face," said Patterson. "Don, get copies of this out to every cop immediately. Brittany, join me at my office and see what we can get from the patrols.

"Yes, boss," said Don and Brittany in near unison.

. . . .

It took the stranger several minutes to recover from the sudden rise of pain in his midsection. At one point the secretary got nervous enough that she asked one of the volunteer doctors to knock on the door. However, by the time the secretary, who left the front of the facility for but a moment, fetched the doctor and they came to the room, the man was gone. Perplexed as they were, the query as to his fate was abandoned as the need to look after the least among them was omnipresent. Eventually, they dismissed the whole episode as a minor curiosity and continued doing God's work.

This mysterious figure, unsuspecting on his surface, was walking on Connecticut Avenue, surveying the shops and the hotels. It was a beautiful day, a little warm but nothing scorching. Since arriving in Washington, the foreigner had to adapt to a sea level land known for its Code Red summers and the fierce backlash of brutal thunderstorms with sheets of rain. This day was better, even as the thick humid air made ambulatory travel less pleasant than if he had been in the mountains.

. . . .

Donald was sending the screengrab image of the suspect to various authorities, including the Federal Bureau of Investigation and Interpol. If this was some out-of-town hired gun or a war criminal from the Balkans, they were going to find out. Meanwhile Brittany and her superior were set up in the commander's office. It offered Ella Patterson more space than the typical detective, though it was nevertheless a modestly dressed cube. One window looked towards the outside world, while a couple of work-related posters dotted the walls. Filing cabinets were pushed to the sides and a generic wooden desk with several drawers, a computer, and photos of children were present. An intercom system that connected to the patrol cars was present, allowing both law enforcers to communicate with those on the beat. For the moment, the intercom was on mute.

"Brittany?"

"Yes, boss?"

"As you know, the three deceased men were hired guns for Viktor Makovnor. This means that this could be bigger than either of us think."

"Yes, boss. You thinking the feds will show up?"

"You know it's inevitable."

"Should that worry me?"

"Depends on who we get."

. . . .

The stranger meandered some as he went about, seeing many of the legions of others going their way in the powerful city. He was divided as to his next location, though he was leaning towards returning to his hotel room. It was not far from his present location, three or four blocks at most. Then again, he was also not far from Farragut Park, a nice small rectangular piece of greenery marked with a statue. After some quiet debate, he simply let his feet make the decision, going as he already was, towards the park.

A loud honking stopped his walking and grabbed his eyes. Turning his head in the direction of the car noise, he saw at the intersection a man with a white cane, sunglasses, and what appeared to be a bandage around his eyes. He had stepped forward into the street only to step back hastily with the annoyed sound of the driver. Plans for the stranger changed as he approached the disabled person.

"Hello there, can I help you?" asked the younger man, taking the blind man by the shoulder and the hand.

"It would be better if I did this alone."

"Maybe," responded the man, "but it does not look like you are used to this type of journeying. Without sight that is."

"You are right," said the blind man, who was in his forties and otherwise healthy. "If it will make you feel better, grab an arm."

"Deal," said the stranger with a wry smile, locking an arm with the blind man and waiting at the corner until the walking icon appeared on the walkway sign.

"I've been practicing some for the past couple days."

"I was about to ask how and when this happened," replied the man.

"My name is Tony by the way."

"Nice to meet you," smiled the stranger. "So what happened, if you do not mind me asking?"

"Well, I work at a place with dangerous chemicals and sure enough, an accident happened and the stuff got into my eyes."

"Horrible. I am sorry to hear that," said the stranger, as the two made their way across the intersection and in front of a stopped patrol car.

"It's not too bad," said Tony. "The company is paying for everything and there is a chance that I can get my sight back."

"That is good to hear."

"I am doing this, just in case. You know, if they cannot get me to see again, at least I will be able to get around."

"How has that been going?" asked the stranger as they got across the street just as the blinking orange hand was cautioning pedestrians to halt their traverse across the asphalt.

"Ah, so-so," said Tony with a laugh. "But you know, as the Good Book says, I'll move by faith and not by sight."

"How about both, Tony?" asked the stranger, whose eyes darkened and lids opened and shut rapidly and then returned to normal. He placed both hands on the head of Tony, finger tips touching the sides of the bandages and the temples. In a moment, a sudden unseen jolt, a blink and then another blink. In a breath of shock, Tony realized that he was seeing the dark shadows of the enclosed bandages. "Say nothing. Do not make a shout. Not yet, at least. Simply know what has happened."

"How is this possible?" asked Tony, the two figures catching the attention of the parked patrol car's driver.

"With God, all things are possible," said the man to Tony, who was overcome yet somehow kept his composure.

"The doctor said it would be a long shot. How can I ever thank you?"

"No need."

"What's your name at least?"

"No need for that and no need to tell people who did this to you. Thank God, for it was His will that I help you."

"What do I tell people? The doctor? My wife?"

"Tell them the obvious," said the stranger. "Once you were blind and now you see."

"I will do that," replied Tony with a growing smile. "I will do that."

"Count to thirty and then remove the bandages. Go in peace."

"Good bye," said Tony, who waited until the count of thirty to see the world in perfect vision once again. The miracle worker walked down the street, nearing Farragut Park. After performing the miracle and evading Tony's renewed gaze, he continued towards the nearby park as he originally planned.

"I have the suspect in view. Do I pursue?"

"Yes, but be cautious," responded Patterson.

The mostly white patrol car slowed to the side of the road near the park. The noise of its engine blended with the rest of the traffic. The man sat down at one of the park benches, looking at the surrounding buildings. From his vantage point, he could see the bustle of people going from the metro station to the major intersection of K Street NW and Connecticut NW. It was a good city to hide in because there were so many people and buildings to get in the way, he thought. Then the police officer approached the seated man.

"Excuse me, sir."

"Yes?"

"You need to come with me."

"For what reason?" asked the stranger as he got up from the bench.

"You are under arrest …" began the officer, whose ritualistic words stunned the man and led many around them to turn and watch.

V.

It was a place too big to be called a village and too small to be a city. Situated in one of the green pastures of England, it was thick with cement streets and man-made structures. Buses and cars drove along its streets, office buildings of glass sat by gothic architecture that had stood since before the Tudors. Victorian Era factories that once blackened the sky with their output were on the skyline; they were now apartment complexes. Instead, a mostly college-educated populace went about typical work weeks and lazy weekends.

Evening draped over this place, similar to so many settlements in the United Kingdom north and south of Hadrian's Wall. Gloomy lights shone through the vesper and mist. Rainfall had once again afflicted the community. The bars were still open, though mostly empty, for the following day was neither Saturday nor Sunday. Most light came from the homes and apartments, opened curtains providing not only bulbs from lamps and ceilings, but also intense pixelated brightness courtesy televisions, laptops, and computers.

Roads and nonresidential buildings remained mostly vacant.

One such dormant facility was the local library. Built in a gothic form, from afar it looked more like a sanctuary, with its vaulted ceiling, stained glass, and spires atop the roof. A sign at the main entrance betrayed its purpose. It had two clear doors that one pushed to open. Inside there were about a dozen computers, each with wireless access if a person had a library card-based code, and two floors of books. There were about 30,000 different titles, mostly classics and new releases. There was fiction and nonfiction, children's, youths and adults, and also some newspapers and magazines.

Two young men were outside. The lights were out and the place was devoid of any human presence. Both were in normal pants and shoes, with raincoats protecting them from the regular precipitation. Standing in front of the main entrance, the one on the left gave a wry smile. He had dark hair and dark eyes, was clean-shaven, and with a broad nose. To his right was another youth, with reddish hair, blue eyes, and a thinner nose.

"Why?" asked one to the other.

"Just in case."

"Very well," replied one to the other as they walked towards the glass doors. As expected, the entrance was not only locked but also had a camera. They both saw it, with the red haired one raising his left hand so that the fingers pointed in the direction of the security device. In a blink the camera ceased recording new information, remaining in a looping process even as its timer continued to move forward with the passage of the seconds. The dark-haired one raised his right hand and with outward splayed pointed fingers directed his attention to the doors. The lock clicked and the doors opened.

Another pair of doors stood between the two as they walked into the facility. To their left was a poster board with various local news and events information put up with thumb tacks. Again the dark-haired man motioned with his fingers and again the doors fulfilled his orders, unlocking and then slowly moving inward to prepare the way. Both sets of doors gently closed behind them and the evening interior of the library was before them. They each surveyed the shelves and shelves of books, some on the ground floor, others on the second floor. They studied the topics until they found the nonfiction section. They walked into that part of the library, going by the unmanned information desk. With some effort they found the section of their choice and then each selected a book to read.

They found a reading area to sit down and digest the ideas of their respective works. It was the children's area where they settled down, as the department had bean bags instead of chairs. When they sat down, the red-haired young man sank deep into the bean bag, prompting some laughter from his companion. After a few moments, the two silently read their respective works. Reading became an odd practice since the happening. Not only were they able to read a work, but the process had an aura of permanence seldom found for people scanning a volume. Maybe it was because a book involved the thoughts of a person being committed to paper, but whenever either of them read a piece in depth, they could remember the text almost verbatim, an instant memorization.

The red-haired stranger decided to read the library's English translation copy of the Bhagavad-Gita. He remembered the exact chapter and verse where he left off at the last time he and the dark-haired stranger visited a library after hours. It was at the eleventh chapter when Krishna, the charioteer, gave Arjuna the ability to see his otherworldly form, with its countless arms, crowns, bellies, and eyes. His presence was described by Arjuna as disturbing, frightening even the demigods of the heavens. With his flaming mouths, the otherworldly charioteer devoured his terrified foes.

His companion took to a more Christian opus, the English translation of The Cost of Discipleship by Dietrich Bonhoeffer. Unlike the other young man sitting in a bright-hued cushy bean bag, he began his reading on the first page. A quick reader, the dark-haired stranger was captivated and troubled by the pain with which the German theologian wrote about the decline of the Church in his country. The culprit was cheap grace. This sense of offering no transformation for the saved soul, of no change in behavior or effort to bend one's own will; this was a curious contemplation for the stranger.

"What are you reading?"

"The Cost of Discipleship."

"Is it any good?"

"I would say so. It makes me think of the Christian life in ways I have not thought about it before. Especially the part about self-sacrifice, of receiving the cross so that one may die."

"Disturbing."

"What?"

"Death."

"I think the author is talking more of a metaphorical death. You know, dying to oneself."

"Sounds more reasonable," replied the red-haired young man as he turned a page in the Bhagavad-Gita and then offered a lengthy yawn.

"Tired?"

"Some."

"Then we should go during regular hours."

"No," said the red-haired young man firmly.

"Why not?"

"Because, I do not like being around people. You know that."

"It's a library, they will be quiet. Or at least quiet overall."

"That is not the issue," said the red-haired man, turning another page as he concentrated both on the conversation with his company and Krishna in his four-armed form. "When I am around them, I feel their pain."

"And?"

"I don't like pain. I don't like suffering. I do not want to have to block out all that misery when trying to enjoy a good book."

"I am not a fan of pain either, but I find it best to confront such matters and resolve them rather than just ignore it."

"It's awkward being around you when you do that," responded the red-haired man, yawning once more. "Giving out money and food to the poor, stopping to remove the addictions from druggies in the alleyways."

"Do you oppose helping the poor?"

"What good does it do?" asked the blue-eyed young man, closing his book and putting it by his side on the floor. "For every one person you help, another faceless thousand are around you. You cannot save them all, Adi."

"You know the story about the star fish on the beach, right?"

"Yes. As I see it, the star fish are on the beach to flee their predators. But rather than leave them alone, some well-intended person throws them back into danger."

"Well, I do not believe that is how the story goes," said the dark-eyed man, having also put his book on the floor nearby his bean bag.

"One day, Adi. There will come a day when you realize just how pointless your desire-driven efforts are and you will relent to a bigger solution."

"Bigger solution? What would that be?"

"I am still reading to find out," replied the red-haired man as a noise drew their attention away from both their books and themselves. The silhouette of a security guard approached the front doors. He took out a flashlight and pressed a button to bring a beam of light into the interior of the library. However, a quick search from without the facility saw no evidence of a hostile party. The lack of financial units being stored in the building generated a lackadaisical approach to verifying things. With the light having been directed to most of the corners and floor of the library, the guard pushed the button, turning the flashlight off and then went elsewhere on his rounds that evening.

. . . .

A plain environment, a small space compared to the other rooms at the office. There were no external windows, but a camera was present in a corner, perched well above any possible reach of someone of average height. The upper two-thirds of the room were painted white, the lower third painted gray. On one side there was a large window, modified so that while the suspect saw only himself, others in the adjacent room could watch him. Two simple metal chairs were present, pushed into a simple rectangular table.

The stranger who was picked up at Farragut Park was waiting in the small interrogation room. His hands were cuffed upon his arrest and remained so as he sat alone in the room. Initially behind his back, following his placement in the room the dark-haired figure dragged his arms underneath his legs to have them in front. They were now resting on the table, elbows hanging off the edge. His expression was stoic, looking at his intently at his surroundings as though it were a great work of art.

Commander Ella Patterson put Detective Brittany Johnson in charge of the interrogation. Brittany wanted the suspect to wait, possibly building up nerves as he remained in the silent small space. She also wanted to wait for the photos of the three decedents to arrive at her desk. Johnson had successfully broken down several perpetrators in the interrogation room. She previously dealt with a couple of suspected collaborators with the organized crime boss Viktor Makovnor, as well as the occasional enemy of said figure. Years had gone by since anyone had tried to move in on Makovnor's territory. Maybe the stranger waiting in the room was a hitman for some usurper. Said usurper could have been the person he talked with on the phone that night when he murdered three Makovnor foot soldiers.

"So how is he?" asked Detective Tracy Ramirez to her friend, each holding a cup of coffee from the break room.

"He's okay. Good looking, sociable," said Brittany.

"What's he do?"

"He works for some company in DC. You know, some nothing office job."

"Does he make a lot of money?"

"Don't know."

"Does he have any siblings?"

"Not sure."

97

"Do you even know his name?" asked Tracy with a critical eye.

"Yes, I know that," replied Brittany with annoyance. "It's Jake."

"Jake what?"

"Are you serious?"

"Sorry," said Tracy, sipping more of her coffee from the paper cup, one of many that had been stacked beside the machine. "I know you are not particular."

"Not this again," said Brittany, rolling her eyes.

"Yes this again. I am worried about you. It seems like you don't really care who you are going out with, or, dare I say, sleeping with."

Brittany gave her a death stare.

"Hey, it's the twenty-first century. I'm not stupid and I'm not judging," said Tracy, "I just think that after a while it gets a little, well, pointless."

"Pointless?"

"Yes," said Tracy, finishing off her coffee. "I mean, great you have a fling and blow off some frustration. But then what? What's next?"

"Tonight."

"Tonight?"

"Yes. Jake and I are seeing each other tonight. My place."

"Okay," said Tracy as the two got up and left the break room, disposing of their now empty coffee cups. "Just be careful."

"I will."

"And I mean more careful than just using protection."

"I will," said Brittany more firmly.

Brittany walked over to the room that bordered the interrogation space, shutting the door behind her and finding Commander Patterson and Detective Donald Patrick. In advance of entering the listening room, Brittany grabbed a folder containing the photo shots of the three victims and held it under her left arm. They were watching the seated stranger, who remained calm as he waited for someone to join him. He continued to eye around the window, acting like he was able to see through it.

"Boss, detective," said Brittany. "Any updates?"

"No, just the same peculiar things," said Patterson.

"Peculiar?"

"I read the police report. Our suspect offered no resistance. He was searched and had nothing on him."

"Nothing?"

"No ID, no money, no credit cards, nothing," said Donald. "Except for a hotel key card, which he freely gave to us and told us where to go."

"What did you find?"

"He lives large," said Patterson. "Very high end suite at one of those luxurious places off of Connecticut. Front desk said he paid with cash."

"Anything at the room? A weapon, paperwork, photos?"

"Nothing," said Donald. "Just a suitcase with clothes, a Bible, and a bag with a tooth brush, tooth paste, and a razor."

"He travels light."

"Name?"

"He refused to give one."

"Even to the hotel staff?"

"He paid them extra for the privilege of anonymity."

"He might be a hitman, someone trying to grab Viktor's business," said Patterson, looking once more at the seated suspect.

"Then again," posited Brittany, "if he was a hitman why is he still in town? Usually they leave when they're done."

"And where is the money he would have been paid with?" added Patterson. "Answers to questions like these are what we need you to find out."

"Sure thing," said Brittany, who opened the door to the smaller room and entered. She had her blonde hair in a ponytail, a black firearm in a holster to her side, and her badge hanging around her neck. Her appearance brought a wry smile to the suspect, who drew back his cuffed hands from the center of the cold table. Brittany sat down, placing the closed folder with photos on the table. Without speaking she opened the folder and placed the three 8-by-12 inch photos in a row before the stranger.

He looked at them in confusion, his smile gone. He studied each photo, much in the same way that he studied the one-sided window earlier. Brittany waited in the silence for a moment, seeing if the alleged perpetrator showed any emotion. Any reflex, any sign of familiarity with the photos of the dead. After a brief period, the man raised his head and looked at Brittany directly in the eyes with his dark-hued irises. Brittany saw no apparent tell that he recognized the dead men. She did not expect such apparent coldness.

"Do you recognize these men?"

"No."

"Are you aware of why you are here?"

"Something about a triple homicide," said the man as he shifted some, his English accent having American touches as he talked more. "I would know more if I could read your mind."

"That will not be necessary, I can tell you –"

"Could I try?"

The request made Brittany straighten up some as she sat. She did not like being interrupted per se, but she also wondered what game the man wanted to play. He was definitely one of the weird ones, in her opinion. She smiled a fake smile as she continued. "Okay then, how about I let you try to read my mind and in return, you give me your name and what you know about these men. Sound like a good deal?"

"I agree to your terms," said the man, who shifted some in his chair. "Now let me take your hands. It is easier that way."

With initial hesitation, Brittany moved her hands to the middle of the table, placing them above the photos of the dead. The man's cuffed hands moved forward and were gently placed above hers. His touch was soft, warm. Brittany noticed that his fingertips had prints, meaning if he was a professional hitman he took no drastic effort to hide his identity. The stranger directed his fingers so that each tip was touching a vein. He then slowly closed his eyes, slowly opened them and then looked into her eyes. He coughed a little, as though attempting to drive away an awkward topic.

"A pity. A great pity."

"Did you fail to read it?" asked a skeptical Brittany.

"You strike me as an attractive and intelligent young woman. I assumed you to be principled. Alas, you are broken inside."

"Excuse me?"

"When will you realize that those men you meet from time to time will offer you nothing in return for your affection?" At that moment, Brittany drew back her hands away from the touch of the stranger. Expressions changed behind the mirrored window.

"Listen if you think that –"

"His name is Jake. Are you even sure of that point?"

"Okay whatever you are doing, if it is supposed to be funny –"

"Funny?" said the man in outrage. "I am trying to warn you. Listen to your friend. Sleeping around is an exercise that offers only temporary pleasure instead of fulfilling relationships. As she said, it's pointless."

"Look you," said Brittany with gritted teeth. "What I do in my time off the clock has nothing at all to do with this case. You follow me!?"

"Detective Johnson!" came in a voice from the intercom system. Patterson held a microphone in the adjacent room and spoke into it. "Come here immediately." Brittany obliged and got up from the table, leaving the photos of the dead on the table and chair pushed out. The door slammed and the man returned to a sense of ponderous peace within his solitude. This time, though, he looked at the photos in addition to the mirrored window. Upon entering the adjacent room, Brittany was met with confused looks by both her colleague and her superior. The latter spoke once more. "If you are going through some personal things that may hinder your ability to conduct this interrogation, now is the time to tell me."

"No, no I am okay," said Brittany. "He just caught me off guard."

"Are you alright?" asked Don.

"Yes, yes I am fine. I just didn't expect him to know about those things. Not sure how he figured that stuff out. But it's probably just some parlor trick."

"You ready to go back in?"

"Yes."

"You want company?" asked Don.

"Not necessary. I got this," said Brittany as she took a deep breath and re-entered the smaller room where the man remained seated. He was calm in his mannerisms as the detective silently sat across from the table. Big eyes, he looked remorseful as he gazed at her, who had a professional demeanor once more.

"Let me apologize," said the man, speaking just as Brittany was about to return to her interrogation. "I know I hit some sensitive areas and you were clearly more inflamed than informed. I am sorry."

"That was nice of you," said Brittany stoically, turning to the folder and the photos of the three dead men, which she spread out a little more to reinforce recognition of their presence. "In many ways it's my fault. After all, I took your parlor trick way too seriously."

"Thoughtreal."

"What?"

"Thoughtreal," said the man with reverence and solemnity. "That is what you encountered when I read your mind."

"Cute. You have a name for it."

"You doubt."

"I've been around people like you, plenty of people like you," said Brittany, staring deeply into the man's dark eyes. "I have sat opposite fortune tellers, magicians, scammers, card readers, and self-professed saviors. You are good at what you do, but it is still a trick and nothing more."

"So you were not convinced?"

"Nice try."

"Let me try again."

Brittany took a deep breath. "I am investigating a triple homicide that has a good deal of politics behind it and if all you are going to do is try and –"

"Adonijah."

"Is that another name for your trick?"

"That is my name. My name is Adonijah. I was born thirty years ago in the Balkans in a country that is no longer on the map. I came to this country only a week or so ago and up until now I have never been in police custody." Brittany looked at him in silence, shifting her hands along the table as she stayed proper in the chair. Patterson and Patrick were surprised at the sudden release of information; their surprise being obscured by the one-sided mirror. "Now may I show you more telling proofs of my power?"

"Will you explain what you know about these men's deaths?"

"Yes. Yes, I will."

"Well," said Brittany as she placed her hands side-by-side in the middle of the metal table, "remove my doubt."

The man smiled, slowly moving his hands to touch hers. Again he fixed his digits to the various veins, making sure each tip had a place along the bloodlines. His breathing slowed, as did his heart rate. Brittany looked at him in confusion as he became very still and then slowly closed his eyes.

......

Sunlight covered them in the valley as they stood there, Brittany and her host. Below her was grass and above her a blue sky. In the background were mountains and clusters of flowers and bushes all around. A village was off in the background with an old European appeal to its architecture. The detective who interrogated some of the most frightening figures of the DC area, who was shot at a few times in the line of duty, and got into a few vicious fights while trying to preserve law and order was beyond stunned. Eyes widened, fear rose. She went for her handgun and pointed it immediately at the man, who was calmly standing opposite her in the otherwise peaceful valley.

"What the hell just happened?! Where did you take me?!"

"You are in the measures of my mind, you are in a world I have created," said the stranger, speaking softly as a shaky handgun was but a couple inches from his left eye.

"Take me back," said Brittany with repressed ferocity.

"Do you really believe that you have any power in my world?" responded the man with a tone to his voice that to Brittany sounded sinister.

"Take me back," she reiterated with greater ferocity.

"Very well."

Brittany all but jumped from her chair in the smaller room, prompting the simple piece of furniture to fall backwards as she backed away from the seated stranger. He remained calm, as sedate as he had been in that mysterious valley. Breathing heavily, Brittany grabbed the knob of the door, opened it, and slammed it behind her as she did her best to explain what had just happened to her peer and her superior. In the small room the ease of mood that the stranger exhibited while waiting returned.

. . . .

Fierce cold defined the land. Snow and ice covered the ground for half the year, preventing floral beauty from abounding. A bleak place, the sun rarely shone through the thick clouds and the limited hours of day. Isolated from grand cities, massive highways, and busy railroads, the terrain remained savage. A last frontier, an untamed country, it was devoid of any structure of civilization. The nearest habitation was at least two hours away on foot, if any dare to make their constitutional in this realm.

Solemn coniferous trees provided shelter from the moon by night and the sun by day. Furry beasts with brutal fangs roamed the wilds in a world where the weak and the wounded die quickly. Herbivores posed impressively, with great antlers and blubbery hides. Packs of wolves had at them, sometimes winning sometimes losing. No mercy for the fallen creatures, picked to the bone by the victorious predators. It was one great struggle, from the cold and the predator, from starvation and deprivation.

Into this untouched wilderness came a single human being. A modern Adam beholding God's creation, he walked amongst the white capped greenery and imposing arboreal canopies. He stepped carefully, wearing thick boots, a heavy jacket, a scarf, and gloves. His occasional exhaling brought a vaporous cloud, as though to blow smoke into the thin night air. No animal approached him, no predator or prey molested him. Most paid him no heed. The rest simply looked and continued with their innate activities. The stranger moved carefully, cautiously going amid the fallen branches, the occasional patch of ice, and the sometimes slippery snow. His desire was solitude, an adventure that made him venture afar from the paths of the paved and comforted.

There was a clearing, the moon shining down upon it. Tall trees seemed to gather round the man, their branches waving in a breeze whose coolness only added to the frigid environment. Despite the cold, he unzipped the heavy coat, tossing it to the ground in front of him. The gloves came next, then the scarf, both placed beside the coat. Underneath it he had on a dark blue long sleeved shirt with bent collar. The shirt was hardly sufficient to keep a man warm in such a time and place as that.

However, the man was not shivering, neither was his body reacting the way a typical human body reacts to bitter cold. There was initial redness in the exposed extremities brought bare that eventide. The man slowed his breathing, slowed his heart rate, and concentrated the pulses of his synapses. The wiring of his mind was changing its current, the waves altering their direction. Soon the reddish hue of his extremities and hands began to disappear, replaced by his usual light pink appearance.

All the while his eyes grew darker and darker, the pupils growing to the point that all white was absent from the sight-giving organs. A line appeared at the very center of his forehead. At first, it appeared like any line upon the compressed forehead, a sign of emotional expression or aged body. But this line was different, being considerably shorter than the other similar aging lines above the brows. It became more solid, overlapping the two sides divided by the line in a manner unseen with wrinkles.

The man stood straight in the clearing, facing the exact cardinal direction south with feet firmly planted upon the cold ground. Both arms were to the sides of the man. From the elbow to the shoulder each arm touched his sides. From the elbow to the fingertips the arms were hanging away from the sides, pointing downward. They were slowly moved to have the palms facing southward like his face, the digits curved and splayed so that no finger touched another and none were straight.

The line upon his forehead curved slightly as the breathing became very slow and paced. Like the eyes, the mouth became a pitch black, the tongue and teeth disappearing in the void. Then the line began to sprout hairs, each pointing downward and moving out to grow. Curved and dark, they stopped at the proper length for an average male. Rounding, the line began to have a rapid pulsing behind it. It seemed as a sphere, rapidly spinning behind it, going back and forth. In a moment the line opened and there was an eye which, like the other two, was a pupil black in its hue. Three eyes gazed southward, beholding the forested wintry surrounding with its wild animals and plants.

The three eyes vigilantly staring, both arms were raised. As though adjusting the wings before flight, from the elbows to the shoulders the arms remained as they were before, touching his sides. From the elbows to the fingertips there was movement, raising them like he was tracing out a circle in the frigid air. The rising of the arms halted upon reaching an angle of about 33 degrees. Everything was in place, everything prepared.

With one final gust of breath, the man shut all three eyes at once, causing a great expulsion of energy. In a split second a great black cloud spewed forth from the head, chest, and legs of the man, spreading outwards in all 360 degrees. Though emanating from the man directly, the ground on which he stood and the clothing which he had discarded by his feet remained untouched. The perimeter was exactly six feet in all directions, with him being the epicenter of the circle.

The black cloud rapidly pushing from his body was a destructive billowing force that consumed all that was beyond the six-foot perimeter as it spread outwards. Thunderous in its cadence, it broke apart trees, rocks, ice, and snow, ripping them apart and exploding them into the finest specks of remnant. Millions of splinters flying all around the outskirts of the cloud were consumed by the dark force as its volume expanded outwards. Snow evaporated and was no more, rocks crushed into miniscule remains, and all nearby animals no matter how large were elementally obliterated.

What creatures could run darted as fast as possible, most realizing in their primitive minds too late that what came was death. Breathing increased, heart rate picked up a wild pace, as fingers twitched and folded. The man kept all three eyes firmly shut as the cloud continued to escape him, like a demon casting a spell upon the helpless world. Faster and faster it went, unfettered by any of the jagged terrain, solid trees, or husky beasts that moments earlier rested, fed, or reproduced. Annihilation was swift and near painless, moving too rapidly to prompt contemplation.

In a sudden breath and hoarse gasp, like awaking from a nightmare, the man opened all three eyes at once. The black cloud ceased its progress and dissipated in the wintry evening. Breathing hard, the man fell to all fours, gripping the discarded heavy coat upon descending. Heart rate became normal; lungs began to pump out the carbon dioxide at a relaxed pace. Three eyes became two. Gusts of white air slowed and then the mouth closed as the nose took over. Rising, the man smiled in awe and wonder. The marvel at leveling all in his immediate vicinity remained on his mind as he gathered up the coat, the gloves, and the scarf, donned the apparel once more, and made the journey back to the nearest human structures. Until he reached them, he wondered if they were also consumed.

....

"If anyone else had said what you just said, I would've considered them insane," said Commander Ella Patterson to Detective Brittany Johnson. With Detective Donald Patrick, they were the only three people in the room adjacent to the interrogation space. Adonijah continued to sit in the smaller, closely-watched room, placid as before. As they talked, their gaze occasionally turned to the one-way window, looking at a figure who claimed to be a man yet performed things beyond the rational.

"And I would agree," said Brittany, still flustered after explaining what happened. "And you saw nothing strange from here?"

"Like I said," noted Donald while scratching his head, "From what we saw, you sat down, he touched your hands, and then you jumped up suddenly and ran in here."

"This is getting way beyond our pay grade."

"Speaking of which," said Patterson, "not long after you went into the room with our person of interest I received a call from the powers that be. A federal agent will be arriving Monday morning."

"I take it they are still working under the assumption that this has to do with organized crime," said Donald.

"You bet. While not as prominent as some mobsters, the Makovnor family has still been under the Bureau's watchful eye."

"But they don't know about this."

"No, they don't," said Patterson in response to Brittany. "For now, we are going to keep it that way. No one in fact, outside of this room, is to know what just happened."

"I can keep a secret," said Donald. "But what about our person of interest in the next room?"

"Solitary confinement," said Brittany. "Give him a cell away from the others. Keep him there until Monday."

"You don't think you should try to get more out of him? After all, thanks to your conversation we now have a name, age, and place of origin."

Brittany took a deep breath. "I'm still trying to figure out what just happened. I am in no state to talk with him now."

"Besides, to your point," interjected Patterson, "this is definitely above our pay grade. Maybe the fed will know something about whatever he is."

"Exactly."

"Sounds possible."

"Okay then," said Patterson. "On Monday we talk with the fed, you talk to Adonijah, and Donald here will grill Viktor."

"Sounds good," said Donald, with Brittany nodding in approval.

"If you won't be needing me before this weekend…"

"Go ahead and have a weekend," Patterson said to Brittany with a faint smile.

"Thank you, boss," responded Brittany before she exited.

. . . .

This time it was her place. White walls decorated with taped-up vibrant posters that added more color than meaning. The mostly wooden furniture with cushions were static, as the pair were not in the living room. Her purse with all its many imprisoned objects was plopped upon the kitchen countertop. No jackets were out, as the day was warm enough and dry enough to not require them. Seven recently-opened, empty beer bottles stood at attention on the floor and small table near the main couch. Two other bottles were strewn along the floor, having rolled some before coming to a stop. The remote was on the couch where the two had been earlier following dinner.

They were in the bedroom, having decided that talking and touching was not enough of an enjoyable evening. Along the carpeted floor there were two pairs of discarded shoes, one of which had extra lift in the heels. Near them were bunched-up clothes, some from him and some from her. These thrown garments pointed in jumbled order towards the bed itself, where Jake and Brittany were present. Clad in their underwear, they had only that basic thin wall of fabric between their bodies and nakedness.

The overhead light was off, but the luminance of a digital clock and a small lamp near it provided vision to the sensual sight. Lips locked and unlocked, arms enveloped bodies, accompanied by the occasional roll. Jake was not as muscular as she had presumed, with a mild pot belly and a thin layer of dark hair on it and his legs. Still, he

114

was available and he was willing and for her that was sufficient. For several minutes they kissed and embraced, her allowing him to grope and fondle, him allowing her to grab and feel. Body heat was not intense enough to cause sweat, but that benchmark was nearing. Breaths between kisses, Jake rose up some, taking his embraced object of sexual desire with him. His embrace became more intricate as he began to undo Brittany's bra, the last line of defense. No resistance from her, a lustful smile appearing on her face as he began to loosen the undergarment. Neither was shocked at him having experience in such matters.

Like a wild earsplitting scream, Jake's phone went off. The hands retracted, leaving the bra looser but still covering her breasts. Both sounded like they had finished a marathon as Jake, wearing only his boxers, scampered off the bed to follow the cue. In his insatiable movement of desire, he had forgotten where exactly he placed the small commanding piece of technology. Embroiled in carnal frustration, Brittany slammed herself down on the bed from her seated position to being on her back. Jake found the noisy device and pushed a couple buttons to check the reason for the noise.

"What is it?" innocently inquired Brittany as she regained her composure and sat on the edge of the bed, her perfectly shaven legs descending to the floor where her toes touched.

"Work," said Jake as he placed the phone by her vanity mirror and hastily went around the bedroom gathering his things.

"We just can't win, can we?" asked Brittany as she fitted her bra back into proper order and got up to slowly gather her clothing items.

"Not this time, anyway," he said, clothes in his arms. "Bathroom?"

"Over there," pointed Brittany as Jake followed the aim of the feminine finger. He nodded with appreciation before shutting the door. She heard the liquid reason for his request. It was fun while it lasted, she thought. She turned on the overhead light and approached the vanity mirror, feeling it best to comb her hair and get back into good order. As she picked up the nearest brush, she saw the message texted to Jake.

Her stomach curled up in knots with those few words, not even a dozen, along with the name of the sender. The bathroom door began to open and she hastily backed away, the carpeting helping to mask the noise of her rapid maneuver. She went towards picking up her shirt, which had landed next to the bed where she jumped towards after seeing the message. Jake came out of the bathroom refreshed and at ease, oblivious to the most recent act of Brittany acquiring knowledge. Hands washed, hair slicked with cool facet water, he now had on his shirt, jeans, and socks.

"Like I said, really sorry but work sucks."

"Yes it does," said Brittany coldly. The tone slightly perplexed Jake as he slipped his shoes on and began to put his belt through the flaps of his jeans. But he brushed it off; reasoning that she must have hated the interruption as much as he did, probably more so.

"How about tomorrow night?"

"Maybe," responded Brittany, whose motions of gathering clothes and putting them back on was slower than her departing guest.

"Alright then. I'll message you about where we could meet up. Maybe my place tomorrow."

"Maybe."

"Anyway," he said as he, now fully dressed, went for his phone on the dresser with the vanity mirror, "I got to get going." She followed him to the door, which she unlocked and opened for him. "Later!"

"Good bye," she said frigidly. He offered a curious look before crossing the threshold into the apartment building hallway, his phone going off again as he walked down the corridor. She closed the door and bolted it, standing there a moment in stillness.

Then her face gradually changed its expression, peeling into a grimace as her fists and teeth clinched hard. Head bowed with her right fist pounding lightly on the door, Brittany suppressed the urge to scream. Instead she took some deep breaths, let a couple tears escape, and then gathered herself mentally and physically. She struggled to pick up the beers, the shared drinks with a man like that. Dropping them into her small yellow recycling bin, placed under the kitchen sink, she again fought a total emotional breakdown with success, though not without another tear and some choked up moments included. Brittany kept trying to remind herself that this was not supposed to be serious. It was never meant to be serious. And yet it still hurt, the epiphany was still painful. She did not expect something permanent, neither did she expect a perfect man; but she also did not expect that. As a result, she struggled to get sleep that night as misery kept her conscious.

VI.

Large numbers of people went to and fro inside the facility, the hard floors constantly pounded by travelers from all over the world. Families with fast-moving little ones, plump white-haired couples in bright shirts, professionals of differing uniforms indicating their responsibilities and ranks. All skin shades were there, all styles of fashion appeared as normal. A great thrown-together grouping channeled through the several gates and their flying machines. Roaring engines were mostly muted by the thick glass walls. Stagnant eyes awaiting the boarding call saw these mechanical birds shrink and grow.

Rows of black seats were found clustered at various points within the main structure, concentrated near the large holes in the wall that at various times led to a docked air vehicle. Every so often one of the portals opened and a stream of people, young and old, male and female, rich and humble, poured into the huge interior of the airport's main building and into the arms of kinfolk and loved ones. Some took photos, most dragged luggage with wheels affixed and handles outstretched.

Another cluster of tourists, businessmen, returning adventurers, and new natives went past Dr. Glen Northside as he continued to look over an academic paper. He leaned forward a little in a black seat that, like the others, had silver arms and legs. It was not the most comfortable seat, but it was not painful either. Dressed in business casual, he had a dark brown tie, brown slacks, black shoes with black strings, and a white long sleeved shirt on. Bespectacled and with mostly gray hair, Dr. Northside looked as much like an academic as he played the part, having years of experience teaching, researching, and being published. A few times his expertise was requested by the government, though it had been a couple of decades since the last time the phone rang for such a patriotic purpose.

Announcements periodically blared over the speakers, echoing throughout the large, long space for travel and waiting. He paid little attention to the remarks, knowing he still had another twenty to thirty minutes before his flight was expected. Weather was nice and the skies clear, so he held little concern for a delay. Forty other people were seated at his gate, again a diverse lot using the same winged machine he was for various purposes. Each person kept to their own, a family talking amongst themselves, some young friends going on an extended excursion together before adult responsibility befell them. He was alone for the time being, silently reading a paper he was scheduled to critique.

He flipped back another page, going to the next heavily footnoted and jargon-laden part of the intellectual opus. Taking mental notes, he had reviewed and critiqued dissertations in the past as part of a panel and even as a professor one-on-one with a student. While it seemed a lifetime in the past, Northside remembered the nerves and exhaustion that came with his own dissertation. There was the note-taking and the draft reviews. Then more note taking, pouring through past scholarship and performing his own research at the campus. He had two major specializations, one being the connection between the mind and health, and the other the various means of clinical treatment for post-traumatic stress disorder. The latter was once called upon for the victims of the human curse of war, while the former was on one occasion more useful than previously assumed. In total, it took nine years including summer classes to complete all the degrees and twice as long to pay off the student loans.

"Glen?" asked a female voice to his left, prompting a halt to the in-depth reading and a turning of the eyes. It was a woman about his age, with shoulder length faded red hair. She had on a modest dress that matched her hair color well and an impressive wedding ring that Glen remembered advising a mutual acquaintance to purchase.

"Brenda," said the studious doctor with a smile as he got up from his seat and put down the dissertation. They hugged. Neither had seen the other in person in about eight years.

"It's been awhile. How are you?"

"Great as always," Brenda said. "What brings you to the airport?"

"Trip to DC. Another one of those combination dissertation review and specialist convention. You remember the drill."

"Oh, very," she said with a laugh. "I'm surprised that Lucy is not here to see you off. Is she doing alright?"

"Yes, of course. But you know how she is with that business of hers. It's taking up a lot of her time. She promised she will be here when I return."

"Let's hope."

"So what brings you here?"

"My son is back in town from college."

"Tommy, right?"

"Yes, Tommy."

"Little freckled Tommy who got misdiagnosed with autism?"

"Yes," laughed Brenda. "That nut case."

"I take it he's doing okay."

"Yes, very much," said Brenda. "I'm glad I got a second opinion on that. Who knows where he would be if I had taken that route, the medications and therapy and all that."

"You would be poorer," smiled Glen as more announcements blared over them. Brenda was more attentive, as she just arrived and was not yet at the proper location.

"Yes, very," Brenda said as she confirmed that the comments were not for her and moved off of the walking area as another large group of people with rolling luggage passed by the two former colleagues.

"It reminds me of how they used to over-diagnose ADHD so that virtually every kid in the country was suffering from it."

"How could I forget? They would say things like 'well, your son has a hard time sitting down in his chair during class.' What kid doesn't?"

"Exactly," replied Glen as the two laughed. A moment passed and the mood, while still amicable, changed a little.

"So," began Glen, "has anything changed with, you know, how you are doing? Do you still have the medication?"

"I do," said Brenda still smiling some, albeit with less enthusiasm. "Every so often I will get a new prescription, just in case."

"But you still don't need them?"

She shook her head.

"Amazing. It's been what? Twenty years?"

"I know," she responded. "I can't even begin to understand."

"None of us could."

"Yes."

"Have you told anyone?"

"No, of course not," she said, lightly hitting Glen's shoulder. "They swore us to secrecy after all."

"True."

"I mean, I know I am not the best keeper of secrets, but when people that high on the totem pole say shut up, I shut up."

"There is that," replied Glen, whose attention like Brenda's was taken by the latest round of announcements. Brenda perked up some at the words.

"That's my son's plane. It's in. Got to go," said Brenda who hugged Glen one more time and gave him a fleeting kiss on the cheek. "It was a pleasure talking to you."

"Likewise. Bye!"

"Safe travels!" she said with a smile as she darted off and minutes later welcomed her son for the semester break.

A few minutes after that, Glen saw his plane slowly wheel its way to the gate. The covered walkway stretched out to connect to the side of the aerial vehicle. He packed the dissertation in his carryon and fell in line, ticket in hand, with the others on their way to the Nation's Capital. As he went down the twisty corridor and into the stuffy plane, he thought about that assignment years back. Brenda was there, as were a few others. There had always been curiosity, wondering, and even the occasional nightmare. There was no resolution, only tragedy. They searched and searched only to find them not. Sitting down and waiting for the machine to leave the ground, he began to go through the same festering unanswered questions about what happened.

....

Brittany struggled to fall asleep. The rush of emotion, lust to disappointment, ecstasy to anger, and with little time to relax in between. She argued with herself as she lay in the same bed that earlier her company had been present in carnal pursuit. Turning to one side, then tossing to another, turning yet again. After a few hours, maybe via the exhaustion of the shifting under the covers, she finally passed out into slumber. No dreams to recall, no magical or horrific images before her closed eyes. Just sleep, just the passing of time from evening to morning. Nothing to look forward to. There was emptiness within.

Sunlight pierced through the window near her bed. Solid curtains prevented a blinding blow of light, but through the bottom of the window and the split between the two wings it did manifest. She regained consciousness with an arm under the pillow and another arm over the top of the covers. Brittany felt soreness in her body. She attributed it to the uncomfortable sleep and positioning rather than any particular health concern. Sure enough, some stretching and walking around, gathering up of clothing and towels for the preparations of the day, these things aided in the removal of such minor pains.

While she had yet to take a shower or eat breakfast, she changed into some sweats and began her routine. Brittany stretched out her legs to make them straight on the faux Oriental rug in the living room. She also stretched each leg by bending them, one at a time, behind her back in a V-shape like soccer players do. Drinking some tap water and grabbing her apartment key, she went outdoors. A little cold but not biting, air lacking wind, as soon as she got to the sidewalk she turned and jogged. A couple of miles later, she returned to the building entrance and went up the elevator to her floor. This morning it was easier, likely due to her mind being on something other than her regimen.

The rest of the morning went normally. Shower completed, she ventured to the kitchen where she got a simple breakfast of orange juice, toast, and coffee. Hair was still wet by the time she got to brushing her teeth. The change was made from sweats to jeans and a short-sleeved shirt. Not flashy, just passable. She turned on her laptop, the device being fully operational within a minute of the start button being pushed. She checked her email and also her phone, seeing if he had left any messages. Why would he? Brittany thought. It's not as though he knows what I know. I need to enlighten him a little.

On her phone she signed into the dating app. It was only available on a mobile device, though it was affiliated with a couple of official dating sites. While she doubted that he was going to be online, to her surprise the icon indicated otherwise. After some hesitation and some worry about contact, Brittany decided to not play ignorant. She needed an explanation. Pushing the icon and opening up an instant chat, she began to type her query with the same thumbs that in youth played video games.

"Who is Jessica?"

There was no reaction at first, making the question seem even more awkward than the discovery. Maybe it was a sister, or a cousin. Brittany once dated a guy who had two sisters who called him regularly. She discovered this fact without the man's knowledge and falsely assumed that they were lovers. They eventually broke up for different reasons, reasons that were petty when reflected upon in the modern day. So maybe it was family; then again, Brittany knew of no sister who would say something like that to a blood relative. The chat message flashed a simple comment in gray lettering at the bottom noting that Jake saw the query and then it changed quickly to note that he was writing.

"What?"

"Jessica," she typed with annoyance. "The person who texted you last night that you said was WORK." Sent. Another confirmation of it being read, a couple seconds passed. Now the confirmation of Jake writing and then the message posted.

"Oh Jessica," said the first message, followed quickly "Yeah her" and then no writing at all. Did he really think that was enough?

"WELL?" typed Brittany in her first response, followed quickly by "WHO is she?"

"A lover."

Brittany's look of shock was reflected in the vanity mirror. Surely this was a typo. He did not mean "A", he must have meant "My" or something.

"What do you mean 'A' Lover?"

"Well," said the first response, all the while the gray comment about him writing maintained itself between posts. "She is a woman I like to see … She's pretty … She's nice … and sometimes we sleep together."

"WTF?" messaged Brittany, adding the question of whether or not they were still together. Seconds passed, it felt longer.

"Hey … This Isn't the 1950s … It's called open relationship … How do you not know about them?"

"So she knows you sleep around?" typed Brittany.

"Yes."

"Does she sleep around?"

"No."

"How do you know?"

"I know."

"So you think it's okay to sleep with me because your girlfriend thinks it's okay?"

"Yes."

"Newsflash," typed Brittany and then immediately sent additional messages: "It's not okay with me … I'm not going to be one of your hos … This is over …"

"You can't judge me," he immediately replied. "I was just a tryst for you also … WTF gives you the right to judge?"

"Because I'm not dating anyone else … It's called monogamy."

"Well I'm doing Ethical Non-Monogamy."

"WTF is that?"

"It's okay when everyone is okay with it."

"WELL, I'm not okay with it. This is over."

"Over?"

"Yes, over. Don't talk to me again."

"Whatever."

Without a farewell, Brittany signed off the dating site and took a deep breath. In earlier years she would have blocked him. Yet since she was a police detective and by extension a gun owner, she knew she was safe from any dangers real or imagined. She tried to take her mind off the matter. Turning on the television all she found were sitcoms that played out much the same angst and tension as she just experienced. Couldn't just one of them not be about sex? Just one, please. She flipped through the news channels, only to see talking heads scream at each other over political disagreements most normal human beings would discuss rationally. Documentaries were boring, so they were skipped through the surfing of the hundreds of channels. Flipping back to one of the calmer news channels, which featured a discussion about the mysterious Siberian explosion, she took out her phone again and called Tracy. After some talking, they agreed to meet in person later.

....

Viktor Makovnor was waiting in the interrogation room. Heavy set and with dyed brown hair, he looked and felt impatient. He remained alone in the small room with a single one-way window. He was wearing a suit, white shirt, black jacket, black pants, and red tie. It was a high quality garment, polished and dry cleaned. A folded red handkerchief rested inside the right breast pocket, its top formed as a triangle. His black shoes seemed to shine as the lights hit them, being blacker than the pants and jacket.

Little trepidation existed in the man. He had been inside police departments in the past and interrogation rooms both in the United States as well as less human rights-friendly regions. Over the years his family both hated and helped law enforcement, creating a complicated relationship with the government. Viktor's father and grandfather were both arrested by American authorities, with the latter going away for a long time under a murder charge. It was a rare legal loss for the Makovnor family, which transplanted itself from its Balkans home to the United States back in the early 1900s. During that time, some men of the family even served in the military, albeit via the draft.

The door swung open and there was Detective Donald Patrick, with his glasses and thick semi-gray mustache. Viktor paid him little attention, but rather was using one fingernail on his right hand to amateurishly clean the nails on the other hand. The sound of the door drew his gaze briefly, but only briefly, as he looked back down at his fingernails. As Patrick pulled back the chair and sat down, Viktor changed actions. Still focused on his own hands, he began to crack the knuckles, making small amounts of noise.

"You know," he said in his deep Slavic accent, "they used to say that doing this would cause arthritis. You remember that? Arthritis. As a young boy, the last thing I wanted was arthritis. The joint pain and all that. So I listen. I stop cracking my knuckles. Now I am an old man and lo and behold, I still get arthritis. Sad. Very sad."

"Mister Makovnor," said Donald stoically. "As you are likely aware, you are not here to talk about arthritis."

"But of course," Viktor said, changing his attention from his hands and turning his sight towards the detective. "We are here about the murders of my three men. That is why you had to speak to me on the same day as my granddaughter's birthday party."

"We did wait until it was finished, as you may recall."

"Yes," said Viktor as he moved in his seat. "I am grateful. As you can understand, my people have not always been so well treated by Americans."

"You are an American citizen, Mister Makovnor."

"I've spent enough time in the old country to note that as a mere formality," said Viktor as he again looked off into the window to adjust his hair with his gliding fingers. "So back to business, correct?"

"About the triple homicide," began Donald, "as you likely know, we are pursuing what leads we can, but we would like your cooperation."

"Cooperation," said Viktor with a laugh. "Your government has illegally monitored my family for decades and you now want help. Why not just take it from all the tapes you have of our personal conversations?"

"Do you have any enemies who may be responsible for this, who may have a motive for wanting your … family … driven out of DC?"

"Yes, you," said Viktor, pointing at Donald, who withheld his emotion. "You are the ones who want me, as they say, behind bars."

"Mister Makovnor, it would help a great deal if you gave us a more legitimate suspect than the US government."

"Overseas, such an allegation would be seriously considered. I had family working for the regime back in the 90s when the American airstrikes began," said Viktor. "Who is to say that such actions are not also committed on American soil?"

"We have video footage of the attack, Mister Makovnor," said Donald with restrained annoyance. "We also have a suspect in custody."

"Then why do you need me?"

"We do not believe he was working alone."

"How did you conclude that?"

"In the footage we have, he is shown talking on the phone with an unknown person. The footage lacked sound so we don't know what was spoken, but I would be very surprised if it had nothing to do with the murders."

Viktor directed his gaze towards the simple ceiling. It was a drab grayish white coloring. Its centerpiece was a simple covered lightbulb that provided luminance within the small room. His eyes seemed to read the ceiling like a book, his chin stroked by his right hand. After a few moments he returned back to the detective.

"Unfortunately, I cannot think of any specific names of any specific enemies."

"Are you sure?"

"Why would I lie to the government?" he replied with a guilty smile.

"Very well," said Donald. "If anyone comes to mind, feel free to call either myself or the Eighth District of Metro PD. You know the number, I assume."

"I have it on speed dial."

"In the meantime, we would really appreciate it if you could help cool down some of the tensions that exist right now."

"Tensions? What tensions?"

"Surely you know that rumors are growing that this was ethnically motivated. Some say a Taran might have decided to kill your men over the whole, you know, the blood feud."

"I see," said Viktor as the two got up from their simple chairs and headed for the exit of the interrogation room. "I will do what I can, detective."

"Thank you, Mister Makovnor," said Donald as they exited. "Just so you know, we might want to talk to you again come Monday."

"How come?"

"A federal agent will be coming."

"You mean take it over."

"Well, um …"

"Regardless, yes I will come in on Monday when needed. Perhaps by that time I will have a few names of possible enemies to give you."

"Here's hoping," said Donald as he escorted Viktor to the outside of the department, past the cubicles and the front desk. Before exiting the building through the glass doors, Viktor stopped and turned towards Donald.

"Is there a chance I could see the suspect?"

"We have him under strict solitary confinement."

"Very well, just asking," said Viktor. "Good day, detective."

. . . .

Brittany waited for her friend to appear at the café. It was part of a much larger building whose awning and shadow helped deprive the sun of beamy influence. Indoors, hipsters and businessmen alike sat down for drinks, cookies, healthy snacks, and exotically-named stimulating potables. Outside, six circular tables with umbrella centers formed two rows of three. The nice weather meant the protective coverings were folded downward, covering the long cylindrical poles. Five of them were occupied by multiple individuals, with Brittany holding down sole ownership over the sixth.

Brittany already ordered a simple cup of coffee resembling the less pricy stuff supplied to division headquarters. She used a thin black straw to stir it so as to pass the time while waiting for Tracy to show up. Every so often she sipped some of the contents. A park lay in front of her, adorned with a statue of a military hero and semi-surrounded by food trucks. Even on a weekend, when so many were at home in Virginia or Maryland, the streets were full of people, some of whom were on the clock.

"Hey!" said Tracy as she approached the café, waving so that Brittany saw her.

"Hey."

"I see you ordered."

"You took too long," Brittany said with a smile.

"I'll try to be quick with my order," said Tracy as she went into the coffee house. Sure enough, she was back in a couple minutes. "So …"

"So."

"You needed to talk?"

"Yes, I do."

"So what happened?" asked Tracy as she sipped her coffee, her badge moving around some via the lanyard.

"He's seeing someone else."

"You mean, he wants to see someone else?"

"No, he is currently, right now, seeing someone else. And he was seeing her as we were dating and as we were in bed."

Tracy looked down into her coffee. "I am sorry to hear that," she said. "So I take it it's over with him."

"Yeah. I am not going to be someone's mistress."

"This is why I quit online dating," said Tracy, putting down the coffee on the rounded table. "You never know what creeps you'll find on the Internet."

"Yeah," said Brittany.

"I mean, how serious was it anyway?"

"Not very," said Brittany, drinking some more coffee. "I mean, I am not a purity freak or anything like that. I'm not a virgin, so I wasn't expecting the same from him."

"I understand."

"But still, still. I have lines and being a pimp is one of those lines."

"True."

"You know what he said to me?" began Brittany, putting down the coffee cup and talking with her hands as well as lips. "He actually said to me that she was okay with it."

"Whoa," laughed Tracy.

"I mean, seriously?"

"What can I tell you, Brittany? There are some people out there who think if it's consensual, then it's okay."

"Well, I sure as hell didn't consent to that."

"Guy must have been a polygamist in a past life."

"Yeah."

Tracy took a sip of coffee to build up to the next question. "So what now?"

"No idea," replied Brittany. "I mean, I probably should cancel my account for that dating app. I won't get my money back, but it was cheap."

"You got what you paid for," said Tracy with a laugh.

"But what's my alternative?"

"The bar scene?"

"I tried that before online dating. Same type of douchebags."

"Church maybe?"

"Haven't gone since teenage years, except for, you know, Christmas and Easter."

"That's more than me."

"I don't think I'd even go that often if it wasn't for my aunt."

"The uber-religious one?"

"Yeah her. Family come in for those holidays and everyone goes to church. I bet half of them wouldn't go if she wasn't urging them."

"She's passionate, at least."

"It can get annoying."

"At least she's not trying to get you in the sack while dating someone else," said Tracy with a finger raised.

"That's disgusting."

"Yeah, kind of is," conceded Tracy, finishing off her cup of coffee before Brittany did. Her phone made noise soon after and she learned that she only ten more minutes before the end of her break.

"Back to work?"

"Yeah. Unlike some people, I still need to catch up on a couple cases before Monday."

"I thought you were already caught up," responded Brittany in sincere confusion.

"You didn't know? Patterson put me on the triple homicide."

"Really?"

"Yeah, she wants as many people on it as she can."

"Did she tell you about everything?"

"Oh yes, and I agree," said Tracy, "it's very weird."

It was not a large church per se. The entire facility safely fit about 200 people. Its main spire, a white structure topped with a golden dome and Byzantine cross, was overshadowed by office buildings that shared the city block. On high holy days like Easter, the church had to hold twice as many services so as to manage the increase in attendance. Baptisms presented a potential crowd issue, though since they were held after worship the risk of traffic was reduced. The parking lot was barely sufficient, but thankfully the clergy received permission to use a lot across the street for overflow.

For a time, the Tayrayan Orthodox community of the area had to rely on a separate worship space across the Potomac in Alexandria. Located on Route 7, the small chapel was already shared by other Orthodox communities. The space had its benefits, since the major road made for quick travel and the close proximity to multiple shopping centers aided in finding dinner afterwards. Still, the sacred facility was small and parking was an even greater challenge there. Also those prideful Tayrayans had a strong desire for a holy place all their own for prayer and supplication.

About twenty years ago, Viktor Makovnor granted such a request. Having made millions from his business affairs both legitimate and otherwise, the patriarch of the Makovnor family shoveled out funds for a new sacred space. At the advice of the parish priest, a place in

Northeast DC was chosen for its proximity to most of the congregants. Viktor purchased it, a foreclosed business whose building was slated to be demolished. He contracted with a construction company known to have ties to the Tayrayan community, further solidifying the authenticity of the ethno-religious endeavor.

Work on the sanctuary was quick but efficient. They modeled the structure off of many of the Eastern Orthodox churches from the old country, complete with multiple golden domes, each topped with a cross, as well as a basic layout of narthex, sanctuary, and altar with iconostasis. One exception from their Eastern European brethren was the inclusion of pews for sitting. In keeping with the ethno-cultural sentiments, the interior was ornately decorated with romanticized scenes from the Tayrayan people's history. Heroes from the past, including those most known for slaughtering Tarans on the field of battle, were portrayed as warriors for the Almighty doing the will of God and Mother Church.

On that Sunday morn, the hallowed chants of otherworldly choral voices echoed inside the church's domed sanctuary. Candles by the altar, placed before icons, and suspended above in two rows of chandeliers lit the holy place. Most of the men were dressed in suits, several mostly younger men in business casual. Women wore dresses and veils to cover their heads while in the holy place. Liturgy was spoken and sung, with a black-robed, bearded priest overseeing the sacred observance. Among the ranks of laity was the Makovnor family. Three generations of Makovnors were present, grandchildren sitting by Grandpa Viktor. He had a son-in-law who was not Orthodox, but still attended the weekly services out of respect as well as a genuine interest in a form of Christianity alien to his own.

The service ended, the Tayrayans gradually exited the church into a warm sunny afternoon. Parents scrambled to get children into their vehicles, various elder members talked with the priest, and a few friends hung out where some light refreshments were provided for minor sustenance. Viktor helped his children with their children, distracting them while others needed attending. As he did so, one of his subordinates approached. Not a particularly religious man, he found little issue with having to work on the Sabbath. Wearing a suit and sunglasses, Viktor saw him from several feet away and told the two of his grandkids he was with to go see one of their uncles.

"Well?" he asked the subordinate.

"I talked with him again and he says that he can meet us tonight."

"Are you sure?"

"Yes, sir. He asked it to be the same place as before."

"Then I guess it was not him."

"Mr. Makovnor?"

"Nothing," said Viktor, illustrating his point by waving off the comment with his hand. "Tell him we can meet tonight. Did he have a specific time?"

"No sir, but he said he was willing to come whenever it was convenient for you."

"My warehouse, 11:00. No later."

"Yes, Mr. Makovnor."

. . . .

Commander Ella Patterson turned the corner and entered into the parking lot for the police division headquarters she oversaw. It was a daunting occupation, at times demanding whole days away from home and the children. However, she took in stride, being a busybody. Curving into the space reserved for her, she easily parked given the lack of automobiles stationed on either side. Key turned and vehicle silent, she unbuckled the seatbelt and opened the door. Walking around to the other side, she pushed the button on the square device that came with her traditional key and unlocked the front passenger door. Opening it, she grabbed a brown suitcase containing various work projects as well as her purse. Door shut, another button was pushed and all the locks were activated at once.

Pushing open one of the glass doors, she found the interior not as chaotic as is typical for the work week. Most likely it was worse earlier in the weekend, with juveniles and young adults lacking sound judgment going about the DC area intoxicated and carefree until the sirens blew. However, most guests in the drunk tank or charged with grave offenses were already sent elsewhere or released. Afternoon was dawning and most were either beginning their day or chilling out.

"Good afternoon, boss."

"Morning, Bob," said Patterson in response to one of the more senior officers on the force that she had known since becoming a commander. As she made her way to her office, she said her greetings to others. Opening her office door with another key on the chain, she got to her desk and turned on the computer. Sifting through some papers on various matters for a few minutes, she found nothing that immediately needed to be dealt with.

As such, she checked her email once the computer was warmed up and then made her way to the holding cells. Closing her office door, she went by the usual scenes of law enforcers busy with the guilty and not guilty. A few more nods of acknowledgement by others as she went to the cells, passing by those still being held with others behind the usual dark gray bars. They were the usual lot of hungover, petty thieves, speedsters, drug users, drug pushers, and delinquents. Rarely did her division get any particular psychopaths, though about once a week an accused murderer might find himself locked away briefly among the cells before being sent elsewhere more long term.

"Good afternoon, Ella," said the guard for the one cell that had a wall rather than long rows of bars. "What brings you here on a Sunday?"

"Have to catch up on some projects before tomorrow morning. Not least of all preparing for the fed's arrival."

"I can see that being fun," said the guard. He had also known Patterson for years and had met her older brothers at social gatherings. Such a masculine upbringing, he concluded, had to explain the demeanor and disposition of his superior.

"How is our guest doing?"

"Surprisingly well."

"Really?"

"You know me, Ella," began the guard. "I have seen my share of men get put into solitary confinement for the weekend. Generally, they break down after several hours. Probably why some groups think it should be illegal."

"What about Adonijah?"

"Quiet and reserved," responded the guard, opening the small window in the door so that Patterson could see. Adonijah was seated on his bed, looking about the interior of the room as he had been while waiting in the interrogation room. "No screaming, no rants, nothing."

"Absolutely nothing?"

"Well," said the guard looking down briefly, "a couple times he had some really bad stomach pains. Spells would go for several minutes each."

"Is he sick?"

"I don't know," said the guard, looking back at Patterson as she kept looking at Adonijah. "One time I asked if he needed to see a doctor, but he brushed me off. He said it was nothing and that it would pass soon."

"Hmmm…"

"Exactly what I was thinking."

"Hopefully we will find out more tomorrow."

"Yes, ma'am."

VII.

It was a slow trip to the warehouse. Starting out from the Magna Colonial after a late dinner, the stranger took the elevator down to the lobby and then walked out of the hotel only to find out that it was beginning to rain. He shrugged and returned to his suite and took a light hooded coat that served to protect him from the oncoming deluge. Returning to the lobby, he exited one of the many doors lined up at the front, initially protected from any raindrops courtesy the awning.

After leaving the rain shield he walked down the busy sidewalk a few blocks before getting to Farragut West metro station. Light rain was beginning to glisten his clothing as he went under the cement covering for the metro station's entrance. As he swung around to go down the escalator, a few less fortunate folks were seated against the wall asking for change. He walked down the moving steps.

Upon getting to the proper platform he waited for nearly a half hour for the Blue line train to come. As it was the weekend, scheduled maintenance was in play and thus delays occurred for a few colors. The stranger worried not, nor fretted with the ire that so many WMATA patrons did. He had plenty of time and no obligation to go to an office the following morning. Rather, he calmly sat on one of the cold hard benches attached to the wall, seeing the diverse cast of waiting characters. The black youths talking about their issues at school, the Latino family talking to each other in Español that seemed rapid fire to the non-speaker, and the middle-aged white businessmen who were hoping to get home to watch what was left of the away game on TV.

Finally, light beamed through one end of the tunnel and in a loud deep-throated honk of the train, nearly everyone halted their activities and approached the end of the platform. The long silver transport zoomed by the platform, gradually slowing its pace and making its blurring interior images clearer. Coming to a halt, five seconds passed away before the doors opened and some people exited. Then those on the platform hastily walked into the various cars, holding a faint fear that the doors might close before they were safely within the transport. The last of the passengers on, including a young fellow who had to make a dashing run to beat the doors, the Blue Line moved on.

The stranger found a window seat near one of the pairs of doors. He looked out at the blurring subterranean world as the train speedily reached the next stop, and then the one after that, and then the one after that. People got on, got off, changed seats, and socialized only with their own, otherwise keeping silent as the stranger remained. The big one was Metro Center, with a large number of people getting off and getting on. Once again, groups that seldom shared the same place in life crowded together and sat beside one another as the long silver machine sped onwards.

As the stops came and went, the number of people dwindled. After L'Enfant Plaza, far more people got off than on. By the time the train reached Eastern Market, only four people including the stranger inhabited the car he was in. The double ring and the robotic announcement that the doors were opening led the stranger to rise and exit the train car. Unlike past stops, no one was trying to enter that segment. Only a few people appeared to be waiting on the platform, with none of them getting up for the arrival. Maybe they needed the Orange Line instead, set to come in five minutes.

Looking at his phone, which doubled as a timepiece, the stranger saw he still had time to spare. The escalator was broken, so he walked up the stagnant gray steps towards the surface. At the surface the rain was plentiful and people sparse. It surprised him to think that any place within the District of Columbia had so few people. Outside of the workhouses, warehouses, and after-hours office buildings, he knew only crowds since coming there. Regardless, he kept walking towards the goal. About fifteen more minutes passed before he made it to the secured warehouses.

Unlocking and opening the door without touching either, he entered the mostly empty storage space and took off his drenched raincoat. Removing the hood, he revealed his black hair and dark eyes, his bulbous nose sniffing the inside air. He tossed the coat to the floor as he found no place to hang it. Standing there all the way across from the entrance, he waited for his clandestine company. Second thoughts germinated within his cerebral passages, echoes of the shimmers of doubt over the bargain. Bowing his head, the stranger even pondered whether or not they will show up.

Then came the noise. The door was being jostled with. A key was inserted and a latch turned. The noises of an opening door and then it swung open. Two men, both in suits, walked towards the center of the warehouse as the stranger had his head lowered. Another two came behind them. Three of the four men resembled the victims of the stranger a couple days earlier. The fourth, however, was older and plumper. He was treated as an authority by the other three, who blindly did his will. As the four men drew nigh, the stranger looked up and saw that Viktor Makovnor had arrived.

"Forgive me if you have been waiting long," said Viktor, who paced as his three body guards remained still. "I would have left a key for you, but as one of my associates assured me, that was not going to be an issue."

He remained silent as Viktor went back and forth in front of him.

"I was very impressed by your work. When the DC police told me about the deaths, I knew it was your doing. Most impressive ... for a Taran."

Still silent, still attentive.

"You do not speak much, do you?"

"Only when necessary," he replied, fixing his gaze upon his older company, who smiled at the laconic comment.

"All seems to be going well," said Viktor, who stopped his pacing and stood beside the man as he continued. "The police do not have any good leads. They do not even know how you killed them."

"You wanted them out of the way, correct?"

"Yes," said Viktor. "Yes, I did."

"Do I ask why?"

"Sure."

"Why? Why would a Tayrayan willingly seek the help of a Taran to kill three of his countrymen?"

"Power, my Taran friend," said Viktor with a smile. "Power to control my internal affairs as well as my external affairs. Power to create fear and paranoia, which will lead more Tayrayans to cling to a paternal influence like me."

"To each his own," responded the stranger. "I did my part, I did as you wanted. Now there remains your end of our agreement."

"Ah, yes," said Viktor, who began to pace again, arms behind his back. "The simple matter of finding someone."

"Someone very important to me."

"Yes, I heard the whole story before. I need not hear it again. But what can a man like myself do to help a man like you?"

"You have men. You have resources. You know this place. Those are three things I do not have," said the stranger with rising emotion. "You have to help me."

Viktor's smile was gone and his posture straighter, his eyes keenly widened. "You must understand one point, Taran. I do not need to help you. I do not need to acknowledge your right to exist. Understood?"

"We agreed that you would help me find him," he said with fire in his belly and his mind, angrily looking at Viktor.

"You young people are all the same, always falling into the same traps," said Viktor as he walked towards his body guards. "As my grandfather told me, never give up something without getting something first."

The stranger's eyes became as fire, causing the three guards to begin moving about in discomfort. The eyebrow ends pointing downward, the stranger slowly shook his head to the negative. "You dare break your word to me." His breathing increased, as did his blinking and his heart rate. "Do you not know what I am capable of?" The overhead warehouse lights began to flicker, random small objects scattered about the work space began to shake as if tremors were hitting the region. The guards became increasingly uneasy, yet Viktor remained fearless and resolved.

"You better cease your trickery, Taran. For I also know that the police have someone in custody for your crime. If they find a crime scene like the one you created they will know they have the wrong man."

The shaking stopped, the lights returned as normal. His breathing and heart appeared regular as before and the guards returned to ease. His head was bowed, his expression full of melancholies. Viktor, still showcasing his confidence, walked towards the stranger and stood before him. The dark eyed man closed his eyes as the family patriarch drew nigh, the mellow noise of rainfall heard in the background. "Your ability is too valuable to be wasted on three of my men," said Viktor. "You will be an excellent weapon for me as I aspire to spread my enterprises. I will compensate you richly for your work. Even a Taran scum like you can appreciate that. Is that understood?"

The stranger raised his head and opened his eyes, the lids revealing spheres that were blacker than the darkest night.

. . . .

Pushing open the glass doors, making way for a small group of coworkers and a handcuffed culprit, Brittany saw her usual surroundings at the station. There were the cubicles, the televisions tuned to news programming, and the constant hustle of people good and bad. One difference was standing with her superior and a couple of her colleagues. He was tall, well-combed hair, and wearing a gray suit. Clean shaven and late thirties with squinting eyes, Brittany already knew it was the federal agent. Nevertheless, she took a deep breath and walked towards the small group.

"Hey," said Tracy, who was in the small group along with Donald and Ella. After their usual greetings, she turned her attention to the newcomer.

"Detective Brittany Johnson," she formally delivered, extending a hand that was in turn shook by the federal presence.

"Agent Murphy Woolton of the Federal Bureau of Investigation," he said in an equally formal voice. "I'm here regarding the triple homicide of the Makovnor Family muscle."

"Yes, of course," said Brittany.

"Your superior just told me that you have a suspect in custody."

"That is correct," Brittany replied. "I was going to interrogate him more this morning, referring any possible questions to your knowledge."

"You're too kind, detective Johnson," said Woolton with a fake-looking smile. "Anyway, which way to the room?"

Commander Patterson led the way as they left the busy and crowded portion of the building into the more silent, secluded site. Inside the smaller room, with its one-way window, was Adonijah. Lacking any tangibly identifiable threat, the handcuffs were not on as before. He kept himself lax, arms resting on the metal table. The four people, three from the Metropolitan Police

Department and one from the FBI, stood in an informal line as they looked at the person of interest.

"You think this is the perp?"

"We are not totally sure," said Brittany. "The surveillance footage we have strongly implies that he killed the three men."

"Is he Taran?"

"Yes."

"That adds to my theory of a blood feud. No way anyone moves on Makovnor territory unless something personal was underneath it."

"We have doubts," said Brittany, causing Agent Woolton to turn his attention to her with a look of confusion.

"You do know that the Tarans and Tayrayans hate each other's guts, right?"

"Yes, sir."

"You know that this guy is Taran and his victims were Tayrayan, right?"

"Yes, sir."

"Then what is there left to prove?"

"Some irregularities."

"Like?" asked Woolton critically.

"You will see them soon enough, Agent Woolton," interjected Patterson, who walked between Brittany and Murphy. "For now, I would very much like it if my detective gets first stab at the suspect."

"She got to talk to him last week, correct?"

"Yes, Agent Murphy."

"Sounds like it's my turn, then."

"We were making progress," said Brittany, by now getting on the nerves of their federal guest. "I need to ask him a couple more questions before you talk to him. I promise if you give me five minutes, you can have him for the rest of the week."

Murphy backed off a bit, thought about the proposal, and then nodded his head. "Alright, five minutes. But no more than that."

"Thank you," said Brittany as she turned and opened the door to enter the smaller room with the seated suspect. He perked up as he saw Brittany arrive and sit down in the metal chair facing opposite his own.

"Good morning, Detective Johnson," he said as he shifted in his seat. "Or can I call you Brittany?"

"Brittany is okay."

"Thank you, then, Brittany. Those close to me call me Adi, by the way."

"Well, Adonijah," she replied, seeming to ignore his previous comment. "What you did on Friday. That weird transportation."

"Yes?"

"Could you do it again?"

"What is she talking about?" asked Murphy from behind the glass, unheard by either party inside the interrogation room.

"I did not tell you earlier, Agent Murphy?" replied Patterson. "Our suspect seems to be able to read minds and take people to places while remaining here."

"I beg your pardon?"

"He had a term for it," Donald chimed in as the three balanced their attention between each other and what was happening in the room.
"Something like thinkreal … mindreal …"

"Thoughtreal," interrupted Murphy. "He called it, Thoughtreal?"

"Yes," said Donald with some surprise on his countenance.

Brittany and Adonijah were in the valley, greenery and flowers gathered in sporadic clusters. There were trees in full foliage, a light wind that cooled as the sun provided a perfect degree of warmth for those below its crown. They were walking through the pleasant scenery, with its sapphire sky and distant villages.

"Unbelievable," said Brittany.

"Amazing what you can appreciate when you don't have a gun to someone's head," replied Adonijah, prompting both to laugh.

"I'm sorry about that, by the way," said Brittany. "You clearly wanted to show me something beautiful."

"Yes, I did," he said as he stopped walking and looked upon a bunch of black peonies rooted in the ground. Kneeling down, Adonijah carefully plucked one of the dark petal creatures and, holding its stem, gave it to Brittany.

"You're too kind," said Brittany, holding the flower with her right hand and looking at it as they continued to walk. "So what is this place, anyway?"

"It is the mental reproduction of my childhood home. You know, back in the old country," said

Adonijah as they went up a small hill. At every point it seemed they were surrounded by forests. Then as they got to the rounded top of the rolling hill, a small town came into view. About ninety roofs and a few spires were present. They went a bit further and saw more homes, small buildings, and a couple of churches.

"What is that place?"

"My hometown."

"It looks like a postcard."

"It does," smiled Adonijah. "Maybe the look has more to do with how I remember it than how it actually was. I was only a child when I left."

"Have you ever returned?"

"I cannot."

"How come?"

"The war."

"This was the war between the Tarans and the Tayrayans, correct?"

"Yes, it was," said Adonijah. "Would you like to sit down?"

"No, I am alright," said Brittany as she glanced at the flower. "You know, my friends are probably wondering why we are just sitting there in the interrogation room, holding hands."

"Doubtful," said Adonijah, who opted to sit down upon the hill, facing his home town. "I've learned through doing this with others that normal time does not apply here. What may feel like hours in this place may be as little as a minute in the real world."

"Interesting."

"It might be because thoughts themselves so often come rapid and fully formed through a mind, therefore time lacks dominion over such matters."

"You speak very good English."

"I speak whatever language people can understand."

"Another one of your powers?"

"Yes," said Adonijah. "Are you sure you do not want to sit down? The bugs do not bite in my world." Brittany obliged and sat next to him, still holding onto the black peony. It was obvious he was being somewhat flirtatious with his words and may have seen this as something more than an interrogation. Brittany did not mind; whatever worked to get answers from this one-named figure. Besides, there was something about him. He seemed different from other strange men she had met in adulthood. This not only included the obvious powers he appeared to have, but his overall personality. Regardless, Brittany prided herself in not letting minor feelings overwhelm her obligations.

"Why did you kill those three men?" she asked, looking down at the flower as she spoke the question as though ashamed.

"Which men?"

"You know which ones."

"Oh, yes, I nearly forgot. The triple homicide," said Adonijah as he looked at the perfect blue sky and the pleasant town below it. Forests flanked the town on either side, which was at the bottom of the hill. "I really do not know what you are talking about. I have no idea who those men were, where they were killed, or anything of that sort."

"You deny doing it?"

"Why would I do it?"

"Ethnic conflict," said Brittany looking at the suspect. "Many people hurt others on the basis of race or ethnicity. In this country, we call them 'hate crimes.'"

"That is a poor motive for me, though," said Adonijah in an amused tone. "As I learned more about being a Christian, I have since removed such enmity for the Tayrayans. As the Bible says, love your enemies."

"Is that so?"

"Let us say these three men were vile. Murder or no, eventually they were going to die of natural causes and face eternal damnation for their wickedness. I have no need to play a role in their demise, for if they are wicked that is what will come to them."

"And if they are decent God-fearing Christians like yourself?"

"Then praise be, for more sinners have come home."

"Look Adonijah," said Brittany as she got up, prompting a concerned Adonijah to follow suit. "You preach a good sermon, talk a nice talk, you have some very special powers, and know your Bible, but facts are facts. We have video evidence that shows you at the scene of the crime immediately after the three men were murdered." Her comments were briefly halted as some thunder and a brief moment of darkened skies came over the pristine terrain. "We know that whoever killed them somehow killed them from the inside out. Someone who probably has some sort of special power, like yours. What we don't know is who you were talking to on the phone that night in the warehouse lot." Adonijah bowed his head in solemnity, appearing in a state of restrained dread. Brittany did not let up, as she felt he was nearing capitulation. "Tell me who put you up to this and we can go lenient on you."

"They doubt, do they not?"

"What?"

"Your friends. They doubt what is happening here."

"You are right. They doubt. They try to believe, but as you expect, they're skeptical."

"How about I help you destroy their skepticism?"

"How so?"

"Hold my hand with your left hand and hold on to the flower." Brittany obliged and they were back in the interrogation room. "Now quickly look at your right hand."

There it was. Her eyes widened as she beheld the black peony, a healthy specimen with sable petals and a green stem, gripped by her fingers. As Adonijah moved back his hands to his side of the metal table, Brittany was in awe. She gathered herself back together and then got up from the table. Entering the larger room where the other three law enforcers were present, she opened and closed the door with her left hand, still passionately gripping the peony with her right. The three semi-surrounded her as they also saw the flower, unaware of what to make of the floral object.

"Can you explain this?" she asked Murphy, staring right at him.

"Wasn't there a serial killer who used to place those on his victims' bodies?" asked Donald with some absence of seriousness.

"He was searched, this was not on him when he was brought in," continued Brittany, ignoring Donald's comment and focusing on the federal agent. "He was placed in solitary confinement. There is no way he could have this in his possession."

"We were just discussing the matter, Brittany," said Patterson. "Agent Murphy has a basic understanding of what Adonijah is capable of."

"But not much, least of all how he got that into the interrogation room," said Murphy as Brittany backed down a little.

"You need to make some phone calls," said Brittany as she looked at the black peony that Adonijah gave her. She held the flower tenderly. "Surely someone like you knows someone who knows something about what he is."

All were jolted a little as the door opened. It was Tracy, who had to look into another matter. She arrived from the door that connected the larger of the two rooms meant for interrogation to the rest of the station. "Hey all, Mike's got something for us to see. He just called and told us where to meet him."

"Remember," said Brittany to Murphy before exiting, "phone calls."

. . . .

The three detectives carpooled to the location, taking one of the official vehicles at the station. Morning rush hour was basically over, making the trip to the warehouse in Southeast DC relatively quick. Parked outside the brick frame of the massive and mostly vacant facility, Brittany, Donald, and Tracy made their way through police security and yellow tape with black letters to get to the gruesome site.

Standing above the four corpses was Michael. Commander Patterson remained at the station to deal with other cases and affairs; FBI Agent Murphy Woolton was making his phone calls. Brittany was still holding onto the flower when they rushed into the car. She placed it on the dashboard and left it there as they exited the automobile for the warehouse interior. They stopped a few feet away from them.

"I thought y'all might want to see them," said Michael as he grimly presented the four bodies, one of which was quickly recognized by the investigators.

"Viktor Makovnor," said Donald, who noted the plump fellow and his cold closed face, as though in a state of deep sleep. A similar look was upon the other body guards. Around them were bullets and shell casings, handguns that once again served little purpose other than to depict what happened.

"Bullets that failed to reach a target, four dead men with no apparent external wounds of their own," said Michael. "Sound familiar?"

"Very," said Brittany, who saw the blood emanating from injuries along the chest yet once again no tears in the clothing. "You'll probably confirm that in the lab."

"I was about to say," said Tracy. "The description of the last crime scene sounded a lot like this. Mike, what was the time of death?"

"I reckon sometime last night."

"It doesn't matter," said Donald. "Our person of interest was in solitary confinement all weekend."

"Then we must have the wrong man," concluded Tracy. "Surely this rules him out."

"Maybe there's a copycat," said Donald. "Someone who knows about the initial crime and carried it out in the same manner."

"How though?" countered Tracy. "We don't even fully grasp how the first three men were killed. How does a copycat killer figure it out without half the analysis we've gotten?"

As Tracy and Donald debated civilly, Brittany was beginning to feel a sense of pain in her head. Hand brought to forehead, it was not a migraine or fever. It was a realization, an annoyed and disturbed realization. She looked at the bodies, those men who fell victim like the others. They died because of a power they were incapable of comprehending and for which no firearm was capable of stopping. She turned to her peers having drawn her own conclusion to what she saw with the latest crime.

"Don't either of you get it?" she shouted, commanding silence from both. "Adonijah has powers. He can create a flower from nothing, he can transport me to some other dimension, and he can read minds. Surely if he can do all that, he can escape solitary confinement and kill more people."

"You might be right," said Tracy. "We don't fully know what we are dealing with in that man. If we can even call him a man at this point."

"So what do we do?"

"I have no idea in hell," said Brittany, who took some seconds to think of something. "But if it's his mind that's doing all this, then we need to knock him out somehow."

"You mean punch him?" asked Donald.

"I was thinking something more concrete, like a sedative or chloroform. Mike, do you have something in your supplies?"

"I do. Ether should do it."

"Then be ready," said Brittany, "because there is a good chance we will need to quickly use it or else end up like them."

....

There were some nerves among those in the automobile that morning. Each of them had experience environments where their lives were endangered. After all, they were law enforcement in a metropolis known for having a high violent crime rate. They all cynically laughed years ago when the late Marion Barry declared with happiness that all crime, save murder, was down. Car parked, they played their roles coolly, not wanting to give off any sense of alarm to others.

There was no agreed upon method of shielding their intentions to incapacitate Adonijah and presumably keep him unconscious. As they entered the building no one knew if he had somehow picked up their intentions and was already halfway across the world or, as they feared, out and about performing his next murder spree. Leading the silent pack as the doors opened, Brittany saw the strange man as sociopathic, if not schizophrenic. Yet there were still more questions to be asked.

Michael broke away from the group as they waited in front of the cubicle, preparing to get the necessary chemical fluid. They had no concrete plan, but the assumption was that being the youngest and fastest of the bunch, Tracy was going to go behind Adonijah in the interrogation room and quickly cover his mouth and nose with a cloth full of ether. Maybe he would pass out before somehow transporting himself to another world or killing them the same way he killed Viktor and the other Tayrayans.

As they waited, Agent Murphy Woolton and an unknown older gentleman approached the pack of investigators. Brittany observed them passing by the cubicles, curious as to the identity of the other person. Wearing glasses, a blue tie, white shirt, and a blue dinner jacket with tan pants, he looked like an academic figure. They both seemed at ease, like all was well. Patterson was not with them.

"Good morning, all," said Murphy to the group. He then directed his words to Brittany. "You told me to make some phone calls, so I made some phone calls."

"Hello, detectives, my name is Dr. Glen Northside. I am a psychiatrist by learning and practice. Agent Woolton here thinks I can help you with a case," said the visitor.

"You're very quick for a federal bureaucrat," said Tracy.

"Dr. Northside just happened to be in town for a convention, so it did not take long to grab him," responded Murphy.

"You might be too late to help us, doctor," said Brittany.

"Oh? Why is that?"

Brittany was tempted to spill it all. She waited a moment for either Donald or Tracy or the returning Michael with his ether to explain the dangerous situation. Maybe she should tell everyone, evacuate the facility before it was too late. Then she started to wonder, she began to think that maybe things were not so dangerous. If Adonijah knew about this conspiracy, his wrath was strangely absent. Then she recalled that he needed to be near her to read her mind. Restrained panic evaporated as she responded to Dr. Northside.

"Just thinking out loud," said Brittany. "We have a person of interest, a suspect in seven homicides."

"How dreadful," said Glen. "What can I do to help you? Do you need me to perform a psychological evaluation?"

"Probably not," replied Murphy. "In fact, we think he is someone you may know from years back. We have him in an interrogation room. I'll lead the way. I am getting familiar with this station."

"We will be with you shortly," said Brittany as the two left for the bigger room of the space allotted for interrogations. Brittany then addressed the others. "We might not be in danger after all. I just realized that its doubtful Adonijah knows what we are up to."

"I am interested in hearing what the good doctor has to say first before I draw any more conclusions," noted Michael as they all joined the other two in the room adjacent to the smaller interrogation room. Everyone was feeling more relief as their sense of security grew. Patterson also arrived, having learned of her subordinates' return and about the four dead including the head of the Makovnor family.

Adonijah was seated at the metal table, arms laying on the bland top as before. It was his typical tranquil appearance and calm demeanor. If he knew of anything nefarious on the part of the investigators, he showed no sign of it. He also did not seem cognizant of Northside, who slowly walked towards the one-way window to behold a familiar face. The reserved nature of the professional psychiatrist melted as he got close to see with spectacled eyes the young stranger from his past.

"It's him," he said in surprise. His eyebrows shifted in the emotional shock, his bottom lip quivered some. "I thought he was dead."

"Who is he?"

"He is one of them," remarked Glen as he kept looking at Adonijah.

"One of whom?" asked Brittany.

"It happened over 20 years ago," said Glen as he finally removed his glance from the man in the smaller room and towards those surrounding him in the larger space. "Back in the late 90s, there was a lot of ethnic violence in the Balkans, you may remember the various crises."

"I do," said Tracy. "I was in elementary school and I remember my class preparing care packages."

"Precisely," replied Glen. "The Tayrayan-controlled government was systematically slaughtering Taran communities. The US became involved, partly because of the international outrage and partly because the Tayrayans had a stockpile of Soviet-issue nuclear missiles. We tried to secure the weapons before they were used, but the Tayrayans launched five missiles before the government collapsed. Three of them were duds and did not get more than several hundred feet before crash landing. The fourth hit its target but miraculously the warhead failed to detonate and so there was only minimal damage."

"You did say they were Soviet issue," interrupted Donald, prompting some laughter from Tracy and Michael. The mood in the room changed once more as Glen continued, recounting memories tearing within him.

"The fifth missile, unfortunately, not only hit its target, but the warhead exploded and everything. It was a small village, maybe seven thousand people. 90 percent of the locals were incinerated within moments of impact; most of the rest died within hours due to the intense radiation poisoning," continued Glen, who took his glasses off and looked down as he spoke. "By the time I got there with the team, only 37 were still alive. All of them were children and teenagers. They had been playing on the outskirts of town, on some of the hills so they were farther away from the epicenter."

"Can I assume he was one of those survivors?" asked Patterson while pointing to the window that showed the seated man. Glen nodded.

"He looks much older, but I have no doubt he is one of them," said Glen.

"What happened next?"

"We commandeered a large hotel located miles away and that was where they were kept for treatment, therapy, and the like," continued Glen as he played with his glasses. "It was within hours of arriving that we began to notice … strange things."

"What kind of things?" asked Brittany.

"It started small. We just dismissed them as forgetfulness at first. You know, a door that was open I could have sworn I closed; a light that was on that I could have sworn I had turned off. Other people had similar tales," said Glen with a pause.

"Soon enough, we figured out that none of these were mere coincidences."

"What were they?"

"They could do things, things that are beyond the norm," replied Glen who put his glasses back on, and had a rise in his voice as he continued. "They could move objects just by looking at them, they could make things appear out of thin air. I remember one little girl who complained constantly about wanting her stuffed animal. There was no way it survived the nuclear blast, but she kept asking for it. By the end of the day, I saw her happily walking around with her stuffed animal under her arm."

"You sure someone didn't just buy her a new one?"

"No, detective. The animal was too worn, aged. She had willed it and so eventually she got it, the very stuffed animal that was lost."

"What else could they do?" asked Brittany.

"Plenty of other things; the exact abilities varied from child to child. Some could touch a person's hand and know their thoughts. Others were able to take people into a different world, like virtual reality. One of them was able to hold a person's hand and actually change their mood, their very psychological makeup."

"What do you mean?" asked Donald.

"I had a colleague with me, she suffered from bipolar disorder and had to take medication. During a therapy session one of the children took her by the hand and smiled," recalled Glen. "That was over twenty years ago and she hasn't needed to take her medicine ever since. We called it Thoughtreal. One word. No space. It was like for them what they thought and what was real were the same."

"So you mean to tell me that there is a whole group of people walking around the world today with these types of powers?" inquired Brittany in amazement.

"Tragically, no," said Glen. "As time progressed … they started to die. One, two at a time. I-I do not believe I will ever get over that. The children … seeing children slip away. Most of them, most of them passed in their sleep and so we would find them in the morning. The only compensation was that none of them appeared to be in pain when they died. They just fell asleep, they fell asleep and did not wake up."

"That had to be troubling," said Michael. "I am sorry you had to see that."

Glen nodded at Michael in gratitude and then continued. "After a couple of months, there were only three remaining. Then one evening, the evening after one of them died, the other two … disappeared. They escaped."

"Escaped? How?" asked Tracy. "If the government was doing this program, they had to have cameras, guards, soldiers …"

"Yes, I know, I know," replied Glen. "But they beat the system, they escaped. No guard saw them leave, no camera got more than a few frames of them before one of them would look directly at the screen, smile, and then vanish." Glen halted his explanation and moved reverently to the window once more, to see Adonijah. "With no one else left, the government closed down the operation. They took brain tissue samples from the bodies, cremated the rest, made us turn in our notes, recordings, and written observations, and then swore us to secrecy lest called upon to divulge such information. The way Agent Woolton spoke about this matter, it sounded like my secrecy needed to be ended at once."

"Yes, it is."

"You have been very helpful, Dr. Northside," said Patterson, speaking in a room with less tension and cooled temperaments, "and for that we are grateful."

"And now we know what we are dealing with," said Donald, "even if it is way past our pay grade."

"Anything I could do to help," said Glen as he stared at the man behind the glass. "I do have one question for you."

"Fire away," said Brittany.

"I know he is one of the ones who escaped, but could you tell me which one he is?"

"Wait a minute. How can you know for sure that he was one of the two that escaped but not know which …," said Brittany, who immediately realized the answer.

VIII.

Elegant drapes were closed. A well painted white door with gold lining was shut and locked. It had a sign on the knob demanding solitude. The lights were out. An overhead chandelier and a lamp by a bed were both in neglect. Only some luminance from the evening city lights seeped into the cracks of the window coverings. Outdoor noise, bustle and hustle of vehicles and men, making their ways in the metropolis, this was the only aspect of the outside world present in the cerebral status.

He was alone. No company, no friends, and no family. Standing at attention, arms were to the sides, legs were touching, and toes were facing forward. His eyes were closed, his heart, mind, and lungs slowly pulsing. The decor all vanished to sable, the chants requesting the consciousness of another were uttered. "Do you see me? …. Do you see me?" calmly repeated at structured intervals. Several feet from him was an empty container that once held a couple of gallons of red ochre sand. It was strewn along the floor in a spiral formation, the figure occupying its epicenter.

172

He was not fully within the hotel bedroom, his consciousness beyond that of the physical. In his sight he beheld a dark forest with bizarre systems of stars revolving above. They appeared at first to be constellations, yet none of the familiar Zodiac signs were among them. No creature devised by culture or science was suspended above him on the sphere. Rather, the shapes made of bright dots were as synapses, floating above and charging in brightened form with every pulse of brainwave. Eyelids fluttered rapidly as a new being was found in the alternate realm, an otherworld crafted by imagination.

He materialized in a lighted figure, his humanoid frame becoming apparent after a few moments. Lines and shapes became multicolored, solid as the man stood opposite the first figure as though in a reflection pool. After a minute, the figure was joined fully by the other, with all the proper form and hue expected of the man if he were standing in the carnal reality of earth. There was silence, the first resident of the cerebral nether region giving a wry smile before his cherished guest.

"You look well," he said, his voice containing a peculiar echo as the waves of sound traveled towards the new man.

"Thank you," he responded, providing a similarly unexplained echo, comparable to a microphone or radio blurring.

"How are you doing?"

"I am well."

As much as he wanted to, the interlocutor who started the communication did not budge from his position. He kept still in both the nether realm and the hotel bedroom. The urge to embrace his peer was restrained; not so much out of preference but rather knowledge as to the fragility of the link. Not only did the man withhold his desire to hug his company, but he did what was possible to restrain his emotions.

"Are you still reading?"

"Yes," responded Adonijah. "Although now I go to the libraries during regular hours and sometimes interact with those present."

"Curing their ills, I assume."

"Yes, sometimes."

"What are you currently reading?"

"I recently completed Brother Lawrence's The Practice of the Presence of God. It is a devotional by a simple uneducated monk who even in mundane matters like dishwashing could see himself doing God's work."

"I see the resemblance very well between you and him, Adi," replied the man with a smile. "You could have written that book."

"How about you? Are you still reading?"

"Yes," began the man. "And I still do so through the night, though as I age it gets more tiring. I may have to go during normal hours and risk being with people in pain."

"What are you reading?" asked Adonijah with concern.

"I am learning about Lord Shiva, a Hindu deity. Shiva, the destroyer, whose power was beyond all mortal weaponry," said the man with a menacing show of joy. "He had three eyes, two that were typical of a humanlike frame and a third for wisdom. When Parvati covered the two with her palms, the Universe was plunged into darkness. Thus the third was formed and yet its power was destruction."

"That is frightening."

"Yes."

"How much of it do you believe?" asked Adonijah, who had long worried about the man's spiritual health.

"To what point is there to believe in Shiva, or Vishnu, or Brahma, or Jesus, or Jehovah, or any other heavenly being?" asked the man, his echo gaining an unusual weight as the sound waves passed by. "It is like being in battle and being struck with an arrow, but refusing treatment until one knew the color of the feathers or the name of the archer."

"I am sorry you think that way."

"Then find me and teach me my errors, that I may commit them no longer," said the man as a thunderous noise roared above them. Neither flinched nor were troubled, as such noises were common in that dark region. They made this world so grim by choice, seeking basic surroundings with the occasional beauty, as with the trees. Sometimes they met on the hills overlooking their deceased hometown, other times within the vaulting of some great cathedral yet to be constructed by the faithful.

"No," said Adonijah firmly.

"I will find you, Adi."

"The world is a big place and it takes more than that."

"Is that so?"

"The wind is ever behind my back and my path rises to meet me at every juncture," said Adonijah with confidence, picking up the paraphrased statement from the surrounding culture. The man figured it out.

"Very well," he said coldly. "There will come a time when I finally find you, Adi. I need to find you for what I must do."

"What is it?"

The man smiled once more, not parting his lips to reveal a perfect two rows of teeth. He deeply blinked and then dematerialized. Inside the dark bedroom, his eyes gained back their whiteness and normal concentric circles and the heart beat as typical for a healthy young man. With the raising of a finger, both the chandelier and the lamp by the bed turned on, giving light to the room. Another thought made and the ochre sand returned to the container. The gliding sands smoothly streamed into it, undoing the spiral as though in rewind. The last speck safely within the container, the lid flipped shut and was pushed into sealing the contents. He grabbed the handle of the container and placed it carefully into a closet where his one piece of luggage lay. Adonijah pondered things within his heart as he returned to the real world, back to noises of high pitched fiddles and pounding drums, of alcohol and revelry, of cobble stones and medieval structures.

....

"Why didn't you tell me you're a twin?" said Brittany to the point of shouting, not waiting to sit down as she quickly entered the interrogation room. Behind her was federal agent Woolton, Commander Patterson, detectives Ramirez and Patrick, and finally Dr. Northside. Adonijah looked beleaguered.

"You never asked."

"Don't get smart with me," immediately replied Brittany, who rather than sitting down opted to remain standing, leaning forward to a seated Adonijah with her hands placed on the metal table. "If you knew there was a possible suspect in these murders and you said nothing, that is withholding evidence. That is a chargeable offense."

"I am aware of American law, detective. And I do apologize for not knowing what you wanted to ask me in advance of asking me," said Adonijah calmly, not noticing the slow moving Glen passing by the others to get a better view of the suspect. "But the fact is, I myself did not know for sure he was here."

"Adi?" asked Glen, who was visible to the seated Adonijah, who then glanced over to where the old doctor was standing. He soon recognized him even after two decades of absence. A smile and a tear came upon his face.

"Dr. Glen," said Adonijah, who rose from his seat and embraced the doctor. "I cannot believe it is you!"

"Nor I, you."

"It has been too long. I should have seen you by now," stated Adonijah, drawing curious expressions from the others within the interrogation room.

"When you and your brother escaped, I feared you had died," said Glen, nearly to tears himself. "How are you still alive?"

"My brother and I were running and at one point we stopped and just realized that maybe we could use our power to heal each other," said Adonijah with a faint laugh. "I guess it worked."

"What then?"

"Well we remained together, traveling through Europe and Asia, doing as we pleased. Nothing horrible mind you, just things like reading books in libraries after hours to avoid people, staying in the best hotels. Eating tons of desserts," continued Adonijah, whose head turned downward and whose tone darkened. "Months back we, well we parted ways and I haven't seen him since."

"It was not an amicable split, was it?" asked Glen, rubbing the right arm of Adonijah as he posited the question. Adonijah shook his head.

"You are correct, it was not," said Adonijah, the law enforcers carefully noting the content of the verbal exchange between the two. "There was something about his outlook, his ideas on the world that troubled me. I decided I could not stay around him."

A pat on the shoulder and the doctor turned to the federal agent, the commander, and detectives. "I must insist, detectives, that you drop what charges you have against Adonijah. You clearly have the wrong man. You are looking for his twin brother."

"Who would that be?"

"Absalom."

Adonijah looked up with dread. Concern flooded his face, a face that up until now was known only for its placidity. He peaceably held both shoulders of Glen after he spoke his brother's name. The young man struggled to find his words and in failing to do so in that immediate moment, closed his lip and looked away, releasing his eased hold upon the shoulders of the doctor.

"Was it your brother who killed those men?" asked Brittany, looking at a man who was looking down at the table.

"I can speak for Adi," said Glen. "It had to be Absalom. When I held sessions with them as children, Absalom always had a certain darkness to his personality. Strange: two twins endure the exact same tragedy. Yet these two virtually identical people could not have been more different."

"Do you know where he is, Adonijah?" asked Brittany, her voice softer than her initial outrage minutes earlier.

"No, I do not," responded Adonijah. "For the past few months I have done my utmost to run away from him. He came close once to finding me, only a couple of weeks ago. At that point, I did not even know he was in the same country as me."

"When the storm clouds and thunder hit when I was inside that world of yours," said Brittany, "that happened right as I told you that we had video footage of you killing those men. You knew then, didn't you?"

"I thought it was possible. I also thought maybe you were lying to get a bogus confession," said Adonijah to the open displeasure of Brittany. "No offense, but it's not like I know you that well."

"Apology accepted," said Brittany stoically. "So we know he is nearby."

"If he is as powerful as we think," said Patterson, "it would be prudent to keep the location of Adonijah a secret between us."

As if cued to enter, Michael barged into the interrogation room, startling everyone inside the crowded room. Through the intriguing discussion, Michael's exact location had been forgotten. Realizing there was no immediate danger he had returned the ether to the morgue and was on his way through the building towards the interrogation space. His face was pale, his breath rapid. At first his lips moved without sound escaping. Then he gathered himself and pointed in the direction of the cubicles where the detectives had their computers and a couple of flat-screen TVs broadcasting local, national, and international news. "Y'all have to come quickly and see what's on the news."

....

It was an old city. A land once inhabited by Vikings and Celts, the barbarians of Western Europe. There they dwelled, having resisted Roman invasion and its claims towards being the one true civilization. However, British aspirations bore another conclusion, invading the emerald realm and subjugating it over a long period of time. The most despised was Oliver Cromwell, whose conquest of the land was total. He was the one who slaughtered those at Drogheda, who displaced countless Catholic nobles, and reshaped the economy in ways that some later declared were genocidal. As Alexander the Great to Iran or William Tecumseh Sherman to the South, so was Cromwell to Ireland.

Still, for all the chaos and invasion, occupation and transformation, the old city persevered. It was a changed city, having gone from an English rule, to a socialist Catholic rule, to a secular cosmopolitan culture. It was by far the largest of the cities, with nearly a quarter of the Republic living among its buildings, Medieval and modern. Whereas on the opposite coast Galway maintained its Gaelic heritage, in Dublin the world dwelt among the columned government buildings, crowded streets, lively pubs, cobble roads, paved roads, stone churches, and centuries-old academic institutes.

Americans, Brits, and Celtic descendants walked amongst one another in acquaintanceship. Southeast Asians manned registers at convenience stores, Nigerians and Romanians worked in the hotels. English and

Gaelic shared the street signs, folk from all over the western world took the tours of statues, Trinity College, the General Post Office, and Kilmainham Gaol. Attendees to that last site got to see the space where the Easter Uprising leaders were executed. Some claimed to have seen eerie presences within the open space where revolutionaries met firing squads.

He was living within the City Centre, where buildings connected to one another, forming a great barrier of different hued walls for broad pedestrian streets. Like any foreigner, he took the tours of the many sites. There were the statues and busts of early twentieth-century nationalists and the Spire of Dublin. He put his finger in the bullet holes along the pillars of the General Post Office, a site that garnered emotion in some even though it had been over a century since the uprising had been violently put down. For rest, he retired to his hotel room within the Temple Bar neighborhood south of the Liffey. At night, whenever he walked the streets, he found the occasional victim of the excesses of the city. Heroin was a major addiction, surpassing the classic potent potables of the pubs in both its usage among the youths and in the damage it inflicted upon the body. Some cruelly joked that the Spire was actually Dublin's homage to its drug of choice.

At various times during the week he worshipped at Christ Church Cathedral, near to the Temple Bar area, where he did most of his work and slept overnight. Founded in the eleventh century by

Vikings, Christ Church saw the upheavals of King Henry VIII and Cromwell alike. Most of its modern appearance came courtesy restoration work performed during the Victorian Era. Its interior included a vaulted ceiling, large pillars connected by arches along either side of the sanctuary, and stained glass windows. Rather than pews, it had rows of wooden chairs with red cushions. The processional to mark the services began at the left side of the front of sanctuary, adjacent to the altar. It then curved past one column of chairs and into the center aisle where it continued its journey to the altar and choir space. He saw these things and during worship felt a connection to the holy.

He brought nothing with him as he came off of the Aer Lingus plane save his ticket and a goodly number of euros in his pockets. Producing whatever official documents needed as he went through the security and the transactions, he hastily exited Dublin Airport and took a taxi about eight miles southwards to the Temple Bar neighborhood. As he saw it, the epicenter was the optimum place to look for him. Upon stopping at one of the hotels, he gave the taxi driver more than double the fare. Slamming the door, he entered the hotel in question and asked if someone with dark hair, dark eyes, a plump nose, and fair skin who was his height and weight had checked in recently.

Adonijah was at worship. The vaulting created an especially elegant echoing of the symphony of choir, congregation, and organ. Some were dressed in business casual or suits; many were dressed in jeans. The service was by no means contemporary, with older liturgy courtesy the Book of Common Prayer and hymns dating from the early modern era. Choir wore robes and clergy wore collars. The Church of Ireland was a high church, proper in its rituals and sacred in its demeanor. Even as the occasional emergency vehicle blared outside of the gothic structure, it eventually passed as the worship went uninterrupted. As though the mortal worlds and their ephemeral trials were but a drop in the bucket and counted as vanity. The sacred process continued.

It was the fifth hotel in the Temple Bar area he had tried. Rapidly walking from one to the next, he wasted little time after a receptionist or manager informed him that no such person was staying at their residence. Whenever one demanded some sort of proof of authority, he was always able to provide one no matter what they wanted. Often he surprised them. With his reddish hair and pale skin, he was mistaken for an Irishman until he opened his mouth and the accent sounded more English. Rushing out the door and nearly hitting someone on the way in, he soldiered on to hotel number six.

The dean of the cathedral ascended to the pulpit, speaking in a monotone as he read from the Bible. It was from the 1st John chapter 4, a passage that Adonijah could recite verbatim from memory. "If a man say, I love God, and hateth his brother, he is a liar: for he that loveth not his brother whom he hath seen, how can he love God whom he hath not seen?" he said along with the clergyman, mouthing his words lest he distract. He thought of his brother, who he left months back. Guilt came over him as the homily was delivered, as he wondered about what he had done. However, it made sense, he thought. For it was not being done out of hate, but love. Or fear. Either way, surely hatred was not a factor.

Then Adonijah began to think more about the last time he and his brother communicated via Thoughtreal. He recalled how much his brother wanted to embrace him but could not, how much it seemed to hurt him to not be near. All I gave in response was a butchered version of an Irish blessing, he contemplated. Then he started to think about what he had said, about his brother's obsession with finding him. He gave an Irish blessing, something he picked up while in Ireland. Maybe he made the connection, maybe he figured out that he was in Ireland and likely in a huge metropolitan area. He kept thinking about it, to the point where he had lost all attention towards the homily.

It was on the fourth floor and kept in good order. The manager gave him a key card to open the door after Absalom explained that the guest was a person of interest in a recent heroin drug bust. The Asian maid service had just left the room. Expressing a nod of gratitude, Absalom turned away from the manager and looked about the rented space. The manager made a passing reference to being needed elsewhere and left the supposed inspector to his own devices. He found the one piece of luggage. In it was what he expected: a few sets of clothes, a Bible, and assorted toiletries.

However, Adonijah himself was absent. He paced around the room, looking for any hint of where the guest was at that hour. There was little evidence to sift through, as he lived simply even in the hotel. No theatre tickets, no written agenda discarded on the end table in the corner. Why would there be? After all, neither the faux inspector nor his brother had ever paid for tickets of any kind. There was never a need to, since by teenage years they had developed the ability to perfectly replicate any handheld item in the genres of money and tickets. Then he remembered it was Sunday morning.

Fortunately for him, he was seated, as was his tendency, in the back row of chairs. So his rising from the seat and moving across a couple of others listening to the homily was not as distracting as it could have been. Saying his goodbye to the usher nearby the exit, he dropped a donation in the box usually used by tour groups during the week. From there he exited the sacred facility, entering into the garden space with its well-trimmed lawn, paved walkways, and the statue of a homeless Jesus. Past the gate and onto the sidewalks, he opted to take the longer route back to the hotel room.

The cathedral was his first guess. Minutes after Adonijah left the property and veered off the most direct route between Temple Bar and Christ

Church, the red-haired man came to the sanctuary. His rushed journey slowed, out of respect for the aura of the holy place. He stopped before the arched doors and then opened them cautiously. He drew the attention of a couple of people in the back row and a few others waiting in the wing. Otherwise, his presence went unnoticed. He nodded with a smile before anyone who kept looking and then quietly walked into the sanctuary.

"Are you looking for someone?" asked an older usher in a hushed voice.

"Yes, I am," said the red-haired man. "Black hair, dark eyes, my height."

"I do not know his name, but I did see a man like that this morning."

"Where is he?"

"You just missed him, he just left."

"Thank you," said Absalom. He turned away from the usher and quickened his step as he opened a door and ventured into the green space. His vision narrowed as he got onto the sidewalk and walked speedily back to the hotel. He was so close. Going across the occasional minor road, he stared at the light system and it remained in his right of way. He made it back to the hotel in good time. Unnoticed by the front desk while they dealt with a vacationing family checking in, the red-haired freckled stranger went up to the fourth floor via the elevator, sharing it with a tourist couple. Once out at the fourth floor, he turned the necessary corners of the carpeted hallway before coming to the room. In too great a rush and with no one else around, he stared at the door and it opened upon command.

Empty. No other person, no piece of luggage. Only him. Breathing hard for his speed and in intense disappointment, he sat upon the bed. Empty. Failure once more. So close. Too close. Minutes, only minutes. How could I miss him by only minutes? He asked himself again and again how he failed. He must have figured it out. But how? It was all coursing through him, the frustration, the rage, the anger, and the sadness. Melancholy mixed with ire as he walked about, bent as though in great physical pain, breathing hard as he fought to suppress the tears that were forming in the ducts.

Hands balled into fists, breathing became enraged. The door slammed shut and locked, drapes closed, and all light escaped the room. His eyes lost all hue, becoming the midnight orbs. Time and matter appeared to pass away, the black clouds blocking all shapes and forms from his presence. The breathing intensified, the heart rate beyond pace to keep. His mouth slowly opened in a scream so deafening yet so muted, eyes firmly shut as the black clouded surrounding became as fire, with tongues of flame consuming all. Eyes opened as tears dropped to the ground of fire, evaporating upon impact. The thrashing of the fire kept its distance from his body, yet tore apart the room in thunderous terror.

Through the anguish, spread to the uttermost reaches of the room, the forehead of the man became the bastion for a new eye, formed from the wrinkles of the forehead. Eye of wisdom, he said over and over, eye of wisdom. Destroy it, destroy it. I must do it now. Must, must, must! It was as black as the other two, its eye lid along with the other two flinching while waiting for the command to close. His body a silhouette behind the walls of fire, the three eyes and mouth turned to the shades of the walls, flame only as his body including his apparel became as black as any vesper.

"Do it, do it," he said over and over, coming ever closer to shutting all three eyes. His posture had straightened, with his feet planted apart from each other. The arms were to the sides from shoulder to elbow and stretched outward from elbow to balled fingers. "Do it, I must do it," he kept repeating, the fingers loosened from the fists and outstretched as well. "No," he said suddenly. "No, I cannot." The thunderous fire began to calm its noise, the blaze gradually ebbing off into darkened clouds. "Not yet, not yet," he said over and over, calmer with each repetition. "Not yet … not yet …"

Clouds that once covered the room were lifted. His third eye folded back into the forehead. The white and hue returned to the pair of eyes remaining on his face, the silhouette regained its normal form and color. The heart rate and the breathing slowed as he mellowed, casually wiping his lachrymose face as though nothing extraordinarily terrifying had just occurred. No burn marks were upon any item in the room. The man walked to the door and left the chamber.

I will just have to try again, he told himself as he walked down the hallway. As he made his way to the elevator, the family that checked in earlier went by him. Sharing the elevator with a few others, he was relaxed. I was close this time, he thought. This time I almost had him. I was closer this time than before. He kept assuring himself even as he knew that with Adonijah gone his brother could be anywhere in the world. A monastery in France, a hostel in the Alps, or even back in the Balkans. He might not even be in Europe anymore, having crossed the Pond to North America, or the Urals to Asia.

"Oh, hello," said the woman at the front desk, a Romanian accent to her English. "I thought you had already checked out."

Absalom paused before giving a response. Fortunately, there was a mirror behind the desk where she was sitting. Apparently in all of his cerebral rage, he forgot to shift into the alternate appearance he created. He collected himself before the desk. "I forgot something and had to return for it."

"Did you find it?"

"Yes, thank you."

"I am glad to hear it."

"Yes."

"Anyway, hope you have safe travels to Washington, DC," she said, creating a wellspring of excitement hidden within the body of Absalom. "I went there once as a child and I'll never forget it."

"Nor will I," said Absalom with a wry smile as he waved good-bye and exited the Temple Bar hotel.

....

Detectives Brittany Johnson, Tracy Ramirez and Donald Patrick, Commander Ella Patterson, and FBI Agent Murphy Woolton were directed to the cubicles area of the station. On the television was a middle-aged news anchor. She was talking about the recent wave of Tayrayan deaths in the area, the perspectives of some local Tayrayan and Taran DC area residents, and then the photo. "Police have a suspect in custody and while they are not releasing further information, a mugshot has been released to media," said the anchor, the photo of Adonijah now taking up space on the HD flat screen.

"Damn," sternly spoke Patterson, verbalizing the discomfort and concern abounding within each of the group that had exited the interrogation room.

At a suite in the Magna Colonial Hotel a man fitting the description of the photo plastered on the television screen watched with interest. He gave a wry smile upon seeing the visage, its curves and hair, its pleasant stare and calm deposition. Doubt was not erased only by the fundamental aspects of hair and eye, nose size and skin complexion. His very personality penetrated through the photograph. A cooler day, the man put on a jacket as he exited the suite with red hair, blue eyes, freckles, and a thin nose.

"He will know I am here, he will be here," said Adonijah with echoes of duress to his voice. "What do we do?"

"Here's what's going to happen," said Patterson calmly. "I am staying here because I have to. Donald, you and Tracy will take a car and see if you can find this Absalom before he finds Adonijah. We know what he's capable of, but we also know he's yet to attack law enforcement."

"Yes, boss," said Donald as he and Tracy hurried out of the station and to their task.

"Where do you want me?" asked Murphy.

"You and Brittany take Adonijah and the doctor to some place safe," responded Patterson. "Brittany, try and find somewhere that isn't an official safe house. Okay?"

"You got it," said Brittany as they went off, leaving Patterson with a hand covering her forehead. Michael was still standing by her.

"May I pose a question, Ella?"

"What would that be, Mike?"

"What if this Absalom fellow does show up here?"

"We act normal and pretend we don't know anything," stated Patterson. "I am not chancing him using those powers in a crowded place."

"I think I'm going to hide in the morgue," said Michael.

IX.

Whizzing by the other vehicles on the lettered and numbered roads of the District of Columbia, the blue compact car containing a federal agent, a Metro PD detective, a psychiatrist, and a mysterious figure went through traffic in a style frantic even by DC-area standards. As soon as he was able to pass a vehicle, Agent Murphy Woolton did so abruptly, simultaneously turning on his signal and turning the wheel. It was not rush hour, so most folk were walking to lunch rather than driving.

In the front passenger side was Detective Brittany Johnson, texting and giving directions to Agent Woolton. She was messaging her aunt, the only other member of the family who lived in the District. The sister of her mother was on a weeklong vacation on the West Coast to see extended family. Brittany wanted to verify that it was okay for her aunt's place to be used as a safe house. It was not the first time Brittany had made this request, with her aunt agreeing every time in the past.

In the back seats were Adonijah and Dr. Glen Northside. Adonijah had returned to a more

193

sedate state of mind, more at ease knowing that at least they were not at a police station any longer. The crazed driving did not seem to affect him; perchance it was due to his familiarity with a host of driving styles found throughout the world. Dr. Northside, by contrast, was ruffled every time Murphy cut into a lane of traffic.

Brittany smiled in relief as her aunt responded within minutes of the text message and said it was okay, including an emoticon smile at the end of her text. Feeling a little guilty of asking for the favor, Brittany texted her aunt between spoken instructions to Murphy saying that maybe they could hang out sometime soon when she got back into town. "Sounds good," replied the kinfolk, adding another emoticon smile to the message. Another turn on another numbered street and they were there.

Parking in a garage, the compact came to a stop at a space delineated by freshly painted white lines. The garage had noticeably improved since Brittany last paid a visit. Since she rarely visited, maintenance had plenty of time to fix things. The engine off, four doors opened and then closed at various intervals as the group left the vehicle. Brittany led the way to an elevator in the corner of a mostly gray garage. Three stories later, the double doors of the elevator opened. They ventured down a simply painted non-carpeted hallway to her aunt's place. Brittany had a spare key on her chain.

It was a plain locale, with white painted walls lacking posters. A set of dark blue plush chairs and couches resided in a living room, semi-surrounding a television with DVD player. A full bathroom with white tiles and blue paint on the walls was near, as was a kitchen space divided from the living room by a wall. Two bedrooms existed, one for her aunt and a smaller one for guests. Since she seldom had company, the aunt stored most of her books and papers there instead.

"This should work," said Brittany as the four panned out from the hallway entrance into the living room. Glen plopped down on one of the chairs while Murphy checked for possible security concerns. Adonijah paced around calmly. "My aunt said it was okay to use it this week since she's out of town."

"It will work for now," said Murphy after completing his security check.

"It's an improvement from the car, that's for sure," smiled Glen as he looked at the federal agent when speaking. All four were in the living room. Murphy doubted how exactly to secure a regular apartment from an individual who had the power to kill people with his mind. With the speed of their lives slowing, the adrenaline of the car ride ebbing, the four all came to occupy the furniture.

"What now?" asked Glen, who was sitting on a chair to the left of the couch, where Adonijah sat down. Murphy sat at the other chair and Brittany opted to sit next to the person of interest.

"If we want to know how to stop this Absalom, we are going to need to learn more about how this, Thoughtreal, works," responded Brittany, who directed her gaze to Adonijah. "You need to tell us everything, everything you can about you and your brother's powers."

"Can't the good doctor tell us all that?" asked Murphy.

"Probably not," said Adonijah. "As we grew older, Absalom and I noticed that our powers got stronger. It was like Thoughtreal matured with us."

"Interesting," said Glen, stroking his chin as he shifted in the comfortable chair. "What can you do now that I did not notice years back?"

"For one, I can speak to you in English," said Adonijah. "Wherever we went, Absalom and I could master the language and eventually the accents. It was like, like our minds adapted to our surroundings."

"How many languages do you speak?" asked Brittany.

"Only English," said Adonijah. "If I go back to my homeland, after a few days it will be only Taran Slavic."

"I remember we had to use translators to talk to the children," noted Glen. "There was no hint of this power years ago."

"What else?" asked Murphy. "If the crime scene report is to be believed, it sounds like your brother can control bullets."

"So can I. Any projectile for that matter."

"More importantly," asked Brittany, "what are the weaknesses?"

"Sleeping was one I remember," said Glen, directing people's attention away from Adonijah. "Once the youths were all asleep, strange things stopped happening."

"It is still the case," said Adonijah. "Whenever Absalom and I were in dangerous places, we always took turns keeping watch."

"Well at least we have one way of stopping Absalom," interjected Murphy, "we literally have to catch him napping."

"What else?" pushed Brittany. "What else can neither you nor Absalom do with this Thoughtreal power?"

Absalom shifted in discomfort. Looking down before he responded, he tilted his head upwards in solemnity. "We cannot raise the dead." A silence went into the apartment before Adonijah continued. "We tried," he continued, pausing once more to gather his emotions. "We tried over and over again. We tried to bring back family, friends. But no matter what, we failed. I do not know why we couldn't, but we couldn't."

"If your powers are restricted to the consciousness, maybe they are also restricted to this life," suggested Glen.

"Maybe," said Adonijah. "I simply concluded that it meant God gave dominion to us only for this life and no other."

"I was just about to wonder," said Murphy, "whether or not you and your brother weren't gods yourself."

"And when I had heard and seen, I fell down to worship before the feet of the angel which shewed me these things," said Adonijah, quoting from Revelation. "Then saith he unto me, See thou do it not: for I am thy fellow-servant, and of thy brethren the prophets, and of them which keep the sayings of this book: worship God."

Murphy being rebuked, Brittany continued her questioning. "Why did you and Absalom part ways and why does he want to find you?"

"A very good question, detective," said Adonijah. "For years and years we traveled, living the high life as we became increasingly able to use our powers to our own advantage. We had no formal schooling since before the missile attack, but my brother and I always loved to read, so we went to hundreds of libraries. Over the past couple of years, he became increasingly dark in his outlook. He kept reading Far East philosophy, literature, religious texts. He was twisting them together to form a worldview that was not to my liking. It became too much; I knew that he wanted to do something, to act upon his beliefs, but I was never sure what. I did not want to find out."

"You knew he was going to do something horrible and you decided to not stop him?" asked Murphy critically.

"All I knew was that whatever it was, for whatever reason, he wanted me to be near him," said Adonijah. "He is still my brother, we are each the only family we know."

"I am afraid you made a bad mistake, Adonijah," said Brittany. "In your absence your brother has murdered seven men. Who knows who else will be killed?"

"I did not think he was capable of that," said Adonijah defensively. "He never hurt anyone before. Not even Tayrayans."

"No ethnic hatred, huh?" asked Murphy, still maintaining some criticality.

"None," said Adonijah in full confidence. "It may seem strange to you, but aside from failed efforts to bring back family, we never talked about the days before the missile attack. We never talked about Tayrayans one way or the other. As far as we were concerned, it was like we were starting a whole new life. No more chores, no more family, and no more petty ethnic conflicts."

"That is how some people deal with intense trauma," said Glen, "they block it out and suppress and it appears as nothing."

Murphy stood up. "Pardon me, I need to make some more phone calls. I think it might be best if I get some federal backup for this one."

"I won't stop you," said Brittany as Murphy went into another room to call up the Bureau. She continued to talk with Adonijah and Glen. "Is there a way you can contact your brother, possibly convince him to turn himself in?"

"No," said Adonijah, "he will not turn himself in, he will not obey any of your commands and you will have no ability to coerce him."

"Not even to see you in person for the first time in months?"

"Are you planning to use me as bait?" angrily asked Adonijah.

"We need to get him off the streets," said Brittany. "He has killed seven men over the span of four days. If he is guilty, then he must be arrested and prosecuted to the fullest extent of the law. If you can help us bring him in …"

Brittany's voice trailed off as Adonijah got up and went towards the window. He was not provoked by any noise, but simply wanted to leave the conversation. He gave a general stare to the outside world, hands resting on the edges of the window. She was annoyed at his dismissal of her words, but she understood the reasoning. Further, Brittany was still a little afraid of what she was dealing with, knowing that the powerful man had the ability to do horrible things. Yet he refused to, and for that, she was amazed. Her respect for him was growing, so she waited a moment. Then Brittany got up and walked to him. It was a careful approach that led the man to look away from the world and see her.

"You don't want to cooperate," she softly stated.

"I have cooperated enough for now," said Adonijah, "I must think more about whether I want to help you ruin my brother's life more than it has already been ruined."

"Adonijah, this isn't about ruining people's lives," said Brittany with conviction, "this is about law and bringing to justice a man who ruined the lives of seven families."

"I believe you," he conceded, looking down at the floor while still positioned at the window. "I just want time to think about this."

"You don't have a choice."

"Yes, I do," said Adonijah, now turning his dark eyes to face Brittany. "You and I both know I do.

I do not need to be here, I can leave whenever I want."

"Then why don't you?" asked Brittany, standing her ground. He hesitated to answer, a placid tension between the two while they looked at each other.

"I need to stop running eventually," said Adonijah, withdrawing away from the window. "Just let me think about this. I promise I will let you know before the day passes."

"Just as well," said Murphy, who interrupted the scene as he quietly reentered the living room. "It's lunchtime and I am starving. Pizza?"

. . . .

He visited every station. Each one was unique in its own imaginings yet tritely common in its fundamentals. Architecture varied, interior design and the overall maintenance was diverse. The people had different faces and voices, accents and skin colors. Yet similar was the overall rush, bustle, chaos both controlled and uncontrolled. Badges gleamed, handcuffs cold, and cubicles stoic with patches of sentiment taped or stapled to their walls. They blurred in his mind as he recounted them all.

Throughout the day, Absalom visited every police station within the Metropolitan system, using his favorite pseudo-image when within the walls of law enforcement and between each edifice whilst on the street. To them he was one of their own, hastily flashing a badge that was created by the synapses of his brain projected into the world. It was as real as any other lanyard flung identification, though its origins were beyond the capabilities of nearly all the world's human inhabitants. They agreed to show him the files on prisoners, to inform him of transfers and witnesses.

Unbeknownst to him, Commander Patterson had opted to keep the whereabouts of his brother off the record. Searching files with the aid of fooled secretaries and duped officers provided no substantive results. By the time he entered the last of the stations, he chose to learn about safe houses and official hideaways for witnesses and persons of interest. Again nothing, as the site for Adonijah's keeping was likewise off the record. Leaving the last station, which was in southwest DC, he had a long time to think about his next move as metro and walking brought him back to the Magna Colonial.

The red-haired man with freckles, glancing at the hotel with his blue eyes, walked back into the elegant facility as the bell hop formally greeted him on his way in. People were going about, some in service economy uniforms and others in t-shirts and shorts. Using the elevator for the vertical journey, Absalom felt drowsy. He had spent several hours going to various divisions of local law enforcement just to come up empty. The doors pulled back and he walked into the carpeted hallway, passing by an older couple opening their door and pulling wheeled luggage into the comfortable place.

Eventually getting to his very own suite, he opened the door and entered in. Portal still open, he added the "do not disturb" sign around the neck of the door knob. With the door latched shut, his red hair turned to black, blue eyes turned dark, freckles vanished, and nose thickened simultaneously in one split second. A deep breath of disappointment billowed out as he slowly went for the bed. Removing his shoes, he collapsed on the sheeted mattress, sinking into it as his eyes closed.

He dreamed, a series of visions that often came to him when lost to consciousness. A dark valley where a full moon suspended above the barren ground was his first stop. The yellowish moon grew in size and then a silhouetted figure seated with legs crossed was before his eyes. In serenity he lifted his right hand and positioned his fingers in peace. He was at ease to behold the wise man filling the rounded moon as it grew larger. Without warning his mind went back to another scene. A pleasant green hill, a village not far off. He knew this helpless land all too well, seeing it again shaded by the shadow of the nuclear missile as it curved downwards and with a rocket's roar crashed into the plaza. From the dark of the shadow came the fire of annihilation, and the strokes of terror awoke Absalom, returning him to a world where he had less limitation to his power.

A check of the clock on the mantle revealed that his late afternoon nap had only lasted a half hour. Feeling rested but groggy, he got up and ventured to the bathroom where he turned the faucet on and splashed some cold water upon his head and neck. Returning to the bedroom, he started to think about what his next step was going to be. It did not take long. He did not like doing it; it always grieved him. Nevertheless, Adonijah was partly responsible. After all, he had the power to stop it.

So Absalom went to the closet door and opened it, grabbing the bucket full of red ochre-hued sand and went to the living room. Removing the lid, he did as he had many times before and began to lead the sand along a circular path that never closed. Dragging his left foot along in the spiral formation, his eyelids fluttered rapidly and his eyes became blacker than coal. By the time he began the sixth and smallest circle, he was drowning out all noise and image from the realm of reality, including the hourly chiming of the bells of nearby New York Avenue Presbyterian Church.

"Do you see me?" he asked, his voice echoing within the darkened vacuum of the innermost thoughts. "Do you see me?"

. . . .

The afternoon went by in a mélange of work and leisure, blurring as they were between keeping watch over the person of interest and overseeing efforts to find another person of interest. Tracy and Donald searched through much of the District, but to no avail. After a few hours of looking about the streets and byways, they delegated their investigation to the patrol cars and returned to the station, as each detective had other cases requiring their attention. Similarly, Commander Ella Patterson had other matters that involved her professionally, which begged activity in light of a cooling trail.

Federal agent Murphy Woolton made more phone calls, a staple of his business it seemed, and soon another four federals appeared at the aunt's apartment. They went through their labors apart from Brittany, who was learning more about Adonijah with the aid of Dr. Glen Northside. Woolton was in charge of the group of agents from the Bureau and they set up shop at an unrented apartment adjacent to the aunt's place. They planned out the logistics of the matter, set up a schedule of watch for the improvised safe house, and discussed other issues regarding how to handle the extraordinary case. Woolton knew the agents, having worked alongside them for years. Therefore, they were capable of openly taunting him with impunity, asking why he was allowing a lowly district cop to have more control over this case than he, the lead federal presence.

It was intriguing to behold the interactions of Dr. Glen and his former patient. Adonijah spoke at liberty regarding his life and times following the escape from the government treatment site. He spoke of the books he read, the times he and his brother stayed up late, watched whatever television or movies they wanted, ate what they wanted, and so much more. As they entered their teen years, they matured. They decided that they needed to educate themselves, take care of their bodies, and learn to hone their powers.

The first few times Adonijah brought religion into the conversation, Brittany would slightly flinch. He seemed to have memorized the entire Bible, quoting it at length and seeming to have a passage for every point he made. As someone who did not even pray before meals, let alone regularly go to church, Brittany felt a little awkward while he spoke. If she had to choose, ultimately she did believe in a Supreme Being, some distant deity that fit the worldview of a Thomas Jefferson or a Ben Franklin, rather than a Billy Graham or a Charles Spurgeon. By contrast, Adonijah's convictions were smooth and he naturally geared his speech into them without any apparent fear of offending a non-likeminded company. There was little private about his faith and how he practiced it. Only clarity of conviction and action, of principle and practice. That much, she was growing to respect.

The discomfort partly came from the fact that much of his religious rhetoric reminded her of her aunt, the owner of the apartment where they were hiding Adonijah. Brittany felt her aunt was pushy at times with her beliefs, often asking her one blood relative in the DC area to church. The most recent request did not go well. Two weeks earlier, the aunt asked right after Brittany had endured two double shifts to tie up some cases. Drowsy and stressed out, Brittany was sharp with her relative. The usually calm detective said she never wanted to follow an institution where she had to obey rules set up by a bunch of old dead men. The aunt countered by pointing out that as an officer of the law and citizen of the United States, she already committed her life to obeying rules from an institution set up by a bunch of old dead men. Not wanting to debate, she instead argued. The fallout was such that over a week went by before the two communicated at all. It was actually the aunt who tried to make amends first, but Brittany was still not in the mood and needed more time.

"Hmmm…"

"What is it, doctor?"

"Just glanced my watch, it is getting late."

"You have an obligation?"

"Oh yes, very," said Glen as he rose from the couch, Adonijah and Brittany standing with him. "I have a dissertation I need to critique as part of a panel." He turned to the detective. "Is it permissible for me to leave the safe house?"

"I think so," said Brittany. "After all, Absalom is not looking for you. I will see about getting one of Agent Murphy's men to drive you back to the convention."

"Thank you," said Glen to Brittany, the three walking towards the door of the apartment. Glen then turned to Adonijah, who was once a mere child and now was two inches taller than him. "Adi."

"Yes, doctor?"

"Take this," said Glen, removing his wallet from a pants pocket and getting a professional business card. "It has my number and email address. Please keep in touch. Out of all my patients, I believe you are the one who has turned out the best."

"I will. Thank you for your kind words, doctor," said Adonijah, who took the card and then embraced Glen. After the hug concluded, the door was unlocked and Glen exited the apartment and then went to his planned professional duties. With the door closed and latched, only Brittany and Adonijah were in the room.

"You've made a very positive impression on him."

"Yes," said Adonijah as he made his way back to the couch. Brittany followed and sat on one of the chairs as he lay on the plush furniture. "He is a good man. I always looked forward to talking with him years ago."

"I think I owe you an apology," began Brittany.

"You owe me nothing," he countered. "You have been doing your job and have been doing it well. All the evidence pointed to me and you drew your conclusions from the evidence. If only all law enforcers were as you."

"Thanks," said Brittany, giving a blushed smile. "You experienced a lot with your brother. Traveling all over the world, looking after each other."

"He's the only family I have. The only one I've ever loved," he continued, the bells of New York Avenue Presbyterian Church chiming in the distance.

"We will find him eventually."

"That is what I am afraid of. For both your sakes."

"Has he ever been violent towards police?"

"Before coming here, he had never been violent towards anyone," said Adonijah, who got to a sitting position on the couch. "I do not know what he is becoming. All I know is that it disturbed me enough to run away. Something tells me, when he finds me, whatever he is going to do he will do it."

"Why would he want you nearby?"

Before Adonijah could answer, his eyes widened, arms gripped his guts, and teeth bit down in intense anguish. Pain shot through the center of his body, slamming into his organs and his midsection. Roaring within him, screaming thrusts of misery. He threw himself to the floor, prompting Brittany to rise from her seat and then tend towards the convulsing man.

"Stay away, stay away!"

"What's happening?"

"Just let me be! It will pass, it will pass," he kept shouting as if to convince himself more than the detective. Adonijah slowly got up, one hand on the couch to balance him and another still holding his sides. He went towards the bedroom, with Brittany cautiously following behind him. He opened the door and collapsed on the bed, wrenching in his discomfort. "Please, close the door, please." Brittany obliged.

He screamed in his misery while Brittany stood right behind the barrier. She was greatly unnerved by his pain. The detective wanted to come in and do something, but not knowing what was happening she stood down. As he continued through the plight, she called up Patterson about the episode of anguish that Adonijah was experiencing. Ella explained that while in solitary confinement he periodically went through identical episodes, adamantly shying off medical treatment. The phone conversation over, Brittany opened the door as the shouts of pain were beginning to decrease. Adonijah looked shocked to see her, like she had caught him in an embarrassing position.

He was fully clothed, laid out on the bed and still convulsing in pain though not with the intensity he was minutes earlier. As she got closer she noticed he appeared to be mouthing words. It looked to be the same four words repeated over and over again. Before she read his lips, he spoke. "What are you doing here? Why did you open the door?" he said it between breaths, desperation infused in the query.

"These pain episodes, you've had them several times since being arrested," said Brittany as Adonijah's anguish faded. "It's not medical, because you keep rejecting treatment. Further, no medications were found in your things when we searched them. Besides, with your power, you could probably heal whatever was causing this, if it was an illness. You don't talk about it. You treat this like I would expect you to treat things about your past or your brother." Brittany asked the question as Adonijah moved himself to a seated position on the bed, its covers rustled. "Does this have to do with your brother?"

He nodded. "You might want to bring in the others, so they know about what you call 'episodes.'" Brittany obliged and got the federal agents including Murphy into the room. Minutes later the suited men of varying ages, each with their badges hung around their necks, stood alongside Brittany as a seated Adonijah explained the matter. "My brother and I can communicate across long distances through Thoughtreal. We found out in our late teens that if we have something like sand or dust present, then we can channel our minds through it and then somehow project ourselves into each other's brains. It's like we are implanting thoughts into another mind."

"How does it work?" asked one agent.

"To work, I need a quiet, secluded space, generally indoors. Dust or sand formed into an image that helps me focus, and then I use Thoughtreal and ask for him to do the same. The alert sent is intense pain, usually centered in the midsection."

"So," said Murphy with some annoyance. "While we've been trying our damnest to find your brother you are telling me that you can find out his exact location with dust and thinking?"

"It's not that simple," said Adonijah. "The communication does not tell you where the person is; you have to figure it out by whatever they mention by mistake. That is why I avoid it, because I fear he will find out where I am."

"Is that why you are here, in DC?" asked Brittany.

"Yes," said Adonijah. "The last time we communicated via Thoughtreal I was in Dublin. Something I said triggered his reason and he figured out I was there. He knew I'd stay in a major metropolitan area and Dublin is the largest city in Ireland, so he searched there first. He almost found me; that troubles me more than any physical pain."

"Wait a minute," said Murphy. "If this, um, calling you, with Thoughtreal causes you so much pain, then why doesn't he just keep calling you until the pain becomes unbearable?"

"Because he does not want me to suffer," said Adonijah, looking down briefly before continuing. "My brother hates pain. He hates it when other people suffer, he hates it when I suffer. I can almost feel him in anguish when he tries to communicate, because I know he knows what's happening to me."

Brittany approached the seated Adonijah, putting one hand on each shoulder. She looked at him in compassionate pity. "You're going to have to contact him."

"I know."

"When can it be done?"

"I cannot have this many people around," replied Adonijah as he surveyed all the agents in the bedroom. "It will be a struggle enough with anyone other than me in the room."

"How about just Agent Woolton and myself?" asked Brittany.

"Yes, that will do," said Adonijah, who then looked deeply into her eyes. "I fear for you. I fear for what you will make me do."

....

"Are you sure this will work?" asked Agent Woolton to Detective Johnson. The two stood near the door of the apartment as Adonijah went about the preparations. He began to center himself as he took a container of sand recently purchased at a local hardware store. The windows were closed and drapes pushed together to avoid most light. The setting sun offered little radiance. With each facet of light covered or turned off, the space became darker. There were only three in the living room, a space big enough so that Adonijah was capable of performing the communication.

"Got a better way to contact our suspect?" responded Brittany, turning to speak to Murphy before turning back to look at the meticulous Adonijah. His humor was gone, his focus was on the task. He seemed already halfway missing from the physical realm, his mind gradually moving away from the regular. With the two looking on he did what was ritual for him: opening the container without touching it, dragging his right foot along the floor with the thick column of sand following, his eyes losing all white and color, replaced by a deep dark black that encompassed the entire ocular sphere.

Adonijah moved with the dragging motion in a straight line, going seven feet forward. His breathing intensified, the heart rate and lungs pumping harder and harder. Eyelids fluttered uncontrollably as he stopped and then made an about-face. Walking with the right foot dragging towards the two, the sand ceased its following and instead began to avoid him, rushing to either side of the seven-foot long line to form a shorter bar that fashioned the design into a Latin cross. He kept moving towards them, instilling some apprehension as they wondered what exactly was happening in the dimly lit room.

....

Knocking on the door alerted him to the service. Absalom rose from his chair in front of the television, keeping a watch on any breaking news regarding him or his brother. Surfing between local news and cable news, he learned much about what was going on in the world and what various personalities felt about it. He hated the segments about starvation, war, and disease, especially when they showed the saddened faces of hungry children or the gruesome carnage of violent extremism. Opening his suite door, he saw a well-dressed waiter who gave him a two-course dinner and liquid refreshment. Handsomely tipping as usual, the door closed and was locked. He set the hearty meal down on a small table before the television and opted to switch to another station to see some action series instead. Staged trauma did not affect him; if he looked deeply, all he found was acting. Utensils present, he carved up his course and enjoyed the sumptuous cuisine.

....

Standing at attention before them, Adonijah then turned in a similar military style about-face and was positioned to view the same wall Murphy and Brittany were looking towards. The two stood in silence, worried their words might disturb their special acquaintance. Murphy was dressed in the usual garb for a federal agent, a dark gray suit including pants and jacket, with white shirt and tie. Brittany wore dark pants, a button-up shirt, and a light jacket. Her hair was in a ponytail while Murphy's was combed over. Both of them had firearms holstered along their waists just in case it was necessary. Adonijah sat down and crossed his legs, stretching his arms out like he was about to embrace someone. His breathing died down, his lungs and heart slowed nearly to a stop. After what seemed a long moment of silence, he slowly opened his all-black eyes and uttered in a loud whisper:

  "Do you see me?"

....

Violent pain ripped into his midsection, the shock of the feeling being such that he swung his arms and tossed much of his dinner onto the floor. Kicking back the chair, which led it to descend to the floor on its back, his arms gripped his sides in a mixture of anguish and ecstasy. Finally, finally, it's happening, it's happening! A joyful burden, a glorious discomfort. The moment had come. He turned off the TV and moved the food both on the table and on the floor to the side of the room simply by looking at both. Absalom rushed towards the bedroom and its walk-in closet where the red ochre sand was found. His agony became such that he screamed in pain as he scampered to the closet, getting the bucket with the red ochre sand and taking it to the next room.

"Do you see me?" solemnly spoke Adonijah, waiting an exact time in silence before uttering it once more. "Do you see me?"

Reddish sand rushed out of the opened bucket, following the dragged left foot of the stranger. The pain was ebbing off. This was typical of their efforts to communicate; the closer their minds were the more the pain weakened. Yet it may also mean his brother was giving up. No, don't give up. Don't leave me. You are so close. I am almost there, I am almost there. Don't give up on me. Don't give up on me! Absalom continued his rush, spiraling the incomplete circles faster than before.

"Do you see me?" repeated Adonijah with two people behind him. "Do you see me?"

"This has been going on way too long," said Murphy, drawing the attention and the angry look of Brittany, but apparently not distracting the process.

"Give it a little more time," said Brittany as Adonijah repeated his mantra. "It could be that we caught his brother while he's in a crowd or something."

"Do you see me?" said Adonijah, repeating the phrase with a softer tone than the first times. He resisted the growing urge to quit himself. After all, nothing good had come of the last time he did this. "Do you see me? ... Do you see me? ... Do you see me?"

Then a rush of wind went through the room, a bellowing noise that came through the apartment and disturbed a few of the various smaller objects situated on a couple of small tables. The wind prompted quiet from Adonijah, his arms drawing back as he remained seated in a cross-legged fashion. He felt it the most intensely, but practice engendered an ability to withstand the sudden arrival. The two investigators waivered in their stances with great unease and growing trepidation. Then they were injected with fear when they heard the loud deep voice offer a reply.

I SEE YOU ... I SEE YOU ... I SEE YOU ... Each statement of the trio of words was slow, the dragging of them with hissing like the voice was a serpent. Then a moment of calm amidst the bellow, a moment where the background seemed filled with the initial incoming presence yet in a more calmed manifestation.

ADI ... I SEE YOU ...

"And I you … Absalom," responded Adonijah, whose arms rested while he slowly got to a standing position. His ascent eerily came like he was levitating and not simply through the force of his legs. "I see you also."

THERE ARE OTHERS … HERE … I FEEL THEM … I SEE THEM …

"They are detectives, Absalom," said Adonijah, who during the mental conversation mouthed his brother's words as they were spoken. It was a tendency performed by both brothers when communicating through Thoughtreal. "They want to ask you some questions about a series of murders. Can you show yourself to them?" There was a silence, a surge of nerves for the two investigators.

YES … YES …

Before them came a glowing light, like a specter or an apparition. The glow was as a blob, but then after moments passed it took the form of a humanoid, the lines and features becoming more proper and solid. Within a half minute the figure had a clearly distinguishable face and body, though the coloring seemed like a photographic negative. The frightened investigators saw the lines of the face and hands become visible, and expressions such as his wry smile became easily visible.

BETTER?

"Yes … Absalom," said Adonijah, whose brother directed his gaze and attentiveness to the two people standing behind his twin.

TELL ME … YOUR QUESTIONS …

With some hesitation over the bizarre sight before her, Brittany calmed her inner nerves and conducted herself professionally. "Last Thursday in the evening at a warehouse complex in Southeast DC three men were killed. They were three adult Tayrayan males who worked for Viktor Makovnor. Were you responsible for their deaths?" Absalom paused a moment before answering.

YES … YES I WAS … THEY FIRED FIRST … I ACTED IN SELF DEFENSE …

"Why were you there?" asked Brittany, still suppressing the urge to run from such a ghostly experience.

VIKTOR SAID HE WOULD HELP ME … HELP ME FIND … ADI … IN RETURN … I KILLED THEM …

"On the evening of last Sunday four more Tayrayan men, one of whom was one Viktor Makovnor, were found murdered in a warehouse. Were you responsible for their deaths?"

Another pause, as though the signal had to travel for a few moments before Absalom received it. The same hissing slow voice, echoing on the walls and ceiling, responded to the detective's query.

YES … YES I DID … VIKTOR LIED TO ME … HE REFUSED TO HELP ME … HELP ME FIND … ADI … HE PROVOKED ME … SELF DEFENSE …

"Then why not just turn yourself in and explain this to authorities?" asked Brittany, getting her response moments later.

219

WOULD YOU BELIEVE … ME? DID YOU
BELIEVE … ADI … AT FIRST?

"No, I guess not."

YOU WOULD DELAY ME … GIVING … ADI …
TIME TO ESCAPE …

Absalom turned his attention back to Adonijah.
His face became hospitable, amiable as his gaze
went towards the man who summoned him. Arms
to his side, standing at almost perfect attention,
Absalom loosened a bit as he saw his family
before him. Raising his right hand, he showed his
palm before the twin as he had years earlier when
they were children, fleeing those including Dr.
Glen Northside. They remembered wondering if
the fallout that killed their peers was going to kill
them next.

I AM … SO CLOSE … TELL … ME … WHERE
YOU ARE … ADI … PLEASE DO NOT RUN
AWAY … AGAIN … PLEASE … TELL ME …

"Let me get this straight," said Murphy,
skepticism somehow present in a situation where
all commonsense notions were in question. "So
none of these murders had anything to do with
the centuries old conflict between your people
and the Tayrayans?"

NONE … NOTHING …

"Then you have no plans to do something like
use your power to kill all Tayrayans?"

Absalom gave a wry smile and then responded.
NO … I DO PLAN TO … KILL … ALL
TAYRAYANS … Perplexed, both investigators
were on the cusp of asking for clarification when
Absalom continued. AND ALL TARANS …

Brittany mouthed the word "What" as Absalom spoke, the roaring background noise growing in its ominousness with each phrase uttered.

… AND ALL EUROPEANS … AND ALL ASIANS … AND ALL AFRICANS … AND ALL AMERICANS … ALL WHO ARE HUMAN … ALL WHO ARE ANIMAL … ALL FISH … ALL BEASTS … ALL PLANTS … ALL MICROBES …

… ALL … LIFE.

The declaration begat another thrust of wind inside the apartment, shaking objects on the tables and even a couple of the chairs. A look of terror came over Adonijah, who stood before the projection of his brother. Brittany's fear grew. Was he telling the truth? Is he capable of this action? He had killed others, but not on a total scale. What little bit of doubt dripped within a perplexed and nervous Brittany contrasted with the criticality welling within the heart of Murphy, who walked closer to the two brothers.

"That's impossible," he declared, almost garnering a chuckle from Brittany amongst her nerves, as she wondered how he can say this given the current situation. "There's no weapon that can do all that."

OH … THERE IS … SUCH A WEAPON … HERE …

Absalom raised his right arm and with the index finger tapped the temple of his head, smiling all the more when making his point. \

THIS … THIS IS THE … MOST DANGEROUS … WEAPON … OF ALL …

"What if I said I remain unconvinced?"

SIBERIA ... SIBERIA ... WHAT HAPPENED ... IN SIBERIA?

"What are you talking about?" asked Murphy.

"Oh, no," interjected Brittany, still having not moved from her place near the apartment's exit. "That mysterious explosion the news keeps talking about."

YES ... YES ... THAT WAS ME ... MY WORK

"Why there?"

I WANTED ... A TEST ... I NEEDED ... A PLACE I KNEW ... ADI ... WOULD NOT ... BE PRESENT ...

"I don't understand," said Murphy, losing his doubts and composure at the realization of what he was dealing with. "Why?"

DESIRE ... PAIN ... SUFFERING ... ALL COME FROM ... DESIRE ... TO REACH ... NIRVANA ... ONE MUST FORSAKE ... DESIRE ... ANCIENTS HAVE LONG STRUGGLED ... TO DESTROY ... DESIRE ... I HAVE THE POWER ... TO DO ... JUST ... THAT ... THE EYE ... OF ... WISDOM!

Upon speaking that last word, Absalom suddenly revealed upon his forehead a dark oval that lit up the room as a search light can for a moment until it returned to the dim darkening interior of before. Such a sudden brightness caused both investigators to jump back a little and led them into a higher realm of fear. The oval vanished from the forehead the following moment as Absalom continued.

THE EYE ... DESTROYS ... ALL DESIRE ... ALL PAIN ... ALL SUFFERING ... FOR SO

LONG ... I HAVE HONED IT ... FASHIONED IT
... STRENGTHENED IT ... AND ITS POWER ...
WAS SEEN ... IN SIBERIA ...

"Why not get it over with?" said a federal agent
dripping with emotion. "Why not just put the world
out of its misery now?"

ADI ... I MUST FIND ... ADI ...

Absalom directed his focus towards his twin
brother. His sadistic appearance transformed into
a compassionate affection for his kin.

PLEASE ... ADI ... FIND ME ... JOIN ME ... I
CANNOT DO THIS ... UNTIL I KNOW ... YOU
ARE SAFE ... I REFUSE TO LIVE ... WITHOUT
YOU ...

"What if I refuse?" said Adonijah, keeping his
fully black eyes affixed upon the glowing
projection of his brother. "What if I resist when we
meet?" A terrible laughter echoed through the
apartment, pummeling all objects with its sound
waves.

ADI ... YOU KNOW BETTER ... YOU WOULD
NEVER ... FIGHT ME ... YOUR OWN FLESH ...
YOUR OWN BLOOD ... YOUR ONLY FAMILY ...

Rather than dispute the point, argue with
rebuttal and opine on his true actions, Adonijah
simply tipped down his head in grief. Brittany saw
only the lowered mind but she knew things had
gotten worse. Murphy, standing a few steps
behind Adonijah, became even more unnerved.
Absalom smiled more gleefully at the concession
and then directed his statements to the
investigators.

223

ADI … WILL NOT FIGHT ME … EVEN IF HE
DID … ADI … WOULD LOSE … FOR AS HE
HELPED THE POOR … AS HE CONDITIONED
HIS POWER … TO AID THE WEAK … I
CONDITIONED MY POWER … TO THE WILL
OF SHIVA … AND HIS EYE OF WISDOM … I
AM BECOME DEATH … THE DESTROYER …
OF WORLDS … HOW FITTING … THE PEOPLE
THAT GAVE US … ZERO … GAVE US THAT
PROVERB … ZERO … OBLIVION …
NOTHING…… ALL … LIFE …

Unable to take in what was being said anymore,
Agent Murphy Woolton drew forth his handgun
and aimed it at the glowing image. A moment
after this action occurred, Absalom beheld the
sight and gave a screeching noise, like a bird of
prey descending upon its meal. His eyes and
mouth darkened and then widened, pulling
vertically to look like thick black lightning bolts.
His two arms became many, each hand bearing a
weapon. The wind that blew became violent, with
assorted objects tumbling over as though the
apartment were experiencing its own earthquake.

"No!" shouted Adonijah knowing what his brother
was capable of. Just as his twin was about to
attack, Adonijah kicked with his right foot the base
of the thick sand cross, disconnecting the bottom
few inches to the rest of the design. The
disruption to the channel was such that in a
moment within a moment the Absalom projection
vanished, what objects were being shaken
became still, and again only three human minds

were accounted for in the living room. The wind was also gone.

Absalom found himself standing in the middle of his red ochre spiral, the room around him still, its only damage being the spilt dinner hurriedly thrown to the wall to make room for the process. The black of his eyes receded, returning to its natural borders in the iris, the other colors regaining their possession. Controlled breaths and standing in good posture, Absalom casually used his mind to pour the red ochre sand back into the bucket and close the lid. He knew he was close. He knew that now the police were going to make an even greater effort to find him. If Adonijah remains in the DC area, Absalom thought, perchance he will use the investigators to his advantage.

Light returned to the apartment as Brittany flipped the switch by the door before approaching Adonijah. Murphy exited the apartment and was outside in the night air. He knew that he needed solitude to cool his head and try to make sense of what happened. He was not alone in this effort. The twin brother was sitting on the floor, slumped over as the sand was mentally moved back to the container. He gently clawed at the floor with his right hand as his left was balling and re-balling into a throbbing fist. She saw him crying when coming down to his level. He lifted his face, showing her eyes that turned pinkish and glassy. He looked down at the blank floor, uttering what he felt was more than relevant scripture for the occasion: "O my son Absalom, my son, my son

Absalom! Would God I had died for thee, O Absalom, my son, my son!"

Brittany sat down on the floor beside him. Filled with pity, she reached out and gripped him by the arm. Slowly Adonijah faced her again, a few thin lines of water along both of his cheeks, and beheld the woman before him. There was a long silence inside the apartment. By now, outdoors Murphy was rallying the troops and doing his best to explain the happenings of the past several minutes. They were alone and together. The tears ceased, Adonijah spoke to the tacit request he knew was coming.

"I have to stay, don't I?"

"Yes."

"He's right by the way," said Adonijah. "He is more powerful."

"You're more powerful than any of us. You are not alone this time, Adi."

The slip of the shortened name drew his attention and he smiled faintly. Brittany realized the informality of the appellation and drew back a bit. She felt a little stupid for calling him that, but it came automatically. Adonijah noted it, but did not make fun at her expense. "You are right, detective Johnson. Or should I say, Brittany?"

"I answer to both," she smiled. They arose from the floor and soon welcomed the others into the space.

X.

They were all gathered at the apartment of Brittany's aunt the following morning. Within the living room were Brittany, Donald, and Tracy representing the Metropolitan Police Department. Also present was Federal Bureau of Investigation Agent Murphy Woolton, along with four other federal subordinates brought in for the case. Via smart phone was Commander Ella Patterson, whose voice occasionally chimed in during the remarks given by Brittany, Murphy, and Adonijah.

The couch was occupied by three federal agents, the two plush chairs occupied by Tracy and Donald, respectively. Murphy and Brittany stood before the semicircle, as did Adonijah. The smart phone with Patterson' voice was on the table in front of the couch. The surroundings were cleaned in response to the minor messes resulting from the act of cerebral communication with Absalom.

Murphy spoke first, since he headed the operation. He explained the strange happenings once more. As before it was met with perplexity. Again, many of the law enforcers present knew that if a source claiming these mad things were a stranger to them, their opinions on the validity of the tale would be different. He told them of the danger, the horrible creature they were going after. "The man's a walking nuclear weapon that can go off multiple times and destroy all life as we know it," continued Murphy. "Needless to say, we will have to be especially careful when tracking him down."

After a few more minutes, Brittany spoke next. A de facto second-in-command, Brittany felt a little awkward since Woolton mentioned most of what she planned to discuss. Regardless, she pointed out certain expected habits of Absalom. This included going out on foot and possibly donning a disguise. This was especially likely thanks to the leaking of the mugshot of his twin, Adonijah. She reiterated the need for caution, especially given what he had done to seven men already. "He is very willing to kill. Further, he will feel that if anything, he's doing the victim a service," said Brittany.

Patterson gave some comments via the small rectangular device situated on the table. She noted that several potential leads were provided by both Taran and Tayrayan individuals regarding Absalom's possible whereabouts. While none of them had proved sufficiently helpful, she was relieved to note that the two diaspora communities were cooperating on the matter and no incidents of hostility were reported. The overall media buzz about the murders and the potential overseas ethnic conflict coming to the

DC area had thankfully died down. This made their jobs easier.

"Anything else we should know, Adonijah?" Brittany asked, drawing all the faces in the room towards the twin of the person of interest.

"Well," began Adonijah, "if this search is around the clock, you might want to have people at the libraries. Absalom and I used to always sneak into them after closing."

"Okay," replied Brittany. "Anything else?"

"I think everything else has been covered."

"Alright then," Murphy interjected, addressing the whole group. "You all know who you're looking for and why. Remember to be cautious and not approach the person of interest. For now, we need to find out where he sleeps at night and go from there. Once we've found the place, be prepared to set up operations nearby and, when necessary, strike. I do not expect our perp to survive the encounter."

Adonijah flinched.

"Now, if there aren't any other questions, everyone get to it," said Murphy, prompting movement among the agents and detectives. Brittany received a text message. Amidst the bustle, no one save her and Adonijah noticed. Her mood visibly soured. Focus was on the task, so no immediate talk of the matter. Temporary headquarters for the operation remained in the apartment, with the various agents and detectives exiting the place save for Brittany, Adonijah, and Murphy.

   He was at ease. The sun shone kindly through
the window, with curtains having been moved
back sufficiently to bring in light. Artificial
luminance was not being pursued nor needed,
given the shiny outdoors. Sounds of cars and
crowds defined the exterior, yet they were mostly
muted by the glass border between in and out.
The television was on, switched to local news.
For the time they were covering a lighthearted
story of some kind, the main anchors periodically
guffawing.

   He was calm. A good night's sleep came within
the comfortable sheets, complimented by the soft
mattress. No interruptions at the door or by the
phone. The temporary one he had used to
contact the Makovnor family was discarded the
same evening as the head of the Makovnor family
himself. No ringing, no knocking, all was well.
Waking under his own power, he pushed himself
out of the comfy bed and into the bathroom. With
a set of casual clothing in arm, he grabbed one of
the fresh towels and entered the white-tiled room.
Twenty minutes later he exited and then ordered
his breakfast.

   A $100 bill was placed to cover the expense and
the tip, a grateful uniformed waiter taking the cash
payment. Put before the television, Absalom
removed the top of the plate to reveal the dish. It
was French toast in its mixture of gold and brown
hues, with a container of old fashioned syrup,
cubes of butter, and a side of reddish brown

crispy bacon. A tall glass of natural orange juice stood beside the meal. He spent little time admiring the elegance with which the various pieces were organized and more time spreading the butter, pouring the syrup, and carving up the toasts.

For the first time in months, Absalom felt relaxed when it came to the pursuit of his twin brother. In his heart, he knew his brother was not going to run away. Not this time. Not when the police are involved; not when deaths were part of the situation. It was different in Dublin, where everyone except some cured unfortunates were ignorant of he and his brother's power. Adonijah made the evening news. While his powers were kept from the public knowledge, Adonijah himself lacked such a camouflage. Now officials from both the local and the federal government were on the case.

It felt good. Absalom felt power when he attempted to strike out at that federal agent, the arrogant one who actually assumed a firearm was going to stop him. He probably still believes it, contemplated the man enjoying his robust breakfast. It was the same kind of pleasurable feeling he felt years back when he first had to use his powers to stop a couple of malevolent folk from harming himself and Adonijah. They thought they were so strong, so intimidating. Not so much following that first blast of brainwave. Unlike those he encountered in the DC area, these rabble-rousers lived to see the future.

After a few minutes, the plate's load was reduced to crumbs and blurry lines of syrup. Orange juice washed down the rest. Rolling the dishes outside of his suite for the help to gather, he returned to the bathroom to complete his preparations for the day to come. Ten minutes later he exited the tiled room once more, cleaner and fresher than before. TV turned off, he pondered his next move. Undoubtedly they were searching for him as never before. Perchance more agents were brought onto the chase. Fleeing was never considered. He and his brother were both in the area. Phase one of his search was complete. Phase two, uniting them in one place, remained to be initiated.

As he planned out his next effort, entertaining ideas of various strands on how to reach out to his brother, a pair of federal agents entered the Magna Colonial. Floors below the pacing Absalom, they asked to see the manager of the hotel. One of the higher ranked figures arrived minutes later to talk with the two men. They showed him a copy of the surveillance image of Absalom at the first crime scene. The clear shot of his countenance was put before the manager, who did not recall such a person entering his business. Per their request, other employees were questioned and they offered the same response. Hiding frustration behind suits and stoicism, the two agents exited the Magna Colonial.

Absalom snapped his fingers when drawing his conclusion. He always doubted this approach, as it caused great pain to his twin. However, it had already gotten him this far and more. Even without a tangible way of telling where he was located within the metropolis, it did inform him about other matters. He was getting to him and this was the best way. Wear him down, coax him as never before. Absalom went for the bedroom and the walk-in closet, where the bucket was situated.

....

At the Aunt's apartment, the duo of federal agent and DC police detective oversaw the grand search. An intercom system was set up on the coffee table by the couch, with intermittent reports from pairs of agents and detectives searching the Nation's Capital. The mellow noise of the technology alerted Brittany and Murphy of the latest calling in and what was always the most recent failure. Beside the radio system for the intercom were sheets of paper, printed out lists of what various websites declared to be the best hotels in the District. Nearly all of them were in the Northwest quadrant, which helped reduce the scope of the search. However, one after the other turned up empty.

Agents made their way into the grand halls of these places, locations of great conventions, meetings, convocations, and dinners. Formality mixed with the casual haste of diverse travelers all coming to the capital of the free world. So it was logical to assume that maybe Absalom had been at one of these spots and was simply unnoticed amidst the constant rush of tourists, foreigners, dignitaries, suits, nuclear families, vacationing youths, reporters, experts, businessmen, and others. If he was in disguise, then the search became even less likely to succeed. Brittany was in idle chatter with Murphy about the state of the coffee he prepared when the tech noise sounded again.

"Headquarters, headquarters, this is Detective Patrick."

"This is headquarters," spoke Brittany into the intercom. "What is it?"

"We've left the Mayflower and it's empty. Repeat, we left the Mayflower and it's empty."

"Got it," said Brittany, her hand grasping at her forehead as she took a pen and crossed out the name. By now nearly every name including the Magna Colonial had several lines of either black or blue ink.

"You need a break," said Agent Woolton as he sat down on one of the chairs, pushed closer to the intercom for convenience.

"I agree."

"Go check on Adonijah."

"Is he okay?"

"Probably," said Murphy as he got more situated and sipped some coffee. "But it is always good to double check."

Brittany walked into the adjacent room, a smaller space that was stocked with plenty of library books. The door was open and Adonijah barely moved from his seat when Brittany entered. It was just enough motion to acknowledge her presence. He was reading, his fingers touching the text and moving down the page as he looked at it.

"Can you read the author's mind when you do that?" asked Brittany with a smile as she sat down at an empty chair in the room.

"Maybe," said Adonijah as he shut the book and directed his attention to the detective. "Something happens. It might be their thoughts; it might be mine."

"You're not sure?"

"I hate to sound clichéd, but this power did not come with an instruction manual. I have no way of knowing exactly everything I can do. Only through testing things do I figure stuff out."

"Maybe I could track that author down for you and we could find out," replied Brittany. "Maybe we can do that after we find your brother."

"What was the text message about?" asked Adonijah, making Brittany a little uncomfortable in her chair.

"That's personal."

"Come on, Brittany," said Adonijah, "If I wanted to I could always just read your mind."

"Not if I don't let you touch my hands."

"I can do it remotely," countered Adonijah in a lighthearted tone. "It's just easier and more detailed when touching the body that surrounds the mind."

"Well," said Brittany as she shifted some. "You already know my bad experiences with men. It was an ex of mine. He sent me a message wanting to reconnect."

"And you said?"

"Nothing. Not yet, anyway."

"What are you planning to say?" asked Adonijah, again encountering a wall of silence. "I only want to help."

"I know," said Brittany, adding hesitation. "But the thing is, this is the type of stuff that only girls talk to each other about. It gets kind of uncomfortable talking about this to a guy."

"How come?" asked Adonijah. "If you are having guy problems, surely the most authoritative expert on the problem is a guy."

"Alright then, I'll buy that for now."

"So what were you going to say?"

"I want to say no, to say it was over months ago. I'm not afraid of him; after all, I own a gun and he knows it."

"But still, you are afraid of something else."

"Yes," said Brittany, getting up and walking about the room. "I am afraid of something else. Brittany Johnson, no fear when bullets whiz by, calmly walks into dark alleys alone for a living, stares down mobsters, rapists, and serial killers. But yes, she is afraid of something."

"Being alone?"

"That might be it."

"So you lower your standards."

"Excuse me?"

"You broke up with him, did you not?"

"It wasn't serious."

"Is it ever serious?" said Adonijah with some strain to his voice. "Have you ever had a serious relationship? Or has it been this leisurely drift from one to another?"

Brittany wanted to respond, she wanted to counter his argument, offer a rebuttal. She tried to think of a man she had ever dated as an adult that she felt committed to. She also attempted to think of any man she was with that acted like they wanted something serious from her. Adonijah sat there patiently, the closed book resting on his left leg, balanced by his hand. She looked back at him, downwards as she stood and he sat, and saw an almost angelic face of patience. His eyes seemed welcoming, a faint smile drained of hostility. She went into the effort, trying to think of any.

"For what it's worth," began Adonijah, "I highly doubt any of those men have given even this much thought to the problem."

"I'll assume that's a compliment."

"It is," said Adonijah. "Deep inside you actually want something permanent. And when it comes to trying, I can hardly compare records. I do not believe I have ever had a date in my life."

"Really?"

"None that I know of. Absalom and I both avoided people after we escaped. We rarely spoke to anyone."

"But you talk to people," said Brittany. "You have probably helped thousands of people with your powers. That required socializing."

"Then I leave," said Adonijah. "I do not stay. I always make sure they do not tell people. I do not want to be known. I do not want people to know me after I have left them."

"Sounds like a very painful way to live," said Brittany. "In fact, it sounds even more disconnected than me."

"Which is why I am reserving judgment," replied Adonijah.

"Adi?" asked Brittany.

"Yes?"

"I was wondering …" began Brittany in hesitation.

"Yes?"

"Well, I mean," stuttered the typically composed detective. "You are alone. I am alone. It seems neither of us hold anyone close. This may sound stupid, but –"

Suddenly a streak of pain went through Adonijah, tearing at his sides and prompting him in his flailing to toss the book on his leg across the room. He fell upon the floor in front of Brittany in a convulsion, stopping her train of thought. Both arms wrapped around his abdomen as the pain grew stronger. "Do you see me?" he uttered between clinched teeth, the message seemingly dripping into his voice box. "Do you see me?" he said again as he shook his head in defiance. In anguish, he looked above at Brittany in fierceness. "Leave me, leave me," he ordered Brittany as his writhing continued on the floor below, causing Woolton to look over to the room through the open door.

"What's happening?"

"Absalom is trying to contact him."

"That again? Okay," callously replied Murphy.

"Leave me," urged Adonijah.

She thought of doing what others had done. Again and again people listened to Adonijah and turned away. The reason for the pain was known, the solution was known. Just wait it out, let it pass away as the twin concludes that he will not reach him this time. Then again, maybe he will keep at it. He won the last round. He might just stay there, keep trying, the misery unending for that man. Brittany was unable to do what he wanted any longer. She was not going to listen to that text message from the shallow man, nor the painful words from Adonijah. So she stood there, wondering what to do.

"Leave me."

Brittany nodded in the negative. She was not an expert on psychology. What little she learned at the academy was not germane to this situation. But she knew basic human nature. So Brittany knelt down and took him into her arms. His back was to her chest as she slowly moved him so that his eyes locked into hers. Brittany stroked his hair, her eyes not leaving his as the pain began to ebb away. Adonijah was surprised as much as he was relieved. The anguish was vanishing sooner than ever before. Breathing improved and his arms, once wrapped firmly around his midsection, loosened.

The black clouds evaporated and the hotel suite reappeared. Absalom stood in the middle of the red ochre sand spiral. His expressions of shock bordered on the comedic as he looked around the room. He was kicked out of the communicative trance. How was this possible? Was the power of Thoughtreal leaving him? Absalom looked at the sand spiral and tried out his nonpareil ability. Stretching out his hand with fingers splayed, he saw the red ochre lines hastily return to the bucket and the lid shut firmly.

"How did you do that?" asked Adonijah as he was seated on the floor, her arms hesitantly moving away from the embrace.

"I don't know."

"Neither do I," said Adonijah as he and Brittany got to a standing position. "God is merciful. I knew He sent you into my life for a reason."

Brittany smiled. Maybe it was because she had been around Adonijah for some time now, maybe it was something he was doing with his powers. Either way, she had become accustomed to his faith-filled rhetoric and was starting to welcome it. No longer did it make her flinch a little or add weight to the postmodern cynicism so ripe in that time and place. He was genuine; even in weakness he was genuine.

"I hate to interrupt," Murphy said while leaning against the doorway arch, drawing the attention of the other two. "But we have a problem."

. . . .

Gathered at the apartment were the disappointed and the tired. A large ordered meal from the nearest Chinese food restaurant was consumed by the federal and metropolitan investigators. They discussed and argued, they pondered and some even made minor jokes to lighten the mood. There was talk of expanding the net, of including more agents in the effort. This was vetoed by Murphy Woolton, who was concerned about too many folks stumbling into the lair of Absalom and triggering something unimaginable. While Brittany Johnson pointed out that Absalom was withholding his destructive solution for when he found his brother, Murphy had his doubts about his sincerity.

Once rested and fed, they returned to work. Murphy ordered his subordinates to explore the streets and check lower quality hotels in the area. Detective Donald Patrick agreed to start looking at better places outside of Northwest. The net was widening to include more of the capital. Brittany, however, decided that she and fellow detective Tracy Ramirez were going to double check some of the better high end hotels. Maybe the first wave of queries came to the wrong shift.

It was midafternoon and the opening volley of rush hour was already starting to thicken the density of cars. On the grid of streets vehicles with tags bearing Virginia, Maryland, and Taxation Without Representation dominated the herds. Honking occurred and hitting the breaks even when traffic lights were green happened frequently. The trips to each of the Northwest hotels took longer, by two or three fold, than the amount of time they took in the morning. Brittany and Tracy returned to the Mayflower only to find nothing but a lawyers' convention in the Promenade Ballroom. Since it was only a couple of blocks from there, Brittany and Tracy decided to walk to the next hotel on their list.

"One down, ten to go," remarked Brittany as she scratched off the Mayflower for the second time that day.

"Can I ask you something personal?" said Ramirez, who walked at a decent pace beside her coworker and friend. "It might be a bit embarrassing."

"No one around us is listening," said Brittany stoically and correctly as plenty of folk went by on either side on the light gray pedestrian walkways.

"Do you like him?"

"Excuse me?"

"You know, Adonijah."

"I knew who you meant."

"Come on, if you are feeling something for him, I'm not judging," said Ramirez as they turned the corner and saw the awning of the Magna Colonial.

"Okay yes, I do," said Brittany as the two walked past the bellhop. "For what it's worth, I'm sure he feels the same way."

"All the better," said Tracy. "He's a good catch. He strikes me as the kind of guy who doesn't expect you to follow the three date rule."

"Doesn't expect?" replied Brittany in amusement. "I'd bet money he doesn't even know what the three date rule is."

The conversation ended there as the two approached the front desk for the large and ornately decorated hotel. There was an older woman there, not quite a manager but neither a lowly shift worker. She smiled at the two women who came before her and became more serious as they both showed their respective badges. The woman nodded and the lanyards returned to their previous hanging position.

"How can I help you?"

"Detectives Johnson and Ramirez. We understand that a couple federal agents came in here earlier looking for a suspect in a series of murders."

"Yes, I was on duty then," she said as she turned her gaze upwards while remembering. "They asked me and others and none of us knew the man."

"Well," said Brittany, "we are just double-checking to make sure." Ramirez took out a copy of the surveillance still and showed it to the hotel employee. "Now that you have had time to think about this, are you sure this man has not been here before?"

"Very sure," said the older woman, who had briefly leaned towards the photo to better look at the facial details. "I remember faces and that face is not familiar. Sorry."

"Well what about strange behaviors?"

"Detective, a lot of strange things happen in DC and a lot of strange people come to DC. It's impossible to remember everything."

"What about current residents?" asked Brittany all the more earnestly. "Something must have been done by someone which was that much weirder than normal. Maybe acted a certain way, did something with the staff."

The woman looked up to the ceiling again, contemplating the wave of suggestions. She seemed dower at first but then lit up a bit, like inspiration was poured into her inner being. "You know what? There is at least one guest here who is kind of strange."

"Yes?"

"Well," said the employee, "he has one of the big suites all to himself, which isn't in and of itself crazy. I mean, we get plenty of rich heirs and bachelor businessmen in our best rooms."

"But?"

"But, as you say, this fellow is strange," replied the older woman. "In all his expenses he always pays with paper money." It clicked for Brittany.

"Do you recall what name he registered under?"

"Smith." It clicked for Tracy. "But he doesn't look anything like that photo you showed me. Not one bit."

"Can you give us a description?" asked Brittany excitedly.

Back at the apartment the agents were all present. Adonijah was among them as the two detectives entered into the living room where the others were seated. There were empty and mostly empty containers of Chinese food, with a fair amount of rice and some extra soy sauce still scattered on the table. Each person looked with interest at the two detectives as they spoke about the finding.

"She gave us a description."

"Our first good lead all day."

Adonijah stood up.

"Before you give it," said Adonijah. "Let me guess it."

"Alright."

Rather than speak his theory, Adonijah blinked and in that moment his entire appearance except for the clothes he wore was altered. His skin was a shade or two fairer, his hair was red, his eyes blue, and his nose slimmer compared to its actual Slavic form. Brittany smiled as she saw the effort. "Almost," Brittany said. "The employee at the Magna Colonial said the man had freckles."

"He must have added that part later."

"No one's perfect, not even someone with your powers," said Brittany as she and Adonijah smiled at each other.

"Alrighty," said Agent Murphy, "sounds to me like we have our guy. He is staying at the Magna Colonial at one of their suites."

"What next?"

"We need to be careful, of course."

"Yes we do, Detective Johnson," replied Woolton. "I was about to say that we will be setting up surveillance first, preferably in a building adjacent to the main entrance. Once that happens, we wait for him to leave the suite and then send in a team to install video equipment. Then when we know he's vulnerable …"

"You strike," deadpanned Adonijah.

"Exactly, my friend."

"Well then, let's get going," said Brittany, who then directed her attention to the numerous discarded small white boxes once containing Chinese delivery. "But first, let's make sure my aunt has less to clean up when she comes back."

XI.

   It was a portion of a wall of imposing buildings.
Parallel to the streets, these structures formed
their lines of battle, ranks pushed closely
together. Some had but a narrow alleyway
between them, wide enough for only a vehicle to
use at a time. Others omitted such a cleaving in
their layout. They were useful in providing shade
at certain times of the work day, with the
occasional awning useful for rainfall. This edifice
had an alleyway on one side and was connected
to a building on the other side.
   They settled for the fifth floor. The office
building was well-staffed and well-stocked, with
firms, companies, and other professionals
claiming their stake of ideal and influential
Northwest property. The ground level had a hard
white floor with simple carpets at the doorways for
sanitary purposes. Four elevators were grouped
in two rows of two, outlined with walls of marble.
Few places were vacant; one was a large three-
room office space formerly rented by the firm
Cooper, Sharp, & Zambo. A legal practice
specializing in corporate law, they were
expanding and sought a larger space. Two

weeks ago, they moved to a good spot in Alexandria, close to Bradlee Shopping Center.

Agents entered the office, which lacked any furniture or equipment of its own, nor any drapes for the windows. Folding chairs were brought up, as well as a couple of metal tables with folding legs. The largest of the three rooms would serve as the headquarters. There the laptops were rolled open and the surveillance devices were concentrated. One of the two smaller rooms, originally the office for the firm's chief legal partner, became the place where lead FBI Agent Murphy Woolton based himself to hold meetings and conduct phone conversations. The final room, slightly smaller than the room Woolton took for himself, was used for rest for those not immediately needed. Adonijah, still troubled by helping people who wanted his brother killed, spent most of his time there.

Detective Brittany Johnson broke away from the group of Metropolitan detectives and federal agents to return briefly to her apartment. The black peony she left on the dashboard of the automobile they had hastily used to get Adonijah to a safe space was looking worn. Hours without proper liquid sustenance were unkind to the tender creature. Getting back to her place in surprisingly good time, she quickly entered her place, found a glass, filled it with water, and placed the peony within it. Just before departing once more she placed the glass with flower on her bedroom window sill.

Getting to the office building took effort thanks to the rush hour traffic. Rush hour, she cynically said to herself, more like "rush shift." Parking in the basement garage of the facility, the receptionist told her where her peers had gone to set up the stake-out. Elevator doors parting open, she walked down the plain hallway, guided partly by the receptionist's instructions and partly by the noise of the agents' business. Entering the headquarters room, she was given a basic nod of acknowledgement as a few peered down into the streets with high powered binoculars and telescopes.

Before her, a federal agent was seated at a rectangular table with metal legs and a dark green top. The surface was crowded with digital flat screens and keyboards, each of the former showing only black screens with the laconic statement "NO SIGNAL" at the center. Woolton was once again on the phone in the room to her left, pacing while the office door was open and he was visible. To her right, behind her was the third room where Adonijah was seated in a folding chair and in solitude.

"Brittany! Glad you made it," said Tracy with a smile and a level of youthful excitement. "As you can see, our federal friends called in more help."

"Yes, I see," replied Brittany as they walked to the windows.

"They have the front of the Magna covered. Woolton was able to get a team by the hotel entrance. When Absalom leaves the place, they'll go in and bug it."

"Sounds good," said Brittany. "And they know who exactly to look for?"

"Yes," said Tracy as they peered out the window, the only two without a technological looking glass to help. "Adonijah was able to recreate the image almost perfectly through that whole shape-shifting power and so everyone knows what they need to know."

"So now we wait," said Brittany.

"He's in there, by the way," said Tracy, pointing to the third room, door open, and a solemn Adonijah sitting down. There was a poker table set up near him, a couple of empty chairs put around it. "I knew you wanted to know."

"Thanks, Tracy."

"He's different, you know," said Tracy.

"I didn't notice," Brittany sarcastically replied.

"I spotted him! I spotted him!" shouted an agent, keeping his eyes within the binoculars. Across the street and several stories in distance, the magnifying visual aid made it appear the suspect was only a few feet away. Another agent chimed in, directing his scope to behold the redheaded Absalom, freckles and all, walking outside.

He veered to their left, going alongside the major road with throngs of others, adding blocks between himself and the Magna Colonial. Oblivious, he walked by an alleyway adjacent to the hotel that included a repair van, complete with bland paint job and generic appellation. "He passed you," said Woolton through the intercom system, his phone on silent. "Go in and give us eyes." They responded in the affirmative. Men dressed in jumpsuit uniforms went into the hotel. They went up the service elevator and quickly reached the correct floor. Walking hastily down the hallway, the three agents were nearing the suite. The sign requesting no disturbance was ignored. The door was opened with a key that the staff gave them. They had two duffle bags with surveillance equipment and tools with which to place the devices throughout the high end suite.

"Situation?" asked Woolton on the intercom. One agent, a microphone embedded in his shirt, responded. "We are in, now planting the cameras."

"So far, so good," said Woolton to Brittany and Tracy as the three stood watching the hotel outside the window, unable to see the work that the team was doing.

"Times like this make me wonder why we didn't just get a court order to access all the feed of the hotel," said Tracy.

"Court orders take time," said Woolton. "And they can draw attention. We cannot afford to lose on either of those fronts."

"Besides, Tracy," added Brittany. "The manager said the best rooms don't have cameras. Something about minding their own business."

"Agent Woolton," interjected the fed seated before the three digital screens, one of which was lit up with a detailed black, white, and gray feed of the living room. The other two still had all-black screens with "NO SIGNAL" statements. Murphy, Brittany, and Tracy left the windows to see what was on the screens. "Progress."

Adonijah slowly got up at the sound of the agent's interjection. He slid through the opening of the portal that was ajar rather than make it wider. He joined the standing group of people as another screen began to have snowy pictures before snapping into a full image of the master bedroom. Another camera was put in the walk-in closet, so the third screen was beginning to have the snowy incoherent display.

"He's coming back!" shouted one of the men at the window, the other spotter directing his scope to confirm the sighting.

"Are you almost done, team?" asked Murphy through the intercom with urgency. "He's only a block away!"

"Yeah, yeah, almost done!" said the agent fixing the camera and hiding it within the closet, accidentally kicking the container with the red ochre sand and moving it a few centimeters in one direction.

"He's at the front!" shouted one of the spotters.

"Get done and out, now!" stated Murphy through the intercom as the third screen finally got a shot of the interior of the closet. The camera feeds showed the three men gathering their things and speedily walking out. Door shut, they were several feet from the suite just as the elevator stopped at the floor. As Absalom walked into the hall, the agents successfully got to the service elevator and operated the lift to descend.

"There he is," said the seated agent, Adonijah welling up as he viewed his brother going about the living room, changing back to his authentic appearance. Casually the figure went to the chair in front of the television and turned it on, removing his shoes and leaning back. He thought about his next moves and did not appear to notice the cameras. Inside the fifth floor office, all were quiet, slow breathing in tense wonderment about whether he was going to notice anything amiss. At one point he seemed to look in the direction of one of the cameras, but then looked away. After about fifteen minutes of him showing only ignorance of the surveillance equipment, the people across the street viewing Absalom began to relax and got to work properly monitoring him.

. . . .

Hours later and the life of Absalom was found to be quite mundane. He watched a fair amount of television, ate his meals in silence, and did pushups for exercise. Other times he just sat there, or lay there with eyes open, contemplating matters. About half of the federal agents who joined them for the installing of surveillance had left the area, leaving four federal agents and Woolton representing the FBI. The one who initially served as viewer to the feed was on break and another similar looking man took his place. They all kind of looked the same, Brittany observed, each with the same basic build, attire, and expressions. Robotic at times, engaging every so often.

"So what do you think?" Brittany asked Murphy in the room to the left of headquarters. Murphy paused a moment before answering.

"In a few more hours, he'll probably go to bed."

"Maybe."

"Maybe?"

"Remember, Adi," Brittany stopped herself with faint embarrassment. "Adonijah said that many nights he and Absalom went out to places."

"Your point?"

"Absalom has irregular sleeping patterns."

"So he might wake up in the middle of the night?" asked Murphy with arms folded.

"Yes, it's possible," said Brittany, who took a brief look at those in the headquarters room looking at screens or through windows. "We need to be cautious. This might take a week or so. Build an understanding of his routine. Things like that."

"In most circumstances, what you said makes sense," replied Murphy, arms still folded. "But this is not typical. Absalom is not typical. We have to get in there and take him out like we were some special ops. And we cannot do it unless he's unconscious. That's something that becomes more possible each passing hour."

"What if he wakes up because he hears you knocking at his door?" `

"Don't get me started on that part," said Murphy. "We can get in there quietly enough. Hotel staff will help with that."

"Gathering information will help also," Brittany responded. "Patterns. I'm assuming the people at the Hoover building still teach that."

As the debate between the DC detective and the federal lead agent continued, across the street and in the monitored room, Absalom was staring at the roof. It was a pure white hue, painted to perfection and occasionally touched up by the management. A square space which was clean and devoid. Along its perimeter were machine-carved designs inspired by popular English Rococo style interiors for gentry homes. Fondly did he view the vacant space, longing for such emptiness to come to earth.

Chiming from New York Avenue Presbyterian Church reminded him that night was coming. Another complimentary image of vacuum for the one seeking to eliminate all that may desire. Inspired by this whim, Absalom jumped to his feet from the couch and made his way to the bedroom where the walk-in closet included the red ochre sand necessary for the Thoughtreal communication. Opening the closet, he entered to find the container right where he always put it. Descending to pick it up, he paused briefly when seeing the slightly crooked angle that it was situated on. With a faint shrug caught by the camera inside the space, he took the container and went to the living room area.

"Guys," said the seated agent in front of the screens. "Guys? Guys! I think he's about to do that weird séance thingy."

Brittany, Adonijah, Tracy, and Murphy joined the agent, standing around the three screens as they all focused on the one recording the living room. They beheld the movement of the sand behind him, following him in his dragging motion. They could just make out the varying and changing breathing pattern of the man, making his circular motion along the hard paneled floor. Adonijah was especially troubled with the sight, as the taped room began to darken unnaturally.

"Things are about to get painful," said Adonijah, looking as the others were at the figure's halting in the center of the spiral. Brittany turned to face Adonijah and opted to take action. She took him by the shoulders, prompting him to look at her instead of his twin brother. She led him to the corner of the headquarters room. Adonijah was slightly confused. "What are you doing?"

"Research," said Brittany bluntly as Adonijah began to mouth the request of Absalom, flinching as the opening bouts of midsection pain began. They descended to the floor. Brittany held him, his back placed upon her legs, their eyes locked, and her fingers stroking his hair. All but the seated agent turned to face the scene.

"Do you see me?" said Adonijah multiple times as the pain came, but surprisingly seemed halted within his frame, unable to spread outwards. This mild misery persisted for only a minute or so and then vanished.

"Guys, check this out," said the seated agent, who directed Murphy and Tracy to the screen where the darkness ebbed away and Absalom stood there awkwardly. Brittany began to help Adonijah up, but he kindly begged her off and rose by his own power.

"I am struggling to understand this," said Adonijah.

"Me too, Adi," she replied.

The two joined the others and beheld a frustrated Absalom, kicking the red ochre sand, hurling it with his mind along the room in fury. Lights flickered as his fists were clenched. Murphy wondered aloud if it was going to happen. But then Absalom calmed down, slowed his anger, breathed hard, cried for several minutes, collected himself, and returned to his methodical ways, directing the sand back into the container. Leaving one screen he entered another, taking the container back to the walk-in closet located in the master bedroom. The remainder of the evening went without incident.

....

Thursday evening. It marked one week since the twins made their presence felt in the District of Columbia. The delivery man brought up some Italian cuisine. Adonijah was the one who answered the door. While Brittany watched, the former stranger pulled out a hundred-dollar bill and gave it to the delivery boy, telling him to keep the change. An openly grateful youth smiled and left. Adonijah and Brittany went into the break room and placed the four pizzas of varying toppings on the table. The two helped set up the place with some paper plates, napkins, disposable cups, and a couple of two-liter sodas.

"You know, Adi," said Brittany as they prepared the break room, "it is a federal offense to privately print money."

"I didn't print that money," replied Adonijah. "If you tracked it down you would find a serial number and could indeed locate its exact pressing machine at a given legal mint."

"Congress should sic you on the National Debt."

Adonijah gave a smile to the thought, but nothing more came of that discussion topic. They were joined by a couple of federal agents and each person took a plate, selected a couple of slices from whichever opened flat cardboard box they preferred, got their drinks and napkins, and then found a place to sit.

Overall, the mood was lax. The sun was setting and the street lights emerged amidst the darkening exterior. They continued to observe the Magna Colonial both from the outside and within. Federal agents provided night vision capabilities for the stake-out. Murphy ate alone in his make-shift office. An agent behind the screens continued to watch while Tracy and Donald looked out the windows.

Absalom was not the same since the latest failed communication. He paced for hours back and forth in silence, he lay on the couch within the living room or on the bed above the sheets for long periods of time. A couple of times he appeared to have finally fallen into sleep. By this point he passed the 48-hour mark of consciousness with nothing more than a single light cat nap. That happened Wednesday evening, with the agents all getting ready and adrenaline abounding. Yet just as they were exiting the office space a shout from Donald stopped them, for he saw Absalom stir.

Debate occurred about moving in closer. The time it takes to go down the floors, cross the street, and then go up to the suite seemed like it had a high chance of error. However, Murphy overruled any effort to move a team closer. There was too much concern that Absalom would notice, picking up on even a faint trace of hostility. They all knew how he had tracked down his brother all the way to Dublin on the basis of a butchered proverb. A mind like that was powerful even without Thoughtreal. Besides, reasoned Murphy, if he is truly asleep, he will be out for hours. Hours made the trip to the hotel suite a quick one by comparison. Yet Absalom still had not fallen asleep.

"Murphy seems very troubled," noted Adonijah.

"He does," said Brittany between bites in her last slice of pizza. By now it was just them in the break room, the other two agents having returned to the headquarters room. "He thought this would be quicker."

"He's not alone," Adonijah said, finishing off his last slice and the sipping more of his soda. "Perchance I am mixing theory with want."

"I respect you a lot for doing this, for helping us," said Brittany, now having only crust on the last slice. "I can only imagine how hard this must be for you."

"There are no other options," said Adonijah, having to work to keep his composure. "I have no choice as to whether or not this will happen. So I must adapt … adapt to him … not being alive." Brittany tenderly touched him as he fought tears.

"I'm so sorry, Adi," said Brittany. The touch became an embrace. Adonijah again felt more peace with the contact from Brittany. The tranquil bliss was not solely reserved for parrying off the pain from the attempted cerebral communication. Something more was present between them.

"Are we interrupting?" asked Donald as he and Tracy entered the room, prompting an immediate termination to the hug.

"A little," said Brittany, causing Adonijah to give a wry smile. The mood lightened and socializing increased among the four.

"Why aren't you sleeping?" asked Murphy in a whispery voice, standing over the shoulder of a seated agent in front of the three screens. Murphy himself could have used some extra shuteye, as the case was wearing him down. He kept visualizing Absalom, full of rage and fury, opting to go ahead and not wait for his brother to be safe. In his dreadful vision, he opens that third eye of his and then shuts the eyelid, causing the destruction of the entire country, then the world. "Go to sleep already."

"You know he can't hear you, Murph," said the agent just in front of him, carefully watching the screen where Absalom was present and ignoring the other two screens.

"His brother said nothing about insomnia being part of the family," said Murphy. "He has to fall asleep at some point."

"You think it's possible he knows we're watching him?"

"No, no," said Murphy with assurance. "If he knew we were watching, he would have done something by now. Maybe even … well he would have done something, okay?"

"Pizza and soda have been in the break room for an hour now," added the agent in a fatherly tone. "You should get some more before the night shift finishes it off."

"He has to fall asleep soon," said Murphy, looking one more time at Absalom pacing about in the living room of the suite. "And when he does, he'll be out."

"And then we take him out," added the agent, who turned to look at Murphy only to find the agent with walking away. Nothing brought joy to Agent Woolton, who became increasingly agitated by the pace of the operation and the demands to be cautious.

…….

Sunrise on Friday and the agents were focusing less on Absalom and more on the door, awaiting their daytime shift. Like his opponent, Murphy seemed to lack good sleep. He chose the room to the left of the office entrance as his space, staying there even when he was technically off duty. He was concentrating his fullest endeavors to taking out what he viewed to be the greatest immediate threat to the country. Like that man on the screens, Murphy had gotten little more than a light laying down of the body, closing eyes yet staying cognizant. No dreams, no loss of time.

As Tracy, Donald, and Brittany entered the headquarters room for the daytime shift, they beheld the five agents getting ready for action. Confused, Brittany stepped forward and asked one of the agents what was happening. "Agent Woolton thinks it's going down today," responded the middle-aged fed as he secured his bullet proof vest. "Our target hasn't slept since Monday. There's no way he's staying awake much longer."

"Are you sure?"

"Have you tried staying awake for nearly a week?" asked the agent as he went to the three screens, which were being watched by the others. "Not easy. Basically impossible."

"They're committed, that's for sure," commented Donald as he and the other representatives of the Metro PD mingled with their federal company. Adonijah entered soon after, saying the usual morning greetings and receiving the same.

"Where were you?" asked Donald.

"Just taking a walk, that's all."

"What if he saw you?" asked Tracy.

"I walked around the alleyway on the other side of the office building," said Adonijah, who then saw the readying feds. "Something happening?"

"Apparently Woolton is convinced that it's going down today."

"Ah," said Adonijah in mixed temperament. "That."

"You should go with us," said the agent nearest to them. He was younger than the first one that Brittany spoke to and not as clean shaven. "If you got his powers, you can help."

"When I agreed to help you find him, I did so under the condition that I do not have to help you kill my last living family member."

The agent nodded in agreement and then went to the window to deal with observation until the command was given. They were meandering as the morning continued. Not just yet, but at least once the moment came they were ready. As ready as any federal agent could be for an assignment this atypical. A couple of them monitored the front of the Magna Colonial, a couple more manned the screens. Others talked with Murphy, sprouting a three-day beard and looking reddish under the eyes. He was also wearing an armored vest, as the others with that dark blue coating emblazoned with the all capital gold letters of "FBI." He was all business, all focus. Brittany and the others felt awkward, useless in many respects as they saw the numbers and intensity of the agents.

Waiting continued. The initial rustling about, the planning out of movements within the hotel and putting on the basic armor for the battle, was completed. They sat around, with three men leering at the digital screens. A couple of them were playing cards to cut the tension. No one was in the break room. It was about an hour before lunch. Sooner or later one of the agents was going to order some more pizza. Walking around his room, Murphy decided to go to the headquarters room. He went to the screens and saw Absalom walking from one screen to another. He began to smile.

"Adi?" asked Brittany.

"Yes?"

"Can we talk? You know, somewhere private?"

"Sure," said Adonijah as he and Brittany got up from their seats in the headquarters room and entered the break room, closing the door behind them. Donald and Tracy saw them doing so.

"I guess they wanted to be alone," said Donald.

"And they will stay that way," said Tracy firmly to the detective.

"No problem for me. I don't think anything is happening today."

The door shut with some loudness. It unnerved the two just for a moment; it had remained open most of the time they had been at the fifth floor office. Adonijah and Brittany both sat down, looking at each other constantly and devotedly. Brittany found the setting a fitting one. After all, she and Adonijah first met in a small room with a simple table, basic paint job, and a set of metal chairs.

"You wanted to talk?"

"You can read my mind."

"Tell me," replied Adonijah. "It feels more valid to hear it spoken."

"It does," said Brittany. They were seated close. She pushed her chair so that they were closer. Adonijah did likewise, the faint jerks of the chairs barely heard with the door being shut.

"You are curious."

"I have only known you a week, Adi, but I have learned so much about you. Your experiences, your beliefs, your actions. I find so little wrong with you."

"I am glad to hear it."

"But I wonder," said Brittany, pausing briefly before speaking once more. "Why aren't you like him? Your brother?"

"Of course, I'm like him," said Adonijah with a bit of a laugh. Brittany smiled some when she realized her phrasing.

"You know what I mean," she replied. "Absalom wants to destroy the world. He thinks it will end all pain. Yet you, you want to save the world. You want to help it work through the pain. Why? Why are you this way?"

Adonijah pondered the question. It was as though he never contemplated it himself. However, it did not take long for a reply. The answer came naturally for him. He returned his impassioned gaze, his eyes to hers, and responded in a soft almost whispered voice. "Do you not know? Do you not know that love is the most powerful force in the Universe? It's more powerful than any weapon, more powerful than any storm, more powerful than even death itself." They seemed to come closer as he spoke, automatically as the gravity of affection pulled them nearer and nearer, withering away the distance. "So few words stand on their own to describe God. Love is one of those few. How can I say no to something that consuming, that creating, that powerful?"

"I believe you," said Brittany.

"You can love. I felt it go from you to me those times when my brother tried to pull me into pain. Do you not know? That is why you can stop it. Affection, tender compassion. That is how his power, no matter how imposing, can be stopped. 'Many waters cannot quench love; neither can the flood drown it.'"

"What then?" asked Brittany, whose response came not with words but with Adonijah slowly moving his right hand upwards, turning it so that the palm faced away from her, and then he carefully moved it down the side of her face, beginning at the temple and journeying down the roundness of the cheek.

"I love you."

She smiled, her confirmation of the feelings both felt within them. Adonijah smiled back and then again brushed the same hand in the same manner against her cheek. Instinctively Brittany placed her right hand on his cheek, the thumb being close to the corner of his lips, the other fingers tucked below the ear. She kissed him on the lips. It felt so strong, so profound, so real. It was more than a kiss. It was a simple yet impassioned statement that this was different. He was different. There was a pause and then

Adonijah did likewise, angling his head slightly as he returned her kiss with another.

"I want to marry you."

She smiled and nodded to his request before kissing him again. He took his hands and placed them on each cheek and kissed her once more. Then he caressed her hair with one hand and used his other hand to grip her shoulder. She kissed him on the lips as he continued to stroke her hair.

Suddenly the door opened with an unlatching even louder than its closing. The two jumped back and looked at Detective Donald Patrick with great annoyance. For his part the detective was blushing as he looked down briefly and then raised his head to face the two soulmates. "Listen, I wouldn't have even thought of coming in if it wasn't really important."

"Well? What is it?" asked Brittany.

"They're gone."

Adonijah and Brittany shifted their focus to the business before them, hastily getting up from the chairs and exiting the small room with Donald right in front of them. They fanned out into a line of three before the digital screens. All the armored and armed FBI agents were missing as the door to the fifth floor office space was wide open. Tracy stood beside the screens. Cameras showed the walk-in closet space devoid of people. Likewise, the living room area was devoid of people. But the master bedroom featured Absalom, covered by sheets, asleep. By instinct Brittany rushed to the windows and saw the agents crossing the street. Miniscule in scale, they were nonetheless the agents led by Woolton.

"They're on their way."

"Then it is almost over," said Adonijah. "'Therefore do not fear, O My servant Jacob,' says the Lord, 'Nor be dismayed, O Israel; For behold, I will save you from afar, And your seed from the land of their captivity.'"

Brittany went back to the screens, leaving the window as the little men seen from stories above the street entered the hotel. She joined the others still in the fifth floor space, beholding the digital images of Absalom and his suite. It seemed so surreal, so anticlimactic. A man able to deflect bullets, able to transmit his consciousness into other spaces, able to destroy existence itself if he so wanted. This was the man who was going to be outsmarted, killed in his sleep by a group of normal government agents. She looked at his slumber, thinking how interesting it was that in a few minutes the scene was going to be very different. She recalled when she first beheld Absalom on the video footage. Brittany remembered how creeped out she and the others were when he gave a wry smile and then vanished. Then the epiphany visited her and she was filled with great dread.

"Oh no," said Brittany, breaking the silence of anticipation.

"What is it?" asked Tracy.

"It's a trap!" responded Brittany while pointing to the corner of the bedroom image, to the closed drape that still showed a slight lining of the outside; an outside where it was still clearly evening.

XII.

"Is there anything else we should do?" asked an old man who handed him the key, concerned expression surrounded by the lines of wrinkle. He was in his polished hotel uniform meeting with the men from the Federal Bureau of Investigation.

"Did you keep the other rooms vacant?" asked Agent Murphy Woolton, taking the key card from the old hand. They were beside the service elevator, away from the front of the Magna Colonial and away from the diverse guests.

"Yes, we directed guests to other floors when they showed up and told them that those rooms were reserved," replied the employee.

"Good, good," Woolton said, his peers similarly dressed and armed nodding in agreement. One of them knew how to operate a service elevator and stood by the controls, waiting for the others. "Well that's all that's necessary. Just get to work and act as though all is normal. This should not take long."

The old man nodded and by instinct saluted, a reflex he developed when serving his country overseas decades back. Going his way, the agents went theirs, filing into the drab service elevator and then ascending upwards to the proper floor. All was quiet as they passed one floor and then another. There was no talk about the risk involved for all knew it. There was no talk of the plan for all knew it. Key acquired, they picked the agent who was going to open the door. Silencers attached, they had their handguns ready to quietly and immediately eliminate the antagonist.

What they did not know was that Absalom knew from the moment he saw the disturbed container bearing his red ochre sand that someone else had been in the closet. The agents nearing the floor of the suite also did not know that Absalom was able to discover the placement of the cameras by mentally picking up the faintest traces of human activity that he was unable to connect to himself nor any of the hotel help. Lastly, the agents were unaware that each night Absalom placed the feed of the cameras on loop before sleeping. The looping continued even while he was unconscious, as it did not require his constant mental attention. Like using his mind to flip a light switch off; leaving the conscious did not flip the switch back to its previous on position.

"We need to warn them, like now!" said Tracy.

"We can't," said Donald. "They told me they were maintaining radio silence for the operation."

"He will find me," said Adonijah in dread, his lower lip quivering. "He will find me and then he will end all things."

"What do we do?" asked Tracy to the general group. There was an absence of words until Brittany looked down at the screens.

"We meet him on our own terms."

Slowly the subordinate dipped the electronic key card into the slot provided just above the door knob. The red light affixed to the side turned green and the latch made some noise with the transition. Carefully the same agent turned the handle and gradually pushed the door into the suite, barring any further commotion. Nodding to the others, each wearing a protective vest and holding a handgun with silencer, the six agents including lead agent Woolton walked into the first room of the suite. Breathing was slow and tense, footsteps were light and cautious. No one wanted to wake him. All they needed was one good shot, right to the head, while he remained unconscious. They were coming within sight of him, still under the sheets of the bed, his head turned away from them.

"Donald and Tracy, stay here and contact Ella," said Brittany as each person in the fifth floor of the office building quickly readied themselves for the coming confrontation. "Tell her we need to get metro to let us take Adonijah through the train without incident. They need to know that a police detective is taking a person of interest via the metro to an undisclosed location on the Blue Line."

"Absalom will follow," said Adonijah.

"That is the plan," responded Brittany, receiving a confused look from Adonijah when she said so.

"We're going to lure him away from the city, hopefully that way if something happens ... anyway I know where to go."

"What about backup?" asked Donald.

"No," said Brittany firmly. "We have to make Absalom think that it is just us and no one else. If there's more force put in ... it's just going to be more bodies."

The agents came into the suite in a curved single-file line. As they entered the bedroom they fanned out, lining along the side of the bed nearest to the entrance. Two of the agents were near his head and pointed their muzzles mere inches away from his hair. Fingers began to pull on the triggers before all went dark. Silence was broken as each agent asked what was going on, whispering for a time. Moments later the lights returned and the bed was empty and perfectly made as if no one had ever slept in it. Woolton and the others, guns still at the ready, looked around briefly before they saw a young man standing in the living room of the suite, giving them a wry smile.

"Absalom," said Agent Woolton, his men shaky and frightened but still approaching the menace with guns drawn. "You are under arrest."

Woolton had no idea why he said that. Maybe he was trying to be funny, maybe it was a ritual of the job that even at this atypical situation merited invocation. Regardless, Absalom bowed his head and maintained the wry smile. He said nothing in return. Then he began to laugh. It was a minor chuckle initially, then it grew more and more guttural. The laughter continued as the agents, not knowing what to do and seeing their exit blocked, crept closer to the guffawing presence of Absalom. Now the belly laugh, the gasps of hilarity and the head raising to reveal eyes that were completely black.

One of the agents, too unnerved and too panicked, began to open fire. The muted noise of the gun was such that the bellowing laughter of Absalom drowned it out. Other agents followed his example, pouring their ammunition into the figure. Shell casings and bullets littered the floor, none of them making their target. Even Woolton, a perfect score on the firing range and but ten feet from his foe, hit him not.

Then Absalom began to rise, his feet leaving the floor as his head slowly turned, yet not fully. Like a cell undergoing mitosis, the head slowly split so that two faces now laughed and then it did this once more. And then again, and then again, going clockwise about the room and adding yet another voice of gaggling in the process. Not only faces but arms, splitting away from the original two, and then splitting once more, also increased. Each new hand had a weapon of some kind, a sword, an arrow, a chakram. A few of the agents reloaded and fired in vain. A couple of them tried to flee but found themselves unable to move towards the door. Fear pounded furiously within each agent.

Then one of the chakrams was hurled, beheading one of the agents. As this one fell into the distance another was thrown, killing another agent instantly. Arrows were tossed and entered the hearts and lungs of a couple more agents. Finally, a curved sword plunged deeply into the body cavity of another agent, their bodies falling dead upon the suite's paneled floor moistened with blood.

Five corpses lay upon the floor as the laughter stopped. The extra arms and faces were gone and Absalom stood before Woolton in an average appearance save his all-black eyes. Without hesitation and with a newly loaded firearm, Murphy drew forth his gun and was set to fire. Arm stretched out with muzzle pointed straight at Absalom, he suddenly stiffened and became immobile. Absalom looked at the trigger finger and with a blink broke it. Moving along the hand the next finger was broken, then the next, and then to the thumb, Murphy grunting in pain at each move. The grip broken, the handgun hovered in the air, suspended by synapse. The hovering gun revolved to face Murphy. Using his thoughts, Absalom ripped off the bulletproof vest, the protective item flung against the wall.

"Very well," said Absalom as he pointed the muzzle to Murphy's midsection. "Your way." With a blink, the levitating weapon fired a single shot, tearing into the ribs and stomach of Woolton. As soon as the bullet struck him, the gun dropped to the floor. Woolton did likewise, writhing in pain as dark red blood emanated from his wound. Gripping his midsection in a hopeless effort to stop the bleeding, he kicked at the floor as a last futile way to flee from an approaching Absalom.

"The wound gives you about twenty minutes of life. Use it well."

"You won't make me talk," Murphy shouted back, getting a wry smile from his company, whose eyes looked normal but whose power was still beyond the laws of nature.

"Not talk," said Absalom, gripping a wrist with one hand and the forehead with the other. "Think!" A minute later he rose up in a gasp, his smile removed and his ecstasy heightened. "That close?"

. . . .

"How much longer?" asked Adonijah, antsy as he was standing outside of the office building and across the street from the Magna Colonial. Beside him was Brittany, who was much calmer in demeanor.

"If he killed them quickly, very soon," she said solemnly, hiding what nerves were within her also.

"When he sees me, so much can go wrong," he said, people walking by them oblivious to the harrowing situation.

"Trust me, Adi," said Brittany, grabbing her soulmate by the hand. The calming feel put away the fretting of Adonijah. Soon after that, he came.

Once he got off the elevator, Absalom quickly walked across the ground floor of the hotel, passing the various guests and staff. He was not in his preferred disguise and so none of the personnel recognized him as he passed by.

Those at the main desk were not present when the police came around with the photos, so they paid little heed to the man who went by and pushed open one of the main doors. Outside on the sunny day, he wore a light jacket of black along with blue jeans and sneakers.

Studying the office building across the street, his gaze turned wide as he beheld his brother amidst the shifting pedestrian crowd. Beside him a woman, looked to be about the same age and judging by the lanyard was a law enforcer. The stare bordered on the fiery in its intensity as they saw one another. Adonijah to Absalom, brother to brother. Only a street and thin streams of people separated them. Smiling he began to walk to his left to get closer, staying on his side of the street for the time being.

"He sees me," said Adonijah. "He knows where I am."

"Come on, let's go," replied Brittany, grabbing her company by the arm. The two proceeded to walk with extra pep as Absalom did, making his way on the opposite end of Connecticut Avenue. Most of his focus was on looking at those two people, especially Adonijah. Between his breaths he mouthed his name. His demeanor was pleasant as he looked at them, rushing away in vain, he thought. Adi is too close to get away. This will not be another Dublin. This will be better than Dublin.

"Is he still following us?"

"Yes," said Adonijah without looking back. "I can feel him; I can feel his words as he tries to talk to me."

"But he doesn't have the sand or anything."

"He does not need it to plant words in my head. When he is this close, his very mental impulses pound me."

"Can you fight back?" she asked as they crossed another block with a group of others. "Can you pound back at him or something?"

"I don't want to," said Adonijah. "I don't need to. He will not control me … he cannot win … I won't let him." Brittany held Adonijah close as they stepped upon the next block of sidewalk. The trio made their way down Connecticut Avenue, getting closer and closer to Farragut West metro station. Adonijah and Brittany were about a block ahead and to the right of the street; Absalom was on the left side. As they reached the intersection with K Street the walk light again flashed for their benefit.

"Well, at least we are getting lucky with the lights," said Brittany with a campy comment as she loosened her grip on Adonijah.

"Do you really think it is luck?" replied Adonijah, smiling at Brittany as she looked at him following his response.

While waiting for his street to clear, Absalom beheld the two people including his twin cross Connecticut Avenue and enter the dark entrance of the metro station. He became nervous as they disappeared courtesy the escalator. About a minute later, he made the same journey, passing a man singing some of the good old spirituals and another more squalid figure begging for money.

Descending into the orange-brown tiled floor and rapidly walking along the curved tunnel, Brittany kept her right hand on the left arm of Adonijah. As they neared the checkpoint for customers, she noticed that there were not many people in front of them. A few WMATA employees wearing highlighted vests and blue uniforms walked along the perimeter, while another sat in the enclosed information desk.

"Metro PD," said Brittany showing them her badge and not stopping. "Have to take this person of interest southwards on the Blue Line."

"Go ahead," said the WMATA personnel nearest to the small black gate placed adjacent to one of the ticket grabbing devices. "Should be coming in a few minutes."

Absalom walked down the escalator, like the duo before him not staying on one step in patience for the descent to be completed. He saw the backs of the two as he curved around the pedestrian tunnel. With a quick flicker of his eyelids he produced a badge that he showed the WMATA employee who had just opened the gate for Brittany. "I'm with them," he said, getting a nod from the oblivious figure.

Yet another Yellow Line train sped by as they walked down the platform. A fair number of people were standing on the tiled floor, periodically looking up at the black rectangular box that displayed the next three trains expected for transport. Blue line to Franconia-Springfield was next on the hopper, a single minute listed by its name. A line of lights at the edge of the platform began to blink. From their end of the platform, Brittany and Adonijah saw the latter's twin walking down the stopped escalator, its moving stairs halted because the other one on that end used for ascending was under repair.

   Light from the far end of the dark-railed tunnel signaled its coming. The loud thrust of the long silver transport cut through the air, giving the audience on the platform a gust of wind and the sight of blurred people seated and standing within the numerous cars attached to one another. Slowing down, the images of commuters solidified. The metro jingle sounded and the doors of each of the cars beside the platform opened, with a small number of commuters leaving their public means of travel and going to their next destination. The passengers entered and either took seats or stood on the old carpeted train interior. Absalom saw them enter a car far ahead of him, but he did not have the time to reach it. Rather he entered a car nearer to the back of the train.

   "Did he get on?" asked Adonijah, seated by the window.

   "Most likely," responded Brittany, sitting next to him. They got the two seats next to the doors, which meant more leg room and a quicker means of exit when the time came. About thirty other people were around them, living and let living as they waited patiently for the train to stop at their destination. "The question is whether or not he will try to get to our car between now and the stop."

"I doubt it," said Adonijah. "He wants to know where we are going. He does not want to make a scene. I feel his discomfort being in such a cramped public space."

With an announcement regarding the next station, the Blue Line picked up speed and flowed through the tunnel. The subterranean realm it moved in on a regular basis darkened and blurred as they sped through it. People slightly adjusted their positions with each fast curve and brief pushing on the brakes by the conductor. In less than a minute they were at the next stop, Foggy Bottom. As the announcer mentioned the place, a few tourists joked at the name. Doors opened, people exited, and a bunch of young people with backpacks entered. Unbeknownst to the duo, Absalom exited briefly, carefully studying the people who exited the train. He was not totally sure that they had stayed on the train, but he was willing to wait it out just in case. Besides, it felt like Adonijah was very near; such a feeling would not manifest if he was ascending above ground to the campus.

"Where are we going?"

"To a place that should be mostly empty."

"Will it do any good?"

"It's better than confronting him in the middle of DC."

"True."

Under the river did the Blue Line go, with a couple of passengers having their ears play havoc with them. Across the Potomac, they were no longer in the District but at the busy station of Rosslyn. The train waited about thirty seconds in the purgatory of the tunnel outside of the station. After another color train left the platform, they were given permission to continue. Doors opened, with more people getting off than on. One more person, a young man, rushed as the warning about the doors closing was sounded and entered the car just as they shut. A harrowing yet common scene.

"Next stop is us."

"He is still here," muttered Adonijah under his breath as he looked blankly forward. Brittany held him by the arm, which broke the stare. He smiled at her for doing so.

"Are you okay?"

"Yes," responded Adonijah. "I've spent months fleeing him, fleeing his essence. Now we are almost there. We are almost together."

"Don't scare me, Adi."

"Fret not, it only leads to evil," he quoted.

"That's more like it."

With a blast of sunlight, the train rushed up to the surface. Fences, trees, cement, railing, the tops of cars on the nearby highway, and finally came the orange-brown tiles of the platform. Black posts with lights attached, operational once the vesper hour drew nigh, had the name of the station printed on their sides. A few families and a few individuals were on either platform. Few people got off or on. Absalom took a few steps from the doors as he had at all the stops before this one.

"There you are!" he said to himself and to his twin, who he knew mentally heard his declaration. He and the detective were walking towards the escalator. She took out her phone and immediately contacted Patterson.

"We're at Arlington Cemetery, boss. Tell metro to close off this station immediately."

"Yes, Brittany."

They descended down the escalator with Absalom in pursuit, all three walking briskly towards the metro station checkpoint. It was as before, with Brittany showing her badge and then Absalom showing his. Another escalator and the two were above ground, before them a sparse broad sidewalk. They went by the occasional monument, seeing easily from their position the gentry house at the top of the hill. Behind them he was walking, staring at his brother and the detective.

"Face me," said Adonijah suddenly, drawing the attention of Brittany. The tone seemed inhuman. "Face me." He was shaking his head no. Brittany held him close while they kept walking.

"Not yet," said Brittany to Adonijah, knowing that Absalom heard her. "But very soon, I promise."

"When?" spoke Adonijah though not of his volition.

"Soon."

The three walked by the workers at the automobile checkpoint above ground. Few cars were arriving. Thanks to the announcement from their superiors, the workers turned away the few that did show up, saying the cemetery was closed due to a minor security situation. Annoyed but understanding, the first driver to get this news simply put on his right turning signal and went to the highway exit. The others did likewise. To their left was the visitor's center, where the announcement from the information desk and ticket booths were the same as for the checkpoint personnel. Brittany and Adonijah turned left into the cemetery.

Speeding up to keep track, Absalom did likewise a minute later.

"Personnel are getting the people out. It should be almost completely evacuated," said Ella over the phone.

"Yeah, I thought it would be pretty easy on a weekday."

"What's happening?"

"He's right behind us."

"Are you sure this will work?"

"I don't even know what I am going to do next. I'll call you back."

Walking on the road, they passed the endless rows of light gray rectangular monuments to the fallen. Green fields were divided by the dark blue streets, with newly installed sidewalks separating legs from wheels. To their left, large colorful tour buses were parked in a line and later to their right they saw the brownstone arch indicating the presence of additional honored dead. Barely inhabited by the living, in the distance a few people were crouched over at certain graves, paying respects and longing to see them once again. Security approached them, kindly explaining that they had to leave the cemetery. Their journey continued, crossing streets named for deceased commanders of past armies.

A cold sensation gripped Adonijah, prompting him to hold Brittany tighter as they walked. She held on in turn as she heard a voice like that on the evening she witnessed the twins communicate. BEHOLD THIS PLACE ... THIS DREADFUL ... DREADFUL PLACE. Again Adonijah blankly looked forward, conveying the words of his brother who was so near.

EVERY MARKER, A TEAR ... EVERY NAME, ANGUISH ... EVERY STONE, MOURNING ... WHY ... ADI ... WHY DO YOU WANT IT TO CONTINUE? ... WHY WON'T YOU FACE ME? ... FACE ME ... FACE ME ...

"Not yet," interrupted Brittany, breaking Adonijah from his trancelike stare. He looked at her with childlike despair.

WHERE?

"There," said Brittany, pointing to the Columbarium. It was an impressive open air building, with stone walls, fountains, and the cremated remains of many armed servicemen. Absalom looked and smiled.

YES ... YES ... THE PALACE ... OF THE CITY ... OF THE DEAD ... THE TEMPLE ... OF THE NECROPOLIS ... I AGREE ... FACE ME THERE ... FACE ME THERE ...

Absalom left the mouth of Adonijah and ceased speaking through him. They turned left and continued the fast walk, creating some more distance between them and their pursuer. Gradually, Adonijah and Brittany loosened their grip on each other and walked separately as they got closer to the entrance of Court 3. With the Pentagon visible to their right they then turned into the solemn structure, with its squared masonry, gray texture, trimmings of shrubbery, black-lettered names, and sparkling fountain. In a last spurt of energy Brittany and Adonijah rushed to the fountain, its water shooting upwards like a beacon. Panting, they passed the rounded structure before turning to wait for his coming. So much went through their minds, still unsure on how to combat the nearing menace.

"Whatever you do, Brittany," said Adonijah while keeping his sight on the archway behind the fountain. "Don't draw your weapon. He'll kill you if you do."

"If I can't use my gun, then what can I do?"

"I don't know."

Silence came between them as the moments turned long, the anxiety burned fully within their frames. Shadowy in his movement, he turned left to walk upon the rising stonework and into the presence of the remains of the departed. Their names and ranks were diverse, the religious icons upon their markers varied, and yet to all came the same fate for the flesh they once inhabited. There seemed a screaming noise within the air, a growing drawn out shriek in the wind as each step was pounded, each segment of the walk echoing through the profound corridors. They blinked with each footstep, with each round of impact upon the light gray surface. Then he entered.

Placed on the opposite side of the fountain, a mirror image of his brother except in dress, he was standing proper and confident. Staring eyes looked at his twin, the rushing soothing waters flowing upwards between them. The blue skies, bluish and beautiful as they had been on that tragic day years earlier, were suspended above them. An occasional airplane marred the natural canopy, its white lines tracking its journey served as mimicry to the clouds. He gave a wry smile before he spoke his peace.

"Adi," spoke Absalom with joy. "I have finally found you. We have come together once more. It has been too long, too far."

"You have seen me, I have seen you," said Adonijah. "And I am begging you, pleading with you to not do it."

"You plead in vain, my dear brother," said Absalom, pacing to one side as Adonijah paced the opposite, as though they were about to duel. Brittany stayed where she was; maybe they can take him if they were split up; a multi-front attack. Then again, the federal agents also assumed surrounding Absalom would work. "I am going to end all desire, all misery, all pain. I will do what no seer or enlightened one was ever able to accomplish. Not Buddha, not Vishnu, none of them. I will shine the eye of wisdom to the whole world. In moments all pain shall be gone and Nirvana shall reign, ending once and for all the samsara of billions of lives. How can you not see this as good?"

"Because you oversimplify pain," said Adonijah sternly. "Pain is not just misery; more can be gained from it than that. People learn through pain, become stronger through pain. Pain is inevitable, but it is also ephemeral. Desire can lead to good things, things that must be and should be pursued. Like love." He looked at Brittany with that last sentence, before returning his focus back to his brother.

"Your opinion is noted, but also unenlightened," replied Absalom, whose eyes began to blacken and whose arms touched his sides. His heart beat grew faster, eyelids flickering as he continued to speak. "Soon you shall understand. Soon you will see what blessing I will give to this existence. You shall no longer be in pain, we shall no longer suffer." His forehead began to shift and reshape and there emerging was the third eye, black as the others. His breathing increased, the lungs and heart as rapidly operating as the two eyes below the forehead ceased their constant movement and remained still.

Brittany did not know what to do. Reason failed to persuade him, even the reason of his own flesh and blood. She thought of calling backup, but feared that reaching for her phone may be misinterpreted by Absalom. Or properly interpreted, as her efforts were meant to stop him from enacting his plan. Hopeless and powerless, unable to fathom what more she could do, these things prompted her to do what she seldom did and pray under her breath for a miracle from the God of Heaven. It was her last bulwark as the dark clouds began to simmer around the strictly positioned body of Absalom.

"Oh Adi, you have but one flaw," said Absalom in his intense aura. "Your compassion is your weakness."

"No," said Adonijah in full faith. "My compassion is my strength."

No sooner had Brittany begun to offer supplications to the Almighty than she felt a jerking at her holster. Then the firearm lifted free from the holster at her hip and flung itself towards Adonijah's outstretched right arm. Spinning around as it traversed through the air and past the fountain, Adonijah caught the weapon with his right hand all without looking away from the menacing presence of his brother. Adonijah shakily pointed the firearm at Absalom as he spoke his final plea.

"I beg you, brother, please … please do not make me do this."

Absalom merely laughed, brushing the threat off as petty. "Come, Adi, you know better. That won't work on me."

"You're right," said Adonijah, the lip quivering more. "It won't work on you … But it will work on me." In a second he turned the gun on himself, pushed the muzzle against his forehead, and then depressed the trigger.

In a millisecond Absalom changed back to his normal frame, his eyes widened and mouth gaped open in great shock. Brittany's expression was similar, remaining where she had been on the other side of the fountain as the loud shot rang out within the hallowed structure. Adonijah fell backwards onto the cold masonry, eyes still open but body stiffening on the Columbarium surface. Absalom shook violently and rushed to the ground to meet his brother. It was impossible, it was not happening. Desperately, he clung to the body of his brother, checking and rechecking. No response, nothing.

"Adi, Adi," Absalom kept repeating over and over as a chant to summon the dead. "Please, Adi. Not this, not this!" When he realized that this was all for naught, he gave out a deafening scream, arching his back almost unnaturally, his face directed towards the sky. Eyes firmly shut, the occasional line of liquid escaping, the wretched wail became as nothing, a muted rupture of sound wave inaudible. He then wrenched back his upper body clockwise and bent over the body.

Brittany was little better, cowering on the stone ground in distress. She did not cry with the ferocity of Absalom, yet she was wracked by severe grief. She saw the brother weeping over his long sought kin. Sobbing and choking up, his mourning gave way to rage. Terrified, Brittany saw the bent figure straighten, his frame rising with the aid of his will more than his legs. Brittany looked up to see Absalom's neck straighten and the figure turn to face her, reddish eyes turning black. Breathing fiercely through his nostrils, fists balled tightly, he walked towards the detective.

Brittany was about to get up, the adrenaline nullifying the stagnation of mourning and prompting her to flight. However, before she could run Absalom stretched out his left hand and un-balled his fist. Fingers still curved, inwards, he raised up the detective until she was three feet off the ground, all the while using his mind to torment her by pressing on her throat. Brittany struggled to breathe as the grip on her wrists and neck tightened. As she looked in terror at her tormentor, the anguished creature spoke.

YOU ... YOU DID THIS .... HE DID THIS ... FOR YOU ... YOU TOOK HIM ... FROM ME ...

Brittany tried to speak, but the grip tightened more, pushing against her throat in such a way that only quick notes of pain escaped. Her face reddened as the lack of oxygen continued, her arms and legs also felt like they were being struck by hammers. She looked at Absalom at first, but as the suffering compounded, she began to look at the body of Adonijah, sprawled on the hard gray floor of the Columbarium.

The expression of anger melted away from Absalom, as did his mental grip on Brittany. Over the course of a half minute, the pain began to ebb and the process of breathing for the detective became easier. Then she was unceremoniously dropped to the ground, landing on her hands and shins before collapsing fully prone before Absalom. Gasping for air, her limbs feeling sore, she slowly turned her gaze upward to see the prominent tormentor, the powerful and sullen man before her.

"No," said Absalom in a voice that was increasingly taking a Slavic accent. "I will not give you release from your suffering." Standing above her, Absalom's eyes became as normal. "You do not deserve it. The world does not deserve it." Absalom turned to his brother. Brittany watched, still laid out on the ground recovering from her physical and mental trauma. The twin brother knelt before his fallen family. "I wanted to give the world peace. I wanted to free it from all its pain. It was my reason and my purpose. In return, all I wanted was the one person I loved. But that was too much. So now, I have no reason and no purpose. No reason. No purpose. No reason …
No purpose …"

Absalom continued to repeat the mantra with each breath. His left hand hovered over the entry wound in the forehead of Adonijah. "No reason … No purpose …" Moving through the wound was the bullet. Absalom stood up and moved the bullet, damaged from its entry into the skull of Adonijah, suspending it in the air. "No reason … No purpose …" the bullet spun as though in a spiral yet it neither moved forward nor backward. Through the spinning he recrafted it, reforming it to its original shape.

"No reason," said Absalom as his fingers began to straighten, which prompted the bullet to move in the air backwards until it was about twenty feet away from him. "No purpose." Absalom quickly moved the four straightened fingers into his palm. This command moved the bullet rapidly forward through the air, entering his forehead between the eyes and out the back of his skull, the projectile landing like a coin in the fountain.

Absalom's body fell beside his brother's, parallel to each other with their faces both tilted towards the sky. Brittany slowly got up, struggling to walk as her body was still recuperating from the mental assault by Absalom. Standing over the two bodies, she took a moment to examine each.

Her phone rang. She picked it up after the fourth ring. It Commander Ella Patterson. Brittany responded: "Yes, boss?"

"What's happening? What's the situation?"

"The situation," Brittany struggled to find words. "Both are dead. Both brothers are dead. I guess … I guess, the situation is safe now."

"Are you hurt?"

"I don't know."

"Stay there. Help is coming soon."

Brittany offered no verbal response, pushing the button on the phone to end the conversation. She sat on the nearby border of the fountain, small drops from the sparkling tower falling upon her back. The daunting clouds vanished, revealing the pure blue expanse. Birds and bugs were chirping and the greens of the plants and small trees decorating the interior of Court 3 felt pleasantly vivid. She looked back at the two corpses, especially at the one who had shot himself.

"Adi," she said in a whisper, tears welling up as the distant sound of sirens could be heard coming through the streets of the cemetery.

293

Evening came to the station. The streaming line
of police, detectives, suspects, press, witnesses,
victims, and others continued at the usual pace.
There was going to be a faint uptick as the
weekend was beginning, however nothing
overwhelming was projected. Within the building,
below the offices and cubicles, the morgue was a
center of activity. Federal agents guarded the
area, some from the FBI, others from an
unnamed wing of the government. Rumors
buzzed amongst the staff and personnel as to the
reason for their presence. Brittany knew why, as
did Tracy. Both were sworn to secrecy about the
things they witnessed. They were to remain silent
on what they knew about the peculiar case of the
two twin brothers from Eastern Europe who had
caused so many strange things to occur.

In a moment of uncharacteristic mercy, breaking
the usual machine stoicism of the agencies of the
free world, the powers that be allowed Brittany a
few minutes in the morgue alongside Tracy. The
two women entered the guarded facility, passing
by Michael who was similarly told to keep quiet.
He nodded at the two coworkers as he continued
to discuss his autopsy report to an agent.
Solemnly and hesitantly they ventured to the two
slabs, each one bearing a body. Toes tagged
and white sheets covering their bodies up to the
chest, Brittany beheld a serene-looking, almost
angelic Adonijah. Only the hole between his eyes
served as evidence that he was deceased.

"He was taking a gamble, you know," said Tracy, standing behind Brittany and next to the corpse of Absalom. "What if Absalom still wanted to go through with his plan?"

"Adonijah knew his brother better than anyone," responded Brittany without turning her eyes away from the body. "He knew himself better than anyone. He knew Absalom could not live without him, and Adonijah knew that he could never hurt Absalom. That left only one option."

She stroked his dark hair and then moved her hand along his cheek. She felt colder as the motions were made and downtrodden as they produced no miracle. Her expression became more melancholy and she took a couple steps back. Tracy walked to face her. "Hey," said her coworker and friend. "You never told him to pull the trigger. He chose to do it."

"I know," said Brittany, "but the result is the same." Tracy hugged her friend, who reciprocated the action. As they let go, Brittany's phone lit up. Pressing a couple of buttons, she saw that she received a text from her aunt. She was back in town and wanted to have lunch soon. Implied in her comment was an invitation to church. "It's better that we leave now. I have paid my respects."

XIII.

  All was still for the moment. The white walls bore various random posters, chosen less for their message and more for their colors and designs. The wooden paneling for most of the flooring was periodically covered with purportedly Oriental rugs. The bedroom was adorned with blue carpeting. The windows were all covered and the door separating the apartment from the hallway was locked and bolted.

  Yesterday was a time of withdrawal and solitude. Requests for socializing were denied and a couple of dating accounts were removed. The bar scene was without her that night, in contrast to many weekend evenings. Before, whenever there was a time she was absent from imbibing in a loud social setting, work was to blame. This time the reason was to simply leave it, to get away and process all that had happened over the course of seven days. So much emotion, destruction, fear, and resolution.

  She was still asleep when the sun rose above Washington, DC. No alarm stirred her, nor any noise from the other apartments in the complex. Restfully she awoke, having turned in early the night before. How unlike her, she thought, her wits returning to the setting of the room. Moving under the covers, shifting as she pleased for she was alone in the bed, her eyelids eventually opened. They closed again for a few more minutes, but her consciousness already won the day. About ten minutes after she first opened her eyes, she got up from the bed and began to get ready.

Shower, coffee, breakfast, doing her hair, finding the right outfit to wear for the occasion, and then doing the last touches of makeup. Yesterday she communicated more with her aunt about weekend plans. They agreed to meet at her aunt's church. It did not reveal itself through the message confirming things, but Brittany Johnson knew her kin must have been elated to hear her decision.

It was not a guilt trip over their past argument, nor was it even so much acquiescing to the merited points made in the past debate. Brittany simply felt it was a good place to be that morning. She felt a stronger urge for spiritual guidance as this time of contemplation continued. The music will be nice, she thought. Also, the kids will be cute and the sermon might not be all that boring. When Brittany first started her adolescent sabbatical from worship, her aunt advised her that the sermon would be less boring if she actually paid attention to the points made. This morning involved testing that theory.

All ready and polished, wearing some of her better work clothes, Brittany found her keys and readied to leave the apartment. She double-checked a couple of things in her bedroom. This included her email accounts both business and personal. Her aunt had the habit of going off the grid on Sunday mornings, but Brittany knew that for her line of work and lifestyle such a habit was impractical. She exited her bedroom, two vibrant black peonies enjoying water and sun on the window sill.

She turned off any lights and climate control, knowing that saving energy was both environmentally and fiscally responsible. There were no nerves or concerns about the trip with her aunt to church. Brittany had no real qualms about going to worship; she had no bad experiences with clergy or laity. No telling episode leading her to conclude all of those in the institution were hypocrites and liars. She believed she recalled most of the prompts and motions. Also her aunt assured her that they pass out bulletins explaining to people the order of things, so she had another crutch to lean on.

As she opened the door her mind again turned to the man that had captured and broken her heart over the course of a week. As with so many people in this day and age, she began to question what she had seen. Surely, she wondered, a man who could move objects with his eyes, create whole worlds within his brain matter, and bend assorted rules of nature could do something unexpected. Brittany thought more in this contrarianism, pondering how for a man as psychologically powerful as he, surely he could simply make it look as though he had committed suicide. Surely this trick was done so that his brother may mistake his actions and then commit the only real suicide of that day.

Exiting the apartment and entering the hallway, she guided the door closed by holding the knob. Returning to her hope-filled playful scenario, she imagined the next steps. Then, assumed dead, he was free from both his brother's pursuit and the authorities who may want to experiment on him. He could return to going about the world, healing the sick, feeding the hungry, and welcoming the foreigner. Locking the door, she dismissed it all as mere curiosity, the typical reaction any person may have when faced with such an emotional tragedy. The door locked, she dismissed any further comprehension as to the question of the authenticity of his death; that is until she turned to face the hallway and saw Adonijah standing there, waiting to go with her to church.

www.ingramcontent.com/pod-product-compliance
Lightning Source LLC
Chambersburg PA
CBHW071307200626
46813CB00015B/573